THIS THY BROTHER

OTHER FIVE STAR TITLES BY ROD MILLER

All My Sins Remembered
And the River Ran Red
A Thousand Dead Horses
Pinebox Collins
Father unto Many Sons
Rawhide Robinson Rides a Dromedary:
The True Tale of a Wild Camel Caballero
Rawhide Robinson Rides the Tabby Trail:
The True Tale of a Wild West CATastrophe
Rawhide Robinson Rides the Range:
True Adventures of Bravery and Daring in the Wild West

THIS THY BROTHER

ROD MILLER

FIVE STAR
A part of Gale, a Cengage Company

GALE
A Cengage Company

LIBRARY OF CONGRESS CATALOGING-IN-PUBLICATION DATA

Names: Miller, Rod, 1952– author.
Title: This thy brother / Rod Miller.
Description: First edition. | Waterville, Maine : Five Star, [2022]
  | Identifiers: LCCN 2022000082 | ISBN 9781432892760
  (hardcover)
Subjects: LCGFT: Novels.
Classification: LCC PS3613.I55264 T46 2022 | DDC 813/.6—dc23/
  eng/20220105
LC record available at https://lccn.loc.gov/2022000082

First Edition. First Printing: August 2022
Find us on Facebook—https://www.facebook.com/FiveStarCengage
Visit our website—http://www.gale.cengage.com/fivestar
Contact Five Star Publishing at FiveStar@cengage.com

Printed in Mexico
Print Number : 1   Print Year : 2022

My brother, Zeb Miller, thought
Father unto Many Sons needed a sequel.
This book is for him.
I only wish he had lived to read it.
Also for editor extraordinaire,
Patricia Burkhart Smith—her final chapter.

It was meet that we should make merry, and be glad:
for this thy brother was dead, and is alive again;
and was lost, and is found.

–Luke 15:32

CHAPTER ONE

Melvin Pate lay on his side with one bleary eye open, watching a fly tiptoe in the drool from his brother's mouth. He sat up, scrubbed his face with the palms of his hands, and looked around. He stretched a leg toward his brother, and prodded him until he groaned, and kept it up, his foot retreating to avoid the arm swatting at it, then poking some more. "Get up, Richard."

Slapping at the air and missing the offending foot with every swipe, Richard's groans turned to a growl. "Leave me alone." He rolled away from his brother. Melvin stood, tucked in his shirt, straightened his trousers, and then landed a gentle kick on his brother's backside. "Get up. Noonin's over. We got work to do." He kicked out again, a little harder this time.

With another growl, Richard rolled to his knees and pushed himself upright. He groaned, his hands gripping the sides of his skull, and flopped back down with a whimper. "My head. Oh, my head. Mel, cut the damn thing off. Please."

Melvin took a twist on the back of Richard's collar and lifted him up, holding him upright until he found his feet and stood swaying, his eyelids squeezing his forehead into rows of wrinkles that disappeared into his hair. "You ought not be drinkin' all that tequila. Even more so, you ought not have stole it off that wagon."

"Leave off with your damn 'ought nots.' You sound like Pa."

"C'mon. We got to get to work."

"I need a drink of water."

Melvin fetched a canteen from where it hung on his saddle horn and handed it to his brother. Richard pulled the plug and tipped up the container, water glugging out of the spout and down his throat as fast as he could swallow. He leveled the canteen and held his breath as the water roiled in his stomach, recalling the effects of the alcohol. He swallowed repeatedly as salty saliva filled his mouth and his stomach lurched. The canteen hit the ground and Richard grasped his knees and heaved up the foul and bitter remnants of the tequila.

"I feel like shit."

"You don't look no better. Now c'mon. I got to go bring up them oxes."

"Oxen, you damn fool. They're oxen—not oxes."

"Well, whatever they are, I need to fetch them. And you ought to be out huntin' 'stead of layin' around drinkin'. You ain't brought in no meat at all since they hired you on."

Melvin watched while Richard sniffed at his rumpled, rancid shirt and screwed up his face in disgust. He walked to where the horses were picketed and Richard scuffed along behind. Richard watched as Melvin pulled the pins and coiled the picket ropes, then snugged up his saddle cinch. "C'mon, Richard. You need to wake up and get to work."

"It ain't been but a couple of days. Shut up your mouth, little brother. Like I said, you sound just like Pa."

"Pa wasn't always wrong, y'know." He spat in disgust and gave the latigo an extra tug. "You figure on ever shootin' that rifle of Pa's? You don't get in some camp meat, you're likely to be let go."

Richard leaned against his horse. "You're still mad I took that rifle, ain't you."

"Darn right I am. It was bad enough we took the horses."

"Well, Mel, you know as well as I do that if I hadn't of took that gun, Pa would've give it to Abel. By rights it's mine, me bein' the oldest. That little bastard don't deserve it."

Melvin shook his head and stared at his brother. "Maybe so. But just because you don't like our little brother, it ain't no call to steal. Besides, Abel always was a better shot with that gun than what you are." He flopped the stirrup leathers down off the saddle seat, stepped into the stirrup and swung aboard the horse. "Sometimes I wish we hadn't never of left Ma and Pa."

"Well, we did. And I'll be damned if I'll go snivelin' back to 'em like a bawlin' calf. You can do as you please."

Melvin rode down the slope to where the oxen waited and started pushing them into a bunch. Some stood, nibbling at the sparse grass; others lay on their bellies, chewing their cuds and watching the horseman. With all the cattle on their feet and bunched, Melvin pushed them toward the wagons to where the bullwhackers waited, yokes and bows balanced on their shoulders or dangling from hands and arms.

One of the drivers was not among them; a man named Goodfellow. He stood atop the tailgate of his wagon, skidding a wooden crate aside and sliding open the lid of another beneath it. He reached inside and pulled out a bottle of tequila, reset the lid and slid the crate atop it back into position. Richard sat mounted behind the wagon, watching out for the wagon master and other drivers. He handed his flask to the man on the wagon and waited for him to fill it. The man handed it back, and Richard took a sip, and handed it back to be topped off before corking it and slipping it into his saddlebag. He turned the horse, with a pack mule on a lead, away from the wagons and rode uphill, following a shallow draw into the timber where he hoped to maybe jump a mule deer and start earning his keep as a hunter for the freight outfit.

The brothers had hired on with the freighters just three days ago, Richard as hunter and Melvin to herd the loose stock. The wagons were bound for the States, lightly loaded with Mexican goods from wool to blankets to buffalo hides—and with Mexican silver coins taken in trade for the goods hauled out from Independence on the Santa Fe Road.

The boys were accustomed to trail life—it had been months since either had slept in a bed or even under a roof. The Pate family left Tennessee under the guidance of their patriarch, Lee. Their father's religious leanings concerning the evils of slavery, fueled by dreams and visions, and sparked by a scheming brother, prompted him to abandon the settled life and strike out for Mexico—much to the dismay of his family.

No sooner had the family reached the exotic new country on the fringes of the Mexican empire than Richard and Melvin lit out on their own. Richard, bitter over what he deemed their father's preferential treatment for their younger brother, Abel, had had enough. He saddled a horse in the dark of night, fingers numbed by alcohol fumbling to tighten the latigo, and rode out of the family camp on the outskirts of Las Vegas, bound for parts unknown. Melvin, indecisive and lacking any driving ambition of his own, opted to tag along with his older brother.

Richard reined up where the draw narrowed to a point to allow his horse and mule a blow. He dismounted, found the flask in the saddlebag, and sat on a boulder sipping the Mexican liquor. When the horse's breathing slowed and steadied, he remounted and chose a ridge heading more or less in the direction the wagons would be traveling, and spurred his horse upward. The mule followed. When he topped out, he rode on downhill just far enough to avoid staying skylined, then stopped. He heard cracking limbs and sliding rocks somewhere below, and then silence for a time.

When the sound of rustling undergrowth again reached him, Richard half-hitched the mule's lead to the saddle horn and stepped down from the saddle, pulling the rifle from its scabbard as he went. He wrapped the bridle reins around a branch of brush, stepped away and sat, his back against outcropping rock. The horse blew, the exhalation ruffling his nostrils in a long, rolling snort. Richard flung an arm toward the horse, and it jerked backward until stopped by the tethered reins, then shifted its hooves until steady, and stood quiet again.

The ruction had upset whatever was below them among the trees. Richard listened to the movement away from him. He checked the seating of the percussion cap on the rifle's nipple and rested the buttstock on his shoulder, eyeing along the barrel the depths of the opposite ridge. Soon, half a dozen deer trotted out of the bottom, climbing the steep ridge at a low angle. Richard spied a buck with a fairly large rack, and another showing two points on each antler. Clambering along behind were two does and their fawns, followed by a lone doe. Settling his sights on the young buck, Richard squeezed the trigger. The white cloud of powder smoke spewing from the barrel blocked Richard's view, so he did not know if his ball found its mark. He waited, his cheek tucked against the rifle, until the smoke drifted clear but saw nothing but an empty ridge before him. The deer, spooked at the sound of the rifle, were nowhere in sight, and he saw no evidence of the two-point buck being down.

"Damn," he said under his breath. He recharged the rifle and slid it back into the scabbard, untied the horse, and mounted. Richard studied the place where the deer had been when he shot, memorizing landmarks, and then spurred the horse into motion. He worked his way down the hill, switching back and forth in the descent until reaching the bottom. Turning up the canyon, he soon spied the hoofprints left by the deer and followed the track as it left the canyon floor and started up the ridge. He reined up where the nature of the trail changed when the deer took flight, and studied the ground. There was no blood to be found—no spatter, no puddle, no drips.

"Damn." He jerked the horse around and gouged it with his spurs, setting off down the canyon. He should reach the road and catch up to the wagons in time for supper. And again, the wagon master would see him ride into camp empty handed. No doubt he would hear from Melvin about his miserable shooting, as if he did not know it already. If Melvin drew any comparison to the skill of their little brother, Abel, he might just poke him in the nose. He was in no mood to hear about it.

Richard cocked his hip in the saddle as the horse worked its way down the canyon and reached back, fumbling with the strap securing the saddlebag. He reached inside and located the flask, uncorked it, and listened to the gurgle as he poured the tequila down his throat in a long draught. He replaced the cork and thought about putting the flask away, thought better of it, and drank again. There was plenty more tequila where this came from.

Melvin, herding the spare oxen and a few saddle mounts along behind the wagon train, was the first to see Richard coming. He had just ridden to the front of the herd to hold the animals as the wagon columns were separating to form up into a camp circle. Once the circle was complete, save a gap at the rear, the reserve oxen would plod through the gap and join up with the animals relieved of their yokes. Melvin would drive the herd to water, then push the oxen back through the gap into the corral formed by the parked wagons to graze and laze the night away. Richard rode toward Melvin to help, but the tame oxen required little in the way of herding.

By the time he arrived, the oxen were already at water, spread along the sluggish stream. Richard rode up and stopped beside Melvin, and the brothers watched the animals drink. In ones and twos and threes, the oxen turned away from the water to crop the grass along the bank.

"I see you ain't got no meat on that mule's back," Melvin said.

Richard did not reply, only looked at his brother as he emptied the last of the tequila from the flask, then held it above his open mouth to shake the last few drops onto his tongue. He put the stopper in place and snugged it with a pop of the palm of his hand.

Melvin said, "You even shoot at anything?"

"What the hell difference does it make? Like you said, I ain't got no meat again."

"Maybe if you'd quit drinkin' so much of that stuff you might be able to hit what you're shootin' at."

"Maybe if you'd mind your own damn business, I wouldn't be so likely to kick the shit out of you."

Melvin reined his horse around, rode around the grazing oxen and pushed them toward the wagons. Richard rode up beside him as they plodded along behind the herd.

"I'm sorry, Mel. Don't mean to have at you like that. Thing is, I don't like to be reminded how useless I am. I had enough of that growin' up with Pa."

"He never was so bad as you think."

"Maybe not to you."

"Not to you, neither." They rode along in silence for a time. "It's just that I'm worried, Richard. I don't know what's to become of us. Or what'll become of Ma and Pa."

Richard laughed, but there was no mirth in it. "Oh, don't you worry none about that. Abel will see it's all sunshine and roses for 'em."

Melvin thought on that. Then, "Well, how 'bout us, then?"

"Hell, Mel, we're on the way to Missouri! Got ourselves a free ride. Better'n that, we're gettin' paid for it. Once we get back to where civilized folks live, we can do any damn thing we please. Just you keep starin' at the shitty end of these oxen for a month or two and it'll be all sunshine and roses for us."

"Maybe so. But I'm thinkin' that if you don't start doin' better at your job, Mister Harlan will cut you loose. Then what?"

Richard smiled and reached out and placed a hand on Melvin's shoulder and gave it a gentle shake. "I ain't worried, Brother. I ain't one to borrow trouble."

The oxen filed through the gap into the wide area surrounded by the wagons which would be pasture and bed ground to them. Melvin pushed them away from where the cookfires were laid, then turned back and looked for Richard. He saw the pack mule turned loose and cropping grass, his brother's horse tied to the rear wheel of Goodfellow's wagon. He rode that way. As he rode up, Richard came out from behind the wagon, licking his lips and slipping his refilled flask inside his shirt.

"C'mon brother," Richard said. "Let's get these horses put up and find us a place to roll out our blankets."

The brothers pulled the saddles, stood them on their forks to dry with the saddle blankets draped over the top, then pulled up handfuls of grass and rubbed down the horses' backs. As Melvin wiped his hands on his pants legs, Art Harlan, the wagon boss, walked up.

"Ba

"E

"Sm

"An

CHAPTER TWO

The tap-tap-tap of a hammer resounded through the camp as a bullwhacker, with help from a pair of other wagon drivers, tapped wooden wedges between the felloes and iron tire of a wagon wheel. The desert air dried and shrank the wood parts of wheels, and the bumps and potholes of the road shook loose spokes, felloes, and tires, requiring constant attention from the drivers to keep the wheels functional.

Another group of drivers stood circled around an ox on the ground, laid down by a system of ropes. A bullwhacker who also served as the train's farrier worked at replacing a lost shoe on the inside sole of the cloven hoof on the animal's right hind leg. Other drivers crawled under and around their wagons, slathering on grease to minimize the grinding of the wheels against the clouts and axles. Elsewhere, bullwhackers slipped under wagon covers and climbed atop their loads, checking to see that nothing had shifted into a dangerous or damaging position.

The camp cook tended to his fires in the fading light of the day, moving from one pile of smoldering coals to another, lifting the lids on the cast-iron ovens to check the food cooking inside.

Melvin stood, weight shifting from one foot to the other, watching the wagon boss. Richard tipped his hat back with a finger to the brim, then leaned and propped his arm atop the front wheel of a wagon and settled his weight against it.

"Mister Harlan," he said with a nod toward the wagon master.

"You know, Pate, we count on your bringing in meat to help feed this outfit."

Richard nodded again. "Yessir."

"Near as I can tell, you have yet to bring in so much as a squirrel."

"No sir."

"You set yourself up as something of a hunter when I hired you on."

"Yessir."

Melvin's head turned back and forth to follow the conversation, along with his shifting weight from one foot to another.

The wagon master turned his head and spat out a stream of tobacco juice. The syrupy string splashed into a puddle on the ground. "Well?"

Richard smiled, but his brother saw through the bluff, recognizing the anxiety beneath. "Game's pretty scarce in these parts. I can't shoot what ain't there."

"I have been through this country many a time, Pate, and there has never been a shortage of deer. Nor antelope. Elk are plentiful if you know how to hunt them. Soon, we shall pass through the buffalo ranges. I expect there are sufficient opportunities to take down game for the pot."

"Yessir."

"Have you even fired that Kentucky rifle of yours?"

"No sir. I ain't seen but one scrawny old doe, and she weren't worth wastin' powder and ball on."

Harlan stared at Richard for an uncomfortable time. "Another thing, Pate. I want you stay away from Goodfellow."

"Oh? Why's that?"

"I have traveled this road many a time with Goodfellow. I do not know if I have never seen the man drunk, or never seen him sober. He may tell himself that I do not know, but I know he is always at the bottle. But, drunk or sober, he is a capable bull-whacker. More than capable. So, I do not concern myself with what he puts into his stomach."

"I don't see what that's got to do with me."

"Do not trifle with me, Pate. I know of a surety that Goodfel-low has been supplying you with tequila. What I do not know is whether or not you can hold your liquor. I cannot be faulted for suspecting that a snootful of tequila may be among the reasons for your failure as a hunter."

Richard said nothing, his head down and watching the toe of his boot tracing meaningless patterns on the ground.

Harlan released another torrent of tobacco juice. "Here is how it will go from now on. You stay clear of Goodfellow. And you stay away from strong drink altogether until you show an ability to perform your duties. Otherwise, I will have no choice but to dispense with your services."

Richard's head jerked up and he found Harlan's eyes. "Who'll do your huntin' then, old man?"

"There are enough men on this train who know the road. They will keep the wagons rolling should I find it necessary to ride out in search of game. I have done so before. I do not wish to do it again, but know that I am capable. Once we reach Bent's Fort, there will be no shortage of men willing to take on the task—and every man of them can shoot."

Harlan said nothing more. He fixed his gaze on Richard for another uncomfortable period, spat again into the slimy puddle in the grass, then turned and walked away.

Richard watched him as he went. His hand, as if it had a mind of its own, reached into his shirt and took out the flask. He pulled out the cork and took a long drink, his eyes never leaving the retreating wagon boss.

"Richard!"

Richard blinked, shook his head, and looked at his brother as

19

if he were a stranger. His eyes came into focus, and he said, "What is it, Mel?"

"Didn't you hear what Mister Harlan said?"

He sipped again from the flask. "Ever' damn word of it."

"Then for heaven's sake, put that there little bottle away. Better still, dump it out and throw it plumb away."

"I ain't one to waste good tequila, Brother," Richard said with a smile. "Not that tequila's all that good in the first place." He held up the flask as if in a toast to his brother, then took another drink. "Still, it beats the hell out of water."

"But you heard what he said! He'll send you packin' if he sees you drinkin' again."

Richard corked the flask and tucked it back inside his shirt. "Aw, hell, Mel, it ain't nothin' but talk. That old man sure don't want to do his own huntin'. You heard him say as much."

"He said he'd do it if he had to."

"Well, as long as he's got me, he don't have to." He clapped a hand on Melvin's shoulder and gave it a shake. "Quit your worryin'. Let's go get us some grub."

The thought of food relieved Melvin's mind of all other concerns. The brothers walked across the corral to where smoke from the fires feathered away into the darkening sky.

Melvin stirred with the first hint of dawn. It may have been the clatter of coffeepots that wakened him, but he did not know. He rolled his blanket and tossed it atop his saddle, then eased out between two of the parked wagons and relieved himself. When he came back into the corral, he prodded Richard with the toe of his boot until his brother groaned and rolled over. He saddled his horse, then poked at Richard until he sat up.

Richard patted and pawed around in his tangled blanket until he found his flask and tipped it up to take a drink, but found it empty. "Sonofabitch," he said under his breath. He stood up, staggered for a moment until finding his feet, shuffled over to his saddle, found his canteen, and gurgled down a long drink of water. He looked around in the dim light. "You seen Goodfellow?"

By then, Melvin was mounted. "Richard, you had best forget about Goodfellow. You remember what Mister Harlan said. Go get yourself some coffee."

Richard answered with a snort, but as Melvin rode away, he looked back and saw his brother shuffling across the corral toward the cook fires and the coffeepots there. There would be only coffee for the bullwhackers until the train stopped in a few hours for the nooning, which always came well before noon. Breakfast would be served to the men while the oxen rested from the morning pull. A bullwhacker had told Melvin that if the train did not stop then and allow the oxen to relieve themselves and chew their cuds for a time, they would not work.

But, for now, the cattle needed to take on water, not let it out, so Melvin gathered the oxen, drove them to the riverbank, and sat in the saddle watching them drink. He wished he had gotten a cup of coffee before setting out. He regretted not saving a biscuit from supper. And he wondered what he would do when Mister Harlan gave Richard the sack. He had little confidence that Richard would suddenly sharpen his skills as a hunter. He had less confidence that his brother would stop drinking.

When he fed the cattle back through the open mouth of the wagon corral, the bullwhackers were waiting, yokes and bows balanced on hips and shoulders. They set out sorting their teams from the herd. Some recognized their cattle by color, having put together teams with similar color patterns and markings. Others tied lengths of colored ribbon or twine to tails or horns for identification. Still others simply knew their oxen by sight, having spent hours and days and weeks and months plodding along

21

beside them on the way out from Independence, and now doing the same on the way back from Santa Fe. Soon, every driver would know his teams just so.

Melvin sipped from his second cup of coffee, working around a tongue sore from the scald of his first cup. He watched the drivers yoking their teams, and cast his eyes about the camp for Richard. He saw his horse and pack mule tied to the wheel of a wagon across the way, but no sign of his brother. Then Goodfellow stepped out from behind the wagon, fetched a yoke and bows from where they sat on the tongue, and started for the herd. He had not walked far when Richard came out from behind the wagon. Melvin watched him tuck his flask, followed by a bottle, into his saddlebags, gather the mule's lead, mount the horse, and ride out through the gap at a trot.

Richard turned down the road in the direction the train would take, figuring to scout the river bottoms in that direction for deer or elk or any other four-legged critter suitable for food. Over the footfalls of the horse and mule he could hear the slosh of tequila in the bottle in his saddlebag. The opposite pouch carried a greasy sack holding a half-dozen leftover biscuits stuffed with cold bacon. The cook begrudged him the food, berating him for not bringing in meat to fill the pots. Richard cared little for the belly cheater's opinions and told him as much.

When the road departed from the river's course, Richard followed the stream, riding through the cottonwood trees that lined its banks. The riverbed was wide, the weak flow meandering among rocks and boulders along its sandy bottom, never nearing the embankment carved by high water during spring runoff. He saw plenty of sign left by deer coming down to drink; sharp-edged tracks likely left that morning, others eroded to varying degrees, all the way down to mere depressions. He saw larger tracks he assumed to be left by elk. Prints from smaller animals and birds pockmarked the bottom. But he saw no living thing save birds flitting about among the trees, and the insects that hovered around in a cloud that followed him, dissipating only when he spurred the horse into a lope to escape them. Eluding the bugs was futile, however. No sooner would he slow the horse to a walk than another fog of insects would form.

Tired of swatting at the tiny pests, he abandoned the river and struck out across the plain. He crossed the road and kept riding into the foothills. Stopping at the base of a ridge, Richard dismounted and loosened the saddle cinch and tied the horse to the limb of a dead cedar tree, and looped the mule's lead rope around a clump of brush. Fetching his flask and the sack of biscuits from his saddlebags, he settled himself in the shade of a cedar and filled his belly. With both the sack and flask empty, he stretched out with a rock for a pillow and his hat over his face, and napped.

Richard knew not how long he had slept when awakened by the pawing and sighing of the horse. He sat up and rubbed his face with both hands to wipe away the drowse, then raked his fingers through his tangled, greasy hair and reset his hat. The sun had disappeared behind the mountains above him, but the plain still shone with sunlight. He stood and stretched the kinks out of his back and shuffled over to the horse. He pulled the bottle from his saddlebag, took a long drink, filled his flask, then drank again from the bottle.

After securing the bottle in the saddlebag and untying the pack mule, Richard shook the saddle into position on his horse's back and tightened the cinch. He lifted his leg and reached his foot to the stirrup, missed, and tried again, finally finding it on the third try. Heeling the horse into motion, he rode slowly down the hill into the brush. He stopped on the road, and read from the tracks there that the train had passed, the wagons spread into four columns.

Kicking the horse into a lope, he set off down the road, the mule keeping pace. From studying the lay of the land from the hillside where he had taken his dinner, he knew the river course took a long bow across the plain, and surmised the freight outfit would make camp a few miles ahead where the road and river again drew close.

The horse ducked and shied when a jackrabbit jumped out from under a clump of brush and ran into the road. Richard, barely keeping his seat, dropped the lead rope and lost his hat when his head dipped to the horse's left shoulder as his right foot lost the stirrup. He grabbed the saddle horn and pulled himself upright and jerked the rein hard, turning the horse in a circle. Reaching out, he slapped the horse between the ears, the blow causing the frightened animal to rear up and toss his head. Richard spurred him hard in the belly and hauled in on the reins when the horse lunged forward.

He sat, gasping for breath, as the horse stood quivering between his legs. He stepped down and retrieved his hat. Down the road a ways sat the jackrabbit, its long hind legs tucked, front legs stiff and upright, ears erect and alert. Richard cursed, walked around the horse and slid the rifle from its sheath, settled it over the saddle, and shot the rabbit. Through the smoke, he saw the rabbit rise into the air and spin around.

The big ball from the rifle nearly severed the jackrabbit. It had ripped a deep gouge through the hare's back, taking out a big chunk of the spine, obliterating bone and organs. Richard picked up the jackrabbit and it nearly came apart, its front and back ends held together only by the skin of its belly. He laid the wasted carcass behind the cantle on the saddle skirt and lashed it down with the saddle strings.

By the time he reached camp, his flask needed refilling, but the bottle that had refreshed it throughout the day lay discarded somewhere in the brush, empty. He entered the wagon corral and rode straight to the cookfires. Art Harlan, the wagon master, was there, drinking coffee and talking with the cook. Richard reined up his mount, closer to the men than horseback etiquette dictated, and dropped the bloody jackrabbit at their feet.

The men looked at the dead animal, then at Richard.

He smiled, tapped the brim of his hat with a finger, then turned and rode away.

CHAPTER THREE

When Melvin shook his brother to awaken him, Richard moaned and groaned and pulled the blanket over his head. Melvin tried to rouse him again after saddling his horse in the dim morning light, but Richard only grumbled and curled himself into a ball. Giving up on the task, Melvin gathered the awakening oxen and drove them out to water.

When he brought the cattle back, Richard was huddled with a few of the bullwhackers at the fire, drinking coffee. His horse was still picketed. Melvin saddled the horse for his brother, gathered up his scattered belongings, such as they were, and stuffed them into Richard's rucksack. He looked for his brother, saw him still at the fire, and took the opportunity to peek into his saddlebags. Seeing a full bottle of tequila inside, he considered dumping it out, thought better of it, anticipating Richard's wrath, and tied down the saddlebag flap.

Melvin mounted his horse and rode past the herd where the bullwhackers were sorting out their teams. He got to the cook-fire in time to pour a cup from the pot just as the cook was preparing to dump it into the fire to douse the coals. The cook and Richard were the only ones still there.

"Saddled your horse for you," Melvin said.

Richard only grunted.

"You don't look so good this morning."

"I ain't surprised. You oughta see how it looks from this side."

"Well, with what you got in your saddlebags, it ain't likely to get any better."

Richard tossed the dregs of his coffee onto the ground. "You been snoopin' in my stuff, Mel?"

Melvin shrugged. "Had a look-see whilst I was saddlin' your horse. I see where you ain't paid no attention to what Mister Harlan told you."

"I see where you ain't learned to mind your own damn business."

Melvin hung his head, shifting his weight from one foot to the other.

Richard said, "I wouldn't put up with Pa tellin' me what to do. I'll be damned if I'll have you or Harlan or anybody else tellin' me."

Melvin offered no reply. He watched the bullwhackers yoking the last of their cattle. Some of the wagons were already hitched with their full complement of teams, the drivers waiting to hear Harlan's call to "Stretch out!" and hit the road. Melvin climbed aboard his horse. "Reckon I had best get to work. You goin' huntin'?"

"That's my job, ain't it?" Richard said.

Melvin reined his mount around and bunched the spare cattle. As he worked, he watched Richard walk across the corral, grasping the pack mule's halter as he went, leading it to where his horse was tied to the wagon. He snapped the lead rope to the mule's halter, mounted his horse, and rode away, the mule in tow.

Richard followed the tracks the cattle had left when Melvin drove them to and from the river for water. He crossed the dry bed until reaching the slowly flowing stream and rode into the water. The horse, never wet above the fetlocks, stopped midstream and dipped his muzzle into the stream, the mule likewise. Richard let them drink for a time, then lifted his horse's head with the reins and spurred him on across the water, across the dry bed, and up the shallow embankment on the opposite side. He turned upstream, angling away from the river, through the willows and patches of cottonwood trees. He stayed near the edge of the narrow fringe of timber along the river.

The band of trees widened somewhat in the bow of the river's course. His horse's ears alerted him of something ahead and he stopped. Following the horse's gaze, he saw a scattering of what he took to be elk, little more than dark flecks in a meadow maybe a half mile ahead. He rode deeper into the trees, almost to the river, and rode on. When he reached a place he thought to be near the grazing elk, he stopped. Tying the horse and mule to spindly cottonwood saplings, he unsheathed the rifle, checked the seating of the cap, and dangled the long gun at his side as he walked slowly through the trees.

Richard saw he had underestimated the distance, finding the elk herd well away from his position, most of them beyond effective range, and with too much open grassland to allow getting any nearer. But there was one sizeable cow near enough to bring down. Slowly, ever so slowly, Richard stepped closer, crouched low and duck-walking toward the only tree large enough to offer any semblance of cover.

Upon reaching the tree, Richard used the palm of his hand to muffle the sound of the rifle's hammer ratcheting into position. He sat flat on the ground, drew up both knees, and propped his elbows on them to steady his aim. He held the elk in his sights until his breathing slowed and steadied, then drew in a long breath, let it out slowly, and squeezed the trigger.

The hammer fell on the cap with a snap. A misfire. But the noise was enough to disturb the cow. She threw her head up, looked for the source of the sound, then turned and trotted away across the meadow. The other elk, sensing fear, also ran away.

Richard dropped the rifle and flopped down flat on his back.

"Sonofabitch!" he shouted, shaking a fist in the air.

He lay there for several minutes, silently cursing the rifle, the elk, his luck, Art Harlan, his father, his brother Abel, and heaven and earth in general. When he sat up, there was not an elk in sight. He stomped back to his tethered horse, opened the saddlebag, and pulled out the bottle of tequila. He sat down on a fallen cottonwood log and drank in long swallows, relishing the burn of the liquor down his throat and into his stomach, and the warmth of its spread from there.

The bottle was much lighter when Richard put it back in the saddlebag, exchanging it for the pocket flask, which was easier to drink from when horseback. He gathered the mule, crossed the river, and rode through the brush until reaching the road, then set out to find and overtake the dust cloud raised by the lumbering freight wagons.

He reached the train late in the day. He stopped where Melvin held the reserve oxen and they sat horseback and watched the wagons form the corral.

"You had anything to eat?" Melvin said.

"No. That cook begrudges me every bite, so I didn't trouble him for no leftovers to take with me this morning."

"I et a good breakfast at the nooning, but it's gone now. I'm likely to eat a bunch come supper time." Melvin looked at his brother, bleary-eyed and wan, sagging in the saddle. "From the smell of you, I'd guess your stomach ain't empty."

The look Richard gave in return forbade asking how the hunting had gone. He fell asleep as they waited. Melvin feared he might fall off the horse, but dared not disturb him. But when the wagons were parked and the teams unyoked, it was time to go to work. He reached out, grasped Richard's arm, and gave him a shake. Richard stirred slowly, looking around through squinted eyes to find his place in the world. With the back of his hand he wiped one eye and then the other. He lifted his hat and reset it, and looked to his brother.

Melvin said, "You think you could hold these oxes here whilst I fetch the rest?"

"I told you before they're *oxen,* not oxes. Can't you get that through your thick head?"

Melvin said nothing for a minute. Then, "Well? Are you goin' to watch 'em, or not?"

"Get on with it—and be quick about it."

Some of the oxen were already wandering out of the corral when Melvin reached the wagons. He rode through the gap, circled the scattered cattle, and drove them out to meet the smaller bunch Richard held. As the oxen mixed, Melvin moved the herd toward the river. Richard helped him start them, then turned back to the camp.

Art Harlan stood waiting when Richard arrived. "I don't see any meat."

Richard stayed mounted and looked down at the wagon master. He looked around the corral as the bullwhackers looked over their wagons, carrying out daily maintenance, effecting necessary repairs, and checking their loads. The cook had fires laid and lit, their blazes dancing amber in air tinged golden by the low-hanging sun.

"Not today," Richard finally said. "Had me a fat elk in my sights. Gun misfired." He shrugged. "Can't do nothin' 'bout such misfortune."

"Well, Pate, we cannot fill our stomachs with misfortune. I have warned you already—either you bring in fresh meat or I will find it necessary to send you on down the road."

Richard wheeled his horse around with a jerk, yanked on the pack mule's lead, and rode away, cursing under his breath. He stopped, pulled the mule close, unsnapped the lead rope, and used it to swat the mule away. As he coiled the rope and hung it on the saddle horn, he looked for Goodfellow's wagon.

He reined up at the wagon. Goodfellow was underneath it on his back, feet and legs poking out. He slid out from beneath the box, stood up and brushed off the seat of his pants with both hands. Richard had dismounted. Without saying anything, he reached out toward Goodfellow, pocket flask in hand.

Goodfellow took a step backward, shaking his head. "Not this time, Pate."

"Why the hell not?"

"Harlan says not to give you any more. Says he's told you to lay off."

"So? Who gives a shit what Harlan says?"

Goodfellow swallowed hard. "I do, for one. Keepin' you in tequila is more than my job is worth. I won't do it no more. Find someone else, or lay off, like the boss says."

Richard dropped the flask and took two quick steps toward Goodfellow. He took another step, shoving the man backward with both hands to his chest, then repeated the attack with another step forward and another push. Goodfellow's back slammed into the wagon box, knocking the breath from him. He gasped, ducked his head, and charged Richard, wrapping both arms around his waist. The momentum carried both men down. Unable to catch his breath, Goodfellow struggled. Richard thrust his hips upward and flipped to the side, rolling Goodfellow off him. He flung a leg over and kneeled upright, astraddle Goodfellow's midsection.

"You sonofabitch!" Richard said. He slammed a fist into the side of Goodfellow's head, and cringed at the pain in his knuckles. Goodfellow tried to roll over, but Richard sat down hard on his belly, further crippling the man's attempts to catch his breath. Goodfellow reached up and grabbed a handful of Richard's shirtfront and swung a fist at his jaw, but Richard leaned back and the blow struck nothing but air. Richard pounded another punch and Goodfellow's nose gushed blood.

He cocked his fist again, but, before he could swing, he was dragged backward off of Goodfellow.

The bullwhacker who had him jerked Richard to his feet, grabbed him by the wrist and wrenched it backward, bending his arm and pinning it against his back. Richard tried to jerk away, but the bullwhacker shoved the arm higher, the pain of it preventing any further struggle. Goodfellow had rolled over and hoisted himself to his hands and knees, drops of blood from his nose puddling on the ground.

As bullwhackers gathered, Harlan elbowed his way through the throng. He looked the situation over. "I do not have to guess what is going on here," he said, his eyes boring into Richard. "Someone help Goodfellow. The rest of you, go on about your business."

The men dispersed slowly, talking in low voices. One of them helped Goodfellow to his feet, held him by the elbow, and led him away. The bullwhacker who held Richard gave his arm a final wrench, then let him go with a shove.

When just the two of them remained, Harlan said, "Pate, this is enough. More than enough. I have always run an orderly outfit, and your presence here is making that difficult, if not impossible. You are welcome to stay for supper and spend the night. But when you ride out of here in the morning, you are not to come back."

"What about my pay?"

Harlan laughed and spat out a stream of tobacco juice. "I will pay you for the days you have been in my employ. Not that you have earned it." He turned and walked away, toward the gap in the wagons through which Melvin would soon be driving the cattle coming back from water.

When the last of the oxen passed through the opening, Harlan hailed Melvin. He rode over and dismounted.

"What is it, Mister Harlan?"

"It is that brother of yours, Mel."

Melvin hung his head. "What's he done now?"

"He attacked Goodfellow. Would have given him a right smart thrashing if he had not been stopped."

Melvin looked up, brow furrowed. "What'd he go and do that for?"

"Goodfellow refused to give him any more of that tequila—on my orders."

Melvin shook his head, then bowed it again, shifting his weight from side to side.

Harlan said, "And, of course, you are aware that his efforts at hunting have not been fruitful. We rely on fresh meat, and he has not provided it."

Still, Melvin stood, head down, rocking back and forth as he shifted his weight.

"Look at me, Mel." When their eyes met, Harlan said, "You are a good man. A willing and reliable worker. I hope you will stay with the train."

"I don't know, Mister Harlan. Richard, well, he's my brother. I kind of feel like I ought to stick with him."

"Richard is headed for nothing but trouble, Mel. And he will take you down with him. I know the type. You would be best advised to stay shut of him."

Melvin said nothing for a time, his eyes and weight shifting as he mulled over the advice. Then, "You're most likely sayin' the truth, Mister Harlan. But maybe if I stay with him, I can keep him out of trouble. Some, at least."

"You must do as you think best. I understand the strength of family ties. I have ordered Richard to leave come morning. Let me know what you decide."

Melvin stood for several minutes after Harlan left. Then he mounted his horse and rode into the wagon corral, looking for his brother.

"Richard, what've you gone and done? What are we goin' to do now?"

"Don't you worry yourself about it none, Brother. We'll be fine."

"But where'll we go? We ain't got nowheres to go."

"Like I said, don't worry. I heard from talkin' to that ornery belly cheater of a cook that there's a town west of here across the mountains, no more'n a hundred miles. Place called Taos. There's lots of white folks livin' there—Americans. Not like all them damn Mexicans we seen in Las Vegas. We'll go there."

Chapter Four

Abel Pate stood slack-jawed in the Plaza at Santa Fe. The arrival of freight wagons earlier in the day had the town in the throes of a fandango. Normally coarse bullwhackers were resplendent in finery laid by for just this occasion, and the men themselves were scrubbed and scoured clean of trail dirt, faces shaved, and hair slicked down.

Likewise, Santa Fe señoritas and eager children, and all manner of local people, crowded the Plaza to fete the arrival of *los carros* and greet *los Americanos*.

The people of the city never wearied of making merry when freight trains rolled into town. Singing and dancing, dining and drinking, and celebratory pops from fresh crackers on bullwhips created an exotic confusion the likes of which Abel had never experienced, or even imagined.

Abel held the hand of Emma Lewis, her younger sister Jane clinging to his other arm. Sarah—Abel's mother—and Mary, the eldest of the Lewis girls, stood aside, unsure of the propriety of such rambunctious behavior in the middle of the day. Or anytime, for that matter, to Sarah's way of thinking.

Even as the fiesta forged ahead, work went on in the streets away from the Plaza. Wagon masters oversaw the unloading of freight into the customs warehouses, administrators collected *derechos de arancel*—duties and tariffs, and *elsorbono*—off-the-books payments to officials in the hope of preferential treatment. Brokers and merchants from the city and outlying communities haggled over prices for American fabrics—cottons, silks, calicoes, velvets, drillings, shirtlings—as well as notions, hardware, preserved foodstuffs, and other goods.

At those same customs warehouses, Lee Pate and Daniel Lewis found their fascination with Santa Fe de Nuevo México. They wandered back streets and alleys, absorbing the furor and flurry of commerce—assessing, anticipating the possibilities of their own entry into trade as a means of providing for their families in this alien land.

The Pate family had traveled a thousand miles to reach this place. Daniel Lewis and his girls had migrated at least as far. The Pates, outbound from Tennessee, met the Lewises—who originated in Missouri—while the families wintered in Fort Smith. Both men, fleeing dissimilar circumstances not to their liking, felt themselves to be refugees. Perhaps the refuge they sought might be found here in New Mexico—or, perhaps, Alta California, or even south, elsewhere in Mexico.

As the day lengthened, festivities at the Plaza grew more raucous, the celebrations more rambunctious. Unfamiliar foods teased Abel's taste buds. He offered tastes of tamales, tacos, burritos, and other savory fare to his mother and the Lewis girls. Corn, beans, and squash in all manner of dishes; beef, mutton, and cabrito—goat—all, it seemed, seasoned with chili peppers. Even with the bite of unfamiliar spices on his tingling tongue and stinging lips, the foods proved irresistible. But, unsure of the contents, Abel declined drinks from the bottles, jugs, jars, glasses, and mugs from which others imbibed freely.

And, always, came invitations for the Lewis girls, and even Abel's mother, Sarah, to dance. Visiting bullwhackers and local celebrants alike offered their hands, some well-mannered and polite, others rude, crude, and ill-mannered. The women refused them all.

With the waning light of the day casting long shadows, a

young man with the intention of a mustache shadowing his upper lip, and wearing tattered workman's clothing and a wide-brimmed sombrero, staggered up to young Jane.

"*¿Quieresbailar?*" he said, miming a dance.

Jane, wide-eyed, shook her head.

"*¡Venga! ¡Vamos a bailar!*" he slurred.

The girl drew back, her fingers gouging Abel's forearm. "No! I do not want to dance!"

"*¡Sí! ¡Bailarconmigo!*" The young man grabbed Jane's arm and tried to pull her away.

Abel stepped in front of Jane and pushed the man's arm away. "She don't want to dance with you. Leave her alone."

The dancer tried to push Abel aside. Instead, Abel put the palms of his hands on the man's chest and shoved him away. He stumbled and fell, bumping into and pushing aside others in the crowd as he went down. The man pushed himself upright and stood swaying with feet wide apart. He swept the sombrero off his head and let it hang down his back, a leather thong holding it around his neck. The hair it released swept down his forehead, dangling in oily strands that fell over his eyes. The people clustered around backed away, forming a circle around the two men.

Abel did not see where the knife in the man's hand came from.

The man tossed his head to flip the hair aside and lunged at Abel. Abel sidestepped the thrust of the knife and, without thinking, landed a long, looping blow on his attacker's jaw. The man went down and was slow to rise. Abel stood, waiting. The man rose to one knee and, without standing fully upright, lunged again at Abel, leading with an upward thrust of the blade. Again, Abel sidled to miss the knife and, again, landed a fist, this one an uppercut, to the chin. The blow stopped the attacker's forward motion and he dropped to the ground. Abel stood over him, breathing heavily, fists hanging at his side.

Pushing through the crowd came a uniformed man. Abel did not know if he was a policeman or a soldier. The man wore a blue tunic, crossed from the shoulders with wide white straps that secured a sheathed dagger and a bayonet on one hip, and a leather ammunition box on the other. A tall, billed cap with a flat top and feather sat on his head, secured by a leather chin strap. He carried a musket in one hand and used the other to push aside onlookers.

The man stepped into the space within the circle of people and stopped. He saw the man on the ground, Abel standing over him. With the barrel of the rifle he gestured for Abel to step aside, then said something in Spanish to a man on the fringe of the crowd. The man knelt beside Abel's attacker and rolled him over. He held his cheek low to the unresponsive man's nose to feel for breath, then laid an ear to the chest. The man sat upright and nodded his head.

Prompted by another outpouring of instructions from the officer, the downed man was lifted to his feet, arms slung over supporting shoulders, and half dragged, half carried away. The officer turned toward Abel, gestured with the rifle barrel, and followed Abel through the parting crowd, the gun at his back.

Abel's mother and the Lewis girls followed, pushing through the crowd as it closed in the wake of the officer and his captive. Once clear of the Plaza and the crushing mass of people, the women hurried to keep up. Sarah told Mary to take Emma and Jane to the wagons, then to see if she could find Abel's father and tell him what was happening. She would follow along to the jail, or wherever Abel was being taken.

The officer pushed Abel through the door of a building, unmarked save the flag flying above it. Sarah shoved her way inside, despite half-hearted attempts to keep her out. The officer pointed to a row of chairs against the wall, and Sarah took a seat. Abel, prodded along with the rifle barrel, walked past the entryway, stopping at a wall with a window and a closed door. A uniformed man behind the window carried on a conversation with the officer who held Abel. Abel understood none of it, as the men spoke in Spanish.

The uniformed man stepped away from the window. Locks clattered and clicked and the door opened. Abel was pushed through. Another man in uniform signaled him to follow. They passed down a long hallway, past a row of offices and other rooms, most with closed doors. The hallway ended at a door built from heavy timbers reinforced with metal straps and bolts, held to the wall with immense iron hinges. An outsized key turned the lock.

The hallway continued beyond the door, lined with locked cells rather than offices. Abel was pushed into the first, largest cell. He looked around the room: three mud-covered adobe walls, the fourth wall a gridwork of metal bands, and a door of the same make. Sitting at random on an adobe bench, built like a tall step along the bottom of the walls, were several men. A few stared at the Americano with hate-filled eyes, some with curiosity, others with no expression. Still others slumped in sleep, or, perhaps, passed out from too much drink.

No one sat on either of the wooden plank benches across the center of the cell. Abel sat astraddle one end of one backless bench and lay down, staring at a ceiling made from row upon row of slender sticks laid across wooden beams that disappeared into the adobe walls. There was nothing else in the holding cell save a clay pot in one corner, the stink of which revealed it as a toilet.

Night had fallen when Lee and Daniel returned to the wagons. Mary was there, having long since given up finding them in Santa Fe's warren of streets and alleys.

Sarah, too, was waiting, eyes red and wet, twisting the skirt of her apron in her hands. "Lee! Thank the Lord you are here!"

"What is it, Sarah?"

"It's Abel. He's been arrested by the Mexicans."

"Arrested? For what?"

"It's my fault," Jane said, stepping out of the shadows.

"Jane—"

"It's true, Missus Pate! It's on account of me!"

Sarah wrapped an arm around Jane's shoulder. "Now, child. It isn't your fault."

Lee said, "Would someone just say what happened?"

Sarah, Mary, and Jane all started talking at once. Daniel held up both hands. "Please!"

The women fell silent. Lee said, "Sarah, you start."

"We was at the Plaza watchin' the goin's-on there. Some fellow in his cups asked Jane to dance—and he weren't the first. We was all fendin' off invitations, Jane and Mary and Emma— even me, if you can imagine. Most all of 'em left off when we told 'em 'no,' but this one, he was in his cups and wouldn't take 'no' for an answer. Then he took aholt of Jane, wantin' to make her dance with him."

Sarah stopped, wiped her eyes and nose with a wadded handkerchief. She pushed a lock of escaped hair behind an ear. "Abel pushed him away. That Mexican was so potted he fell down. When he come up, he come at Abel with a knife. Abel busted him one and knocked him down, but he didn't let up. That boy come at Abel again, and Abel walloped 'im again. Knocked him out colder'n a wedge."

Daniel moved beside Jane and cradled her in his shoulder. He whispered, "Jane, are you all right?"

She nodded.

Lee said, "Then what happened, Sarah?"

"This Mexican come along, wearin' one of them peacock uniforms you see paradin' around. He took Abel away."

"Where did he take him?"

"Just some place—I can't say what kind of place it is. Everything there was written in Spanish. Wouldn't nobody talk to me. They just let me sit there for the longest time. Then they shoved me on out the door once it was comin' on dark. Guess they was closin' up for the night. I gave 'em what-for, but they didn't pay no mind."

"Can you find this place, Sarah?"

"I sure as hell can!"

"Now, Sarah, coarse language will not help the situation. Come along. Show me."

"I'll be coming with you," Daniel said.

Lee thought for a moment. "Maybe you had best stay here with your girls. Could be it ain't safe to leave 'em."

Emma stepped forward. "Papa won't be staying. And neither will we. Come along, girls."

"Now, wait a min—"

"There is no use arguing, Mister Pate. I will not stay here a minute longer worrying what has happened to Abel. We are coming, like it or not."

Lee shook his head. "Lead the way, Sarah. I can see good sense won't change anything."

Sarah snorted. "Good sense! What in God's name would you know about good sense, Lee Pate? If you had even a smidgen of it, we wouldn't be in this godforsaken place."

"Now, Sarah . . ."

"Don't you 'Now Sarah' me! Not that long ago I had me three boys. Now I ain't got a one—and it's all owin' to you and your fool notions."

Lee hung his head and said nothing.

The Lewises looked on, not knowing how—or if—they should respond. Finally, Daniel cleared his throat. "Well, come along, then. Let us see about getting one of those boys back. We will

41

accomplish nothing standing here."

Sarah found her way back to the building that held Abel. "This is it. This is the place."

Lee stepped up and tried to open the door, but found it locked. He knocked. After a moment, he pounded harder. And again.

Light spilled out of the building when a peep window, cut into the door, opened. A face appeared, dark against the light from behind. "*¿Quién es?¿Quédeseas?*"

"Let me in. You got my boy in there."

"*¿Qué?¿Quédeseas?*"

"My boy's in there. Abel Pate. Let me in."

"*Vete,*" the man said, and slammed the window shut.

Lee pounded on the door again, and the peep window opened.

"*¡Vete! Vuelve mañana,*" the man inside shouted. And again, the window slammed shut.

This time, no amount of pounding would open it.

The families traipsed back to the wagons and turned in. Sarah did not sleep, fitful through the night. Her agitation awakened Lee repeatedly. With the first hint of dawn, he abandoned their blankets and stirred up the fire. The coffeepot had just come to a boil when Sarah joined him. She picked up the pot, filled a cup, and handed it to Lee. He sat down on a box and stared through the steam into the cup.

"Do you think they'll let you into that place this morning?"

Lee shrugged. "Can't say. I aim to try."

"Maybe you need someone along who talks Mexican."

"Maybe so. If there ain't no one there who can understand me, I'll find me one of them bullwhackers or a wagon boss that talks their lingo. Or maybe knows someone who does."

Daniel stepped into the firelight. "I concur. We must, at the very least, establish communication if we are to extricate Abel

42

from this mess."

Lee nodded.

"Let us be off, then."

"Ain't no need for you to come, Daniel."

"I tried to tell my Emma that very thing. She was having none of it. Perhaps you would like to try telling her. She is mightily concerned about the boy, and insists I accompany you."

Lee smiled. "No thanks. I don't reckon I could change her mind. I am obliged for your company." He sipped at the coffee, now cooled enough to drink. "Sit down, Daniel. Sun ain't nowhere near bein' up yet. Have yourself a cup of coffee. Then we'll be on our way."

CHAPTER FIVE

The door was still locked when Lee and Daniel arrived at the place Abel was being held. As he had done the night before, Lee pounded on the door. As before, the peephole window opened. The man's face flashed recognition, then annoyance.

"*¿Qué es lo que quieres ahora?*"

"Anybody in there talk English?"

The man screwed up his face in disgust. "*Un minuto,*" he said, and slammed the window.

Lee raised a fist to knock again.

"Wait, Lee," Daniel said. "I do believe that whatever he said says someone will be with us in a minute. Perhaps it is best that we do not antagonize him further."

Lee hesitated, then lowered his fist. "I'll wait. But I ain't waitin' long."

Shortly before Lee lost his patience and pounded the door again, the peep window opened to reveal another face. Lee assumed the man to be of greater importance, as his face was freshly shaved, his air oiled and neatly combed, and his moustache sharply trimmed.

"What is it, Señor?"

"I see you speak English. Thank the Lord."

"What is it you want?"

"You-all have my boy in there. Abel Pate. Been in there since yesterday."

The peep window closed and the lock on the door ratcheted

and clicked as it turned. The door opened.

"Come inside, por favor," the man said. "I am Francisco Guzmán. Follow me."

The three men walked past the chairs in the entry room. The man at the reception window, the same man who refused them entry last night and answered their knock this morning, stood behind the reception window. Guzmán said something to him and he unlocked the door to allow them entry into the secure area beyond. Lee and Daniel followed along the hallway, at the end of which stood the heavy, fortified door leading to the cells. They followed Guzmán as he turned through a doorway into an office.

"Have a seat, por favor." Then, "I have some knowledge of your son's situation, but have not been fully informed." He smiled. "I have only recently arrived, you see. If you will allow me a moment, I shall learn the particulars." The man smiled again, and bowed slightly. *"Perdóneme,"* he said, and closed the door as he left.

"He seems a reasonable fellow," Daniel said.

Lee sniffed. "We'll see."

The official returned after a few minutes carrying a paper. He sat at the desk and placed the paper before him. He took a sheet of paper from a drawer and laid it atop the other. "Now, gentlemen, how may I be of service to you?"

"Like I said, I've come about my boy. Abel Pate."

"Yes, Señor. And what is your name please?"

"Pate. Lee Pate."

Guzmán dipped his pen and took down the name, then smiled at Daniel. "And you?"

"Daniel Lewis."

After writing that down, he asked Lee his understanding of the situation.

"Way I heard it, he—Abel—was protectin' our womenfolk

from uncouth and untoward advances by a drunken Mexican boy when one of your policemen arrested him."

Guzmán put the pen in its holder and leaned back in his chair. "First, Señor Pate, the man who 'arrested' your son was not *policía*—he is *un soldado,* a soldier of the army. On occasion, to assist us in enforcing the laws, soldiers will take suspected lawbreakers into custody, and we will hold them for investigation." Guzmán shrugged. "So, you see, Señor Pate, your son is not under arrest at all."

"Then I can take Abel with me? You're lettin' him go?"

"That I cannot say, Señor. We will hold him until such time as we are convinced of the facts."

"Seems like to me the 'facts,' as you call them, is pretty easy to understand."

"Perhaps. Perhaps not."

"What's not to understand? That drunk Mexican boy was vexing our womenfolk. Young Jane, in particular."

Guzmán leaned forward and placed the palms of his hands on the desktop, then leaned farther toward Lee. "It is important for you to keep in mind, Señor Pate, that 'Mexican boy,' as you call him, is a citizen of Santa Fe. You, on the other hand, are merely a visitor in our city." He sat back and inhaled then exhaled loudly, shaking his head. "You Americanos—you come here and act as if we are savages, barbarians. That we, who have resided here for hundreds of years, must adopt your ways, must recognize your supposed superiority in all things."

Lee held up a hand. "I assure you, Mister Guzmán, I don't think no such thing. The only savage I'm talkin' about is that boy as was botherin' Jane. Far as that goes, it could be he's a fine boy, when he ain't drunk. But from what I was told—by my wife and both of Jane's sisters—is that he was told by Jane that she did not want to dance with him but he kept after her. When he took ahold of her, meanin' to drag her away, my boy stepped in. Kid come at him with a knife. What Abel done wasn't nothin' more than defend himself. That, and defend Jane."

Guzmán listened to it all, working at his teeth with his tongue. From time to time he dipped his pen and wrote something on the paper.

Daniel cleared his throat. "If I may say something, sir, I believe I can add to your understanding."

Guzmán nodded.

"My family consists of three daughters—four, actually, but one remains in Fort Smith." He waved his hand. "That is neither here nor there. My three daughters, the three with me, are twenty, sixteen, and fourteen years of age, more or less. Jane is the youngest. As we were making our way here, we encountered an encampment of traders. Comancheros, I am told they are called. I am also given to understand that their trading activities with the native tribes are not always in concert with the laws of commerce in your country." He waved his hand in the air again, as if wafting away the words.

"Be that as it may, one of those ruffians followed us, covertly, when we moved on. A day or two later, our Jane ventured away from the camp—for reasons it would be indelicate of me to mention—and was seized by him. He attempted to abuse Jane, forcing himself upon her despite her protestations. She was rescued in time, thank the Lord. But, as you might imagine, the experience resulted in severe distress, and, it is sad to say, the girl has yet to fully recover."

Daniel sniffed, and wiped a tear from his eye before it could fall. "Although I was not present during the incident at the Plaza now under consideration, I believe the young man may have reminded our Jane of her attacker—as I understand it, they are not dissimilar in appearance. Her fear, you see, was real, and not without cause."

Guzmán studied Daniel for a moment, then started writing.

As the pen scratched its path across the page, Daniel said, "It may bear mentioning, sir, that during the aforementioned circumstance with the Comanchero, it was Abel Pate who saved our Jane from certain molestation and, most likely, murder."

The official sat for several minutes, occasionally adding to his notes on the page. He asked a few follow-up questions. Then he placed the pen in its holder and leaned back in his chair, interlacing his fingers behind his head. He looked from one man to the other. Lee shifted in his seat again and again, bending down with elbows on knees, sitting upright with arms folded, propping an ankle on the opposite knee, crossing and re-crossing his legs.

Guzmán leaned forward and folded his hands atop the desk. "Mister Pate, what are your intentions here in Santa Fe, in Nuevo Mexico?"

Lee, with wrinkled brow, considered the question. "Don't rightly know as yet, Mister Guzmán. We only just got here and ain't had time to get our bearings. Could be we'll stay here if we can see our way clear. Daniel and me, we've discussed goin' into trade—maybe open up a store or some such. Soon as I can, I'd like to find me a piece of land and take up farmin'. Or stock raisin'. I done both back in Tennessee." He shrugged. "Mayhap there won't be no chance for us hereabouts. Could be we'll have to move on—maybe go on to California."

Guzmán said, "In either case, you will be in the provinces of Mexico. Americanos do not always find Mexican rule agreeable."

Lee chuckled dolefully and slowly shook his head. "I have had my fill of the American government and its ways. The United States are mired in the sin of slavery and unless I miss my guess, they are soon to suffer the Lord's wrath."

Guzmán arched his eyebrows at the explanation. He turned to Daniel. "And you, Señor Lewis?"

"While my daughters and I have lived in America these past few years, we are English. We came here—to the States, rather—to join with Joseph Smith and the Latter Day Saints in the establishment of Zion. An endeavor much more in keeping with my late wife's wishes than my own, you see. But we Mormons came under attack in Missouri, as the old settlers feared our presence there. Most of the Saints fled eastward to Illinois. I, feeling refuge there would be temporary at best, resolved instead to seek opportunity in Texas.

"We took up temporary residence in Fort Smith to wait out the winter and add to our coffers. There, we met the Pates. Lee and I discussed the situation, and he convinced me, rather easily, I must say, to try Mexico rather than Texas. While my feelings for the United States are, perhaps, less resolute and entrenched than Mister Pate's, I feel no particular loyalty to a government that refuses to shield its citizens from religious persecution despite its constitutional duty to do so."

Guzmán sat leaning back in his chair studying the Americans. Lee and Daniel sat, listening to the sounds of activity beyond the door. As the morning lengthened, more people had, it seemed, come to work at the jail, or police station, or whatever the precise definition of this place may be.

The Mexican official sighed, then leaned forward in his chair and reviewed his notes. He set that page aside and scrutinized the sheet below. Taking up the pen, he shook his head and sighed again, then wrote something on the page. He sat back and read what he had written, then wrote something more on the bottom of the page with a flourish that implied a signature. He picked up the paper and blew the ink dry, then studied the page once again. He said, "I have authorized the release of Abel Pate."

"Many thanks, Mister Guzmán," Lee said. "I'm glad you saw fit to do the right thing."

Guzmán held up a finger. "*Un minuto,* Señor. It is fortunate for your son that the other boy was not seriously injured. The boy is known to us—he is not an established criminal, but we have our suspicions regarding some of his activities.

"And now, Señor, your son is likewise known to us. A penchant for violence will not endear him to the authorities, or to the people of Santa Fe. We will be watching. Should another unfortunate incident occur, it will not go well with him."

Lee stood and started to say something, but Daniel placed a hand on his arm and advised him to be quiet.

"If you will be seated, Señor, I will see to Abel's release." Guzmán left the room, closing the door behind him.

Back in the cells, Abel sat, still on the backless bench where he had spent the night. Elbows on knees and head in hands, he waited. And wondered.

Two guards appeared outside the cell, one carrying a tin pail, the other dragging a metal ladle across the iron grid, raising an infernal ruckus. The locked-up men rushed forward, shoving each other out of the way and crowding toward the cell door. One of the men shoved stacks of clay bowls through a pass-through port in the door, and the prisoners handed the bowls to one another. Abel sat and watched. A ragged, dirty man at the rear of the throng turned and held a bowl toward him. He stood and took the bowl, stepped back, and waited.

The prisoner nearest the door held his bowl out through the port and waited while the guard with the ladle stirred the mess of watery beans in the bucket.

Before he dipped out the first serving, an officer came through the big wooden door. "*¡Espere!*" he said.

The guard dropped the ladle into the bucket and stepped away from the door. The prisoners groused and grumbled at the interruption.

"*¡Tranquilo!*" the officer causing the delay said. "*¡Aléjate de la puerta!*"

The prisoners backed away from the door, grasping their bowls and glaring at the officer. The officer stepped up and stared through the grid, his arms clasped behind his back. He studied the prisoners one by one until fixing his stare on Abel.

"*Tú, gabacho,*" the officer said. "*Ven aquí.*"

Abel's head and eyes darted back and forth, looking for understanding. A prisoner behind him put a hand to the small of his back, and gently, but firmly, pushed him forward.

The officer took a ring of keys from his belt. He selected the proper key and unlocked the cell door and held it open. Abel stepped through and into the corridor. The officer locked the cell then opened the heavy wooden door and nodded toward Abel, gesturing for him to go out.

Down the hallway stood Francisco Guzmán, waiting outside his office door. He opened the door when Abel drew near. "In here, por favor, Señor Pate."

Abel stopped, uncertain of what fate lay inside the room. The officer behind him propelled him forward with a hard shove to his shoulder blade. He walked into the room and relief flooded through him when he saw his father and Daniel Lewis waiting there.

CHAPTER SIX

When Lee, Daniel, and Abel returned to the family encampment, Emma ran to Abel and threw her arms around him with such momentum that the two of them almost tumbled to the ground.

"Abel! Are you well? Were you mistreated? Did they harm you?" She grasped his shoulders and stepped back to arms' length. "Let me have a look at you. Tell me! Have you—"

"Emma! Please! I'm fine!"

Emma again enfolded him in her arms. Red-faced, Abel gently separated himself from her. "I'm fine, Emma. Honest."

Color rising in her face, Emma lowered her head. "I am sorry, Abel. I have been so worried." She turned and walked away.

Sarah hugged him. "Oh, Abel, I'm so glad you're all right."

"Yes, Ma. I'm fine."

She took him by the arm and led him toward the cook fire. "You must be hungry."

Abel nodded, and sat down on a box. No sooner was he settled than Sarah put a plate in his hands. "Eat. I've kept it warm for you."

The beans on the plate, thick with chunks of bacon, looked more appetizing than those in the bucket at the jail.

"Thanks, Ma."

"Eat. I'll get you some bread. And there's rice pudding."

Jane handed him a tin cup filled with water. "Are you sure you are all right?"

He smiled at the girl. "Yes. I'm as fine as frog hair." He sipped the cool water. "Thanks, Jane. This tastes right good."

"Tell us what-all happened, Lee," Sarah said as she dropped a biscuit on Abel's plate. "I'll get a plate of food for you and Mister Lewis."

Lee carried a cup of coffee to Daniel, then sat on the wagon tongue beside him and sipped from his own. "Well, they was a man there that spoke English, thank goodness. Name of Francisco Guzmán. He was some kind of in charge, seems like. Leastways them others there done what he said. From what he told us, that boy that handled Jane and attacked Abel ain't the worst they got in Santa Fe. But he sure ain't one of the best, neither. He—that Guzmán—don't think that boy'll be botherin' us anymore."

Emma said, "What about Abel?"

"Oh, he didn't have much to say about Abel in particular. Painted him and most all Americans with the same brush— seems most folks hereabouts don't take too kindly to 'Americanos.' They all think that we all think they're a lower-down kind of humans or some such. But, he could see why Abel whomped that boy, once Daniel told him why young Jane was so afeared of him. That, and because that boy come at him with a knife."

Sarah asked Daniel if that was his understanding of the conversation.

"Indeed. I believe that sums it up rather well."

"All except for one thing," Abel said.

All the families turned to Abel. Mary asked the question.

"He said the police would be watchin' me. Said I must have a bad temper, and was likely to cause more trouble."

Sarah scoffed and swept a lock of hair aside, tucking it into her bonnet. "But you never caused no trouble! It was that damned Mexican boy that caused the trouble!"

"Even so, he said they'd be keepin' an eye me." He shook his head. "I ain't been in this town a week, and already I got folks against me." He looked from one parent to the other. "I'm awful sorry, Ma. And Pa. I never meant to be a burden."

"Don't you worry none, Abel. Like your Ma said, you wasn't behind this. There ain't no need to borrow trouble—you just go on about your business and don't worry none about the police. They ain't likely to find cause to bother you no more."

Lee stood and handed his empty plate and coffee cup to Sarah. Daniel did the same. Lee said, "Now, Son, Daniel and I are goin' on over to the Plaza to the Governor's Palace. See if we can see this fellow named Armijo about what we need to do to improve our situation here and start earnin' us some money. I'll be obliged if you'll stay here and keep watch over the womenfolk and whatnot."

"Sure, Pa."

The portico of the Palace of the Governors, Palacio de los Gobernadores, lined the north side of the Plaza. Vendors sat in the shade of the portico, their wares spread before them on blankets. Inside, and within the palace grounds, were offices, ceremonial and reception rooms, living quarters for the governor, servant's quarters, barracks and an arsenal for the military, as well as stables and vegetable gardens.

Lee and Daniel attempted to talk with several of the functionaries who insulated the governor and other high officials from having to deal with people. They failed numerous times in finding one who spoke English. Someone finally directed them to a secretary or clerk of some kind who understood English, and spoke the same with a heavy accent. Under an embroidered vest, the man wore a brilliant white shirt stiff with starch, with protective sleeves over the cuffs. Lee got the feeling he and Daniel were keeping the man from more important work.

"How may I be of help?"

"Well," Lee said, "we ain't rightly sure. We—"

"If you do not know what you want, I do not know how to help you," the man said with a sniff.

"Beggin' your pardon, Mister, we would like to see a man named Armijo. I believe he's the governor."

The man sniffed again. "Of course he is. Why would you like to see Gobernador Armijo?"

Lee felt in his pockets and found a scrap of paper. He unfolded it, read what was written on it, and put it back in his pocket. "We seen a fellow over in Las Vegas, man name of Hilario Gonzales. We seen him in his office, and he said we needed to see this Armijo once we got here."

Another sniff. "I know of this Hilario Gonzales. A minor functionary."

Lee shrugged. "All the same, he's the one told us to see Armijo."

"And?"

"And that's why we're here."

The man shook his head and *tsk-tsk*ed. "Surely you do not expect to see Gobernador Armijo without . . . without . . . how do you say? . . . *la cita* . . . the appointment."

"Well, that's why we come here—to see Mister Armijo. If we need an appointment, then put us down in his book, or whatever you need to do to get it done."

The man shook his head, pressed his lips tight, and sighed long and slow. "But, sir, it is not I who keeps the *gobernador*'s calendar."

"Listen here, you. I'm doin' my level best to be polite and mind my manners. But my patience is wearin' mighty thin. We ain't got nothin' but the runaround since we got here. You're the first one they've trotted out that speaks English, and you ain't said nothin' but 'no.' Either you help us out here, or find somebody who will—else I'm likely to do something we'll likely both be sorry for."

The man tipped his head back and stared down his nose at Lee. Their eyes locked until Daniel interrupted the silence.

"I say, sir. Begging your pardon. We wish only to see Governor Armijo—or, perhaps, Guadalupe Miranda, who Mister Gonzales also named—in relation to acquiring a license to trade, or perhaps obtain land for cultivation and grazing. We are family men, and hope to make our homes here. That is our purpose. Should you be able to assist us in our inquiries, we would be most grateful."

The man thought for a time. Then, "I see. This is a matter most complicated. That which you seek is not always easily accomplished. If I might make a suggestion . . ."

"Certainly."

"There is a man. He is a representative of the Americano government—not altogether formal, you see, lacking the proper *exequator* from Ciudad de México, the City of Mexico. Even so, Gobernador Alvarez permits this man to act as consul. His name is Manuel Álvarez." The clerk told the Americans where to find him.

"I swear, Daniel, I come right close to takin' that fellow by the throat. He sorely tried my patience," Lee said as they made their way through the streets.

Daniel chuckled. "He was an officious little git, for certain. At long last, however, he may have charted the proper course for us."

"I surely do hope so. My Sarah, she's gettin' mighty testy waitin' on me to get us settled."

The seekers were somewhat stymied on reaching the place they were told they would find the American Consul, Manuel Álvarez. Rather than an office, it was a commercial building, a store. The largest store, in fact, they had seen in Santa Fe.

Inside, displays of goods filled the area between the entrance and the long counter that crossed the breadth of the building. Three men worked behind the counter, outfitted in aprons over white shirts. Farther back, in the dim recesses, were rows and rows of high shelves stocked with goods. From time to time, workers bustled into and out of sight, pulling stock off or piling it onto the shelves.

Lee and Daniel watched customers come and go as they waited a turn with one of the clerks. They chose one who looked to be American, with a pale, freckled face and hair a sandy color tinged with what Daniel called ginger.

They stepped up to the counter as he wrote in a ledger book, recording the previous customer's transaction. He said, without looking up, *"¿Le puedo ayudar?"*

Neither Lee nor Daniel knew how to respond. The man finished his entries in the account book and looked up, eyes widening at the sight of the two fair-skinned men before him. "Yes? May I help you?"

"Well!" Lee said. "You speak English!"

The man nodded. "I do. I seldom do, though. Don't see many of your kind here, except when a freight train makes town from the States."

"I don't suppose you would be Manuel Álvarez."

"You suppose right. Señor Álvarez is my employer."

"What would a man have to do to see this Álvarez fellow? Over there at the Governor's Palace, they told us we should talk to him."

The clerk closed the ledger book and slid it onto a shelf beneath the counter. "I believe Señor Álvarez is in his office. Let me see if he is busy."

Gone only a short time, the clerk returned to say Álvarez would see them in his office, then directed them to the end of the counter, where he lifted a hinged section of the countertop to allow them through. After turning around the corner of a short wall, the men saw the storeroom was much larger than what was visible from the front of the store, with shelves and tables receding into the dimness. The clerk opened a doorway and gestured for the men to enter the room beyond.

Lee stopped inside the door and looked around the room. The office was a large one, which made the expansive desk behind which a man stood seem small. On the wall behind the desk was an American flag, its blue union with twenty-six stars and the thirteen stripes of red and white the brightest colors in the room. Spines of books lined up in ranks and rose in tiers on the shelves of a glass-fronted bookcase. A buffalo hide, tacked to the opposite wall, blended with another robe of its kind, draped over the back of a couch. Two stuffed chairs faced the couch, with a long, low, table between. On the adjacent wall hung a sun-bleached buffalo skull and some stretched animal hides—Lee recognized beaver and raccoon and wolf, and believed another skin to have once dressed a mountain lion. Woven wool blankets hung over the chair backs, and a rug of similar make covered the plank floor beneath the table and chairs.

The man standing behind the desk allowed the visitors a moment to take in the room, then said, "Gentlemen—I am Manuel Álvarez. I am told you wish to speak to me. Please, have a seat." Rather than invite them to sit in the soft chairs, he indicated two wooden chairs facing his desk.

Before sitting, Lee reached across the desk to shake hands, and Daniel followed suit. Álvarez took each hand in turn, a forced smile and a nod accompanying each handshake.

"If you don't mind my sayin' so, Mister Álvarez," Lee said as he sat. "You don't look like you've come from the States."

Álvarez shrugged. "That is so. I was born in Spain. I left the country of my birth for Mexico as a young man. I traveled from there to Cuba, then to Saint Louis—do you know Saint Louis?"

Daniel said, "Yes, yes—Saint Louis. I passed through there, only briefly. Our family emigrated from England and settled in Missouri—in a city called Far West, in the northwestern part of the state, in Caldwell County. Caldwell County would not have existed during your tenure there, I expect. It was established in 1836; 1837, perhaps."

Álvarez shook his head. "You are right. I do not know Caldwell County. To continue. After Saint Louis, I came here, to Santa Fe, when Nuevo Mexico was yet a province of Virreinato de Nueva España—New Spain. But, alas, I was expelled from my home and business after the Spanish rulers in Ciudad de México capitulated to the insurgents and Mexico declared independence from Spain, leading to the eviction of Spaniards such as myself.

"For a time, I trapped for furs. I was a 'free trapper,' if you know the meaning—an independent agent, coming and going when and where I pleased. Later, I led a brigade for the American Fur Company. Hence, the décor you see," Álvarez said, with a wave toward the skins on the far wall. "A few years ago, the government in Washington appointed me to serve as consul here, and I returned to Santa Fe. As you have seen," he said with a wave of his arm toward the store beyond the walls, "I have been fortunate to re-establish myself in trade here. Alas, my tenure as consul has not been as successful. The Mexicans do not offer the formal recognition due a representative of a superior nation such as the United States of America. Gobernador Armijo allows me to perform my consular duties to some extent, but makes it clear I do so according to his pleasure." He sighed and raised his hands, palms upward.

After a moment, the consul continued. "Still, there are certain things I can do to further American interests here, despite the incompetence of the Mexicans. Now, what is it you wish of me?

But first," Álvarez said with a waggle of his finger, "how came you gentlemen to be in Santa Fe?"

CHAPTER SEVEN

Daniel Lewis related his tale. He told how he left his home in Manchester, England, with his family to join the Latter Day Saints in America after converting to the faith. He told how his wife took sick and died aboard the ship that carried them across the ocean, leaving him with four daughters to raise.

"Praise be," he said, "the girls were well past the need for diapers or I do not believe I could have coped. Martha and Mary, in fact, were all but grown women—Martha around about sixteen or seventeen then, with Mary but two years behind. Martha married in Fort Smith during our journey here, and is no longer with us. Mary—near twenty years old now, she is—is still with me, as are her younger sisters—Emma, a young woman herself now at sixteen, and Jane, who has turned fourteen, I believe, or will soon do so." Daniel smiled and shook his head. "They grow up so quickly, I cannot keep pace."

Álvarez studied Daniel for a moment, then turned to Lee. "And you, sir?"

"The Pate family hails from Shelby County, Tennessee. I was a planter and stockman there, like my father before me."

Álvarez's brow furrowed as he waited for Lee to continue. "But no longer, it would seem."

Lee nodded. "What with the way things was there—and elsewhere in the States, leastways the South—it had become such that I could no longer abide bein' a part of it. I had come to believe, through manifestations from the Almighty, that slave-

61

holding is evil. It will be the downfall of the nation. Finally, it come to mind to be shut of the place."

The wrinkles and ridges in the consul's forehead were even more pronounced. "So you sold out and came to this place?"

"More or less. I've got—had—a younger brother, you see. Ben. He was my brother, bless his heart, but he was not a man who lived by God's word. Greed and pride infected him. Seemed like Ben couldn't ever own enough of anything—including slaves. He and I did not see eye to eye on much. He resented my holdin' the Pate farm—never mind his sharp wheelin' and dealin' had give him more land than mine, twenty times over.

"We had a disagreement, Ben and me, over his abusin' of one of his darkies. I cleaned his plow, and he vowed to put the law on me. Which he would've. And they'd have done his biddin', what with him havin' most of 'em, from the sheriff to the judge, in his pocket. My sharin' of my opinions on bondage didn't set well with folks thereabouts, neither."

Lee sighed long and slow. "But all that's behind me. Left the whole of it back in Shelby County."

Álvarez sat with his elbows on the arms of his chair, fingers interlaced beneath his chin. He turned the rotating chair slowly back and forth. "And your family?"

"Sarah and I was blessed with three sons. The two eldest, Richard and Melvin, left us back in Las Vegas to make their own way—they didn't countenance my bringin' the family out here. It pains me to say they came to think ill of their father, and wanted no more part of me or my ways."

Lee bowed his head and sighed, then met the eyes of Álvarez. "The youngest boy—Abel—he's near growed up himself. A good help to his ma and me, Abel is."

"And this Abel—he is the one involved in the unfortunate incident in the Plaza?"

Lee sat back in his chair and his eyebrows arched upward. "How'd you come to know 'bout that?"

"Francisco Guzmán, of the *policia*, informed me."

"I hope he told you that it wasn't none of my boy's fault."

With a shrug, Álvarez said, "Señor Guzmán did not share the details. He only informed me as a 'courtesy'—which he does not hesitate to do at every opportunity. The presence of Americanos in Santa Fe does not please him. He apprises me of every indiscretion, real or perceived, by a citizen of the United States."

"Well, just so's you know, Mister Álvarez, what Abel done wasn't no more than defend himself." Lee turned and nodded toward Daniel. "And protect Daniel's youngest from the unwanted advances of that Mexican boy."

Álvarez nodded. "And now, to business." The consul slid open a desk drawer and removed a sheet of paper. Scrap paper, it appeared. Writing covered one side, lined through and with insertions and notations in the margins, as if a draft of a letter or document. He placed it on the desktop, clean side up, then, from another drawer, took a stub of a pencil and rolled it across his tongue and laid his forearms on the desk, framing the paper. "What is it you wish of me?"

Lee and Daniel exchanged glances, and Lee nodded at Daniel to speak. "It is like this, you see. We are looking for opportunities to make a life here—or elsewhere, perhaps California, should it prove impossible here. We have our families to provide for. We were told in Las Vegas that we should consult with Governor Armijo, or, perhaps, Guadalupe Miranda. But, at the Governor's Palace, we were refused an audience with either man. A man who appeared to be an ordinary secretary or something, but seemed to consider himself a person of consequence, suggested we see you."

Álvarez leaned back in his chair and studied his guests. "And what is it you wish to do, precisely?"

Lee spoke. "As I said, I was a landholder back in Shelby County. Raised crops and livestock. Gettin' back to that kind of life would be to my liking."

"We have discussed, as well," Daniel said, "the notion of going into trade. Much as you have done, Mister Álvarez."

The consul tapped the lead of a pencil against a front tooth, looking from one man to the other. He settled on Lee Pate. "You will find farming and stock raising a much different proposition here than in Tennessee. We live in a desert, you must understand. Crops do not thrive as you are accustomed to them doing in your country. Here, irrigation is required. Which requires water. And so, you see, water is the commodity most valuable—land without water is of no value for cultivation."

Lee nodded. "I saw some of how farming works hereabouts, back around Las Vegas. Looked to be mostly small plots in the bottomland."

"You have observed well, Señor Pate. It is the same families who have, for many generations, tended those small holdings. You will find nothing of the 'plantation' methods here. It is a subsistence way of farming for the most part, with enough surplus to supply the needs of the local community.

"As for the raising of livestock, it, too, is not in keeping with the order of things in the States. Again, I mention the desert. You have no doubt noticed the scarcity of growth on much of our land. Brush, such as *chamisa,* and bunchgrass, will not sustain livestock as the lush pastures of the East will do. The sheep and goats, and the cattle—which are not as numerous—must be driven into the mountains to graze in spring and summer.

"The sheep and the goats are kept in small flocks and herds by the farmers. There are some large *estancias* in the outlying areas where rancheros keep sizeable herds of cattle and sheep. However, much land is required, and for one whose family is not a traditional landowner, obtaining a sufficient number of leagues to establish a rancho will be difficult, if it can be accomplished at all. Land is granted at the whim of the officials—Armijo, the *gobernador,* and Guadalupe Miranda, *el ministro,* as you have been advised."

"Well, what would a man have to do to get some land?"

Álvarez shrugged. "Who can say? Some days, Armijo is inclined to welcome Americanos and is most generous in providing land grants. The next day, it is the opposite. It is as unpredictable as the shifting winds. I have been told that dinero, *elsoborno,* the bribe, is a consideration. But this, I cannot say for a certainty." The look on Álvarez's face said otherwise.

Lee sat in silence, working his tongue and jaw, brow wrinkled and foot jiggling against the floor.

"I can tell you this, Señor Pate. There are certain requirements in the law for an Americano—or anyone who is not Mexican by birth—to own land in *Nuevo Mexico.* You must commit to obeying the laws, which differ from what you are accustomed to in the States. You must learn to speak the language, *lengua Española.* And you must convert to Catholicism. Do these things to obtain citizenship, and perhaps—perhaps—*el gobernador* will consider your petition."

Crestfallen, Lee sagged in his chair.

Álvarez watched his visitors for a time. Then, "There may be another way—if I may make a suggestion."

Both men perked up, eyes fixed on the consul.

"Mister Lewis, it is true that you are yet a widower?"

Daniel nodded.

"It is the law that any man who marries a Mexican woman is granted citizenship as a matter of course. Perhaps this is something you might consider."

Daniel said nothing. Álvarez waited. Lee looked at Daniel. Daniel looked at the floor.

A knock at the door interrupted the silence. At Álvarez's word, the door opened and the clerk who had escorted the visitors stuck his head through the gap. "*¿Un momento,* por favor, Señor Álvarez?"

Álvarez walked to the door and engaged in quiet conversation with the clerk. The talk went on for some time. Lee and Daniel sat silent, Daniel staring at the floor and Lee fidgeting. Daniel raised his head when Álvarez returned to his seat behind the desk.

Daniel cleared his throat. "Tell me, Mister Álvarez, are the procedures for obtaining a license to trade as burdensome?"

Álvarez smiled and shifted the sheet of paper on the desktop and picked up the pencil, even though he had yet to write a single word. "I am certain you will find the procedures for engaging in trade less onerous. If there is one thing in which *el gobernador* is always in favor, it is the money. With the tariffs and taxes imposed, encouraging trade is a definite means of enriching the treasury, and Armijo is an advocate of adding to government coffers." Álvarez smiled again. "And should some portion of the money taken in find its way into his *bolsa,* his pocket, I would not be surprised."

Trade was not restricted to citizens, Álvarez told Daniel and Lee. Among successful merchants were men who, like himself, had been engaged in the fur trade—men such as Robidoux, St. Vrain, and Jeantet. He explained the *derechos de arancel* and *derecho de consume,* the tariffs on imports and consumption. And he explained the acquisition of goods, most all of which arrived on freight trains from the United States, or from Mexico City, Durango, Chihuahua, or elsewhere deep in Mexico via Camino Real de Tierra Adentro, the Royal Road of the Interior.

"You must understand that most of the trade goods from the States are contracted merchandise—ordered and purchased by merchants such as myself," Álvarez said. "Still, there are wagons and trains carrying merchandise on speculation—traders who believe a buyer will be found and a profit will be made at the end of the road. When still many miles from Santa Fe, these expeditions send *avant couriers*—what you might call 'runners'—who seek buyers, bargain for better terms with customs officials, and so on. These men you must make acquaintance with if you wish to obtain the best price on goods. Otherwise, Señor Lewis," he said with a smile, "you will be forced to purchase from me, or one of my counterparts, and include our profit in the price."

Daniel nodded his understanding, but his wrinkled brow and pursed lips betrayed a mind still reckoning with the onslaught of information. Lee asked about storing and selling the merchandise—the availability of warehouse space, and buildings suitable for displaying and retailing goods.

"Aah, yes, Señor Pate. A most suitable question. I, myself, own buildings here in Santa Fe other than the one you see around you. I am confident we can come to some accommodation for rental—or even purchase, if you have the means. And, if I might suggest, there is opportunity to be found in other communities for enterprising men such as yourselves. A small store in San Juan, Abiquiu, Bernalillo, Albuquerque—who can say where fortune lies?"

The silence that followed, with Lee and Daniel deep in thought, held until interrupted by a knock on the door. Álvarez left his seat to answer the appeal. He exchanged a few hushed words with the ginger-haired clerk. Then, "Gentlemen, I am afraid my presence is required elsewhere. If you will pardon me, my man here will show you out."

Álvarez walked away with his guests, who were lost in their thoughts, barely aware of his leave-taking.

CHAPTER EIGHT

Richard and Melvin followed the stream into the valley. The passage through the mountains had taken longer than anticipated—Richard thought they may have lost the track somewhere along the way. The travelers followed Rio Pueblo de Taos, although they had no way of knowing it. Smoke hanging in the sky said people occupied the valley, and the thought of it set the saliva flowing in Richard's mouth. It had been more than a day and a night since the last of the tequila from his flask made its way down his throat, and his quivering hands and sweat-beaded brow felt the lack.

"What the hell is that?" Melvin said, jerking his horse to a stop.

Richard's horse bumped into Melvin's, jarring him out of his reverie. "Mel! Watch what you're doin', dammit!"

"Look! What is that?"

Richard followed the direction of his brother's pointing finger. "Looks like a building of some kind. Ride on ahead, and we'll see soon enough."

The river flowed on toward the building. Another like it, nearly as large, appeared as they rounded a bend. Then other structures appeared beyond.

"I ain't never seen nothin' like that," Melvin said. "Looks like a whole bunch of boxes all stacked up."

"It's somethin', all right."

"Lookee there! There's Indians around. Them buildings must be theirs."

Indians working in fields of corn and squash, and other plants the brothers did not know, stopped what they were doing and watched the riders, as did others around the pueblo. No one waved or smiled or otherwise greeted the horsemen, only stared.

"Look at that!" Melvin said. "There's people up on the tops of them buildings!" He studied the adobe structures as they rode along the creek. There were two sizeable buildings, one on each side of the river. "Them's the biggest buildings I ever seen. Weren't nothin' that big back in Memphis, even. And damned if it don't look like they're made out of mud."

The mud-plastered adobe structures rose in tiers and layers and steps as they reached skyward. "Rich, what do you reckon them big buildings is for?"

Richard craned his neck from side to side, studying the structures as they rode. "Don't know. I guess they must be houses—like a hotel, maybe, with all different rooms."

"But how do they get inside? I can't see no doors or windows anywheres."

"Damned if you ain't right, Brother. But look at all them ladders everywhere up there on the tops. Could be there's holes in the ceilings that lets 'em in."

The other buildings in the complex were not as impressive, save what looked to be a church across the way with a bell tower. It, too, was mud-covered adobe. Beyond the church, the brothers followed the river and a few miles later reached Taos. The town looked to be an architectural polyglot. As in the pueblo, adobe was at the core of most buildings. Some resembled the Indian way of building, others showed Spanish, or Mexican, influence. Others were assembled from logs, and a few from sawn lumber. Whitewash covered the exterior of a few buildings, and there were splashes of color in places.

The brothers left the river to follow a well-worn trail through the town. They soon reached the town square, or plaza, where people as varied as the architecture moved about. Richard reined up and looked around, and Melvin followed suit.

"I believe a man could get hisself a drink yonder," Richard said, with a nod toward a cantina on a side street running into the plaza.

"Ain't you hungry? Don't you think we ought to find somethin' to eat? I'm awful hungry, I am."

"Don't you worry none, Mel. There'll be plenty of time to eat later on." Richard touched his spurs to the weary horse's belly and the animal ambled across the plaza, weaving through the foot traffic and dodging mounted horses and mules and burros, halting when carts drawn by donkeys blocked the way. The riders reached the cantina and dismounted.

As they wrapped bridle reins around a hitch rail, the door of the *taberna* crashed open and a man reeled out, missing the single stone step, moving backward faster than his feet could keep pace. He fell on his back and rolled, then lifted himself to his hands and knees, wagged his bowed head back and forth and attempted to fill his lungs with ragged breaths. Drool hung in strings from his mouth and drops of blood rained from a wound on his forehead.

He stood, unsteady on his feet, and grasped the hitchrail for balance. The man was dressed in buckskin, from a band around a greasy head of hair to the soiled and stained moccasins that covered him from the knees to the soles of his feet. He wiped the blood dribbling into his eyes with the back of a hand, and, with a shake of his head and the growl of an angry animal, he started for the door.

Leaning against the jamb, filling the gap between that and the broken door, held up only by the lower hinge, was a bearded man. In one hand he held a stained and splotched wide-brimmed felt hat; in the other he carried what looked to be a club of some kind.

"You had best stop right there, *culero.*"

The door-crasher stopped, seething. The man in the doorway sailed the felt hat toward him, and he caught it out of the air.

"You go on home. And don't come back here till you learn to mind your manners, or I'll beat the hell out of you worse than what I already have."

With the hat, the man swiped the dust off his pants legs, then jerked it into place on his head, wincing as it touched the cut on his forehead. Through eyes near aflame, he stared at the man in the doorway.

"Go on. Leave now, and there won't be no hard feelings. *¿Comprende?*"

With a low growl, the man walked away, his gait unsteady. The other man hopped out the door and lowered himself to the stone step. The brothers noticed his left leg ended somewhere near the knee.

"Give me a minute to get myself put back together and you gents can c'mon inside. You look like you could use a drink." He then proceeded to strap what the Pates had thought was a club onto the stump of his leg. He finished the job, scooted backward off the step into the doorway, grabbed the jamb, and hoisted himself to his feet—rather, one foot and the peg leg. "Well, boys, don't stand there gawping. C'mon in."

Richard and Melvin ducked past the broken door and paused inside to allow their eyes to adjust to the dim light. The bearded man with the peg leg was already seated at a table, his wooden appendage propped on another chair.

"Sit," he said.

Richard stood a fallen chair upright and sat. Melvin stood, staring at the peg leg.

"Sit down, son. That wooden leg there don't bite. Howsomever, was I to unstrap it, it may well take a lick at you," the man said with a laugh.

On the table were a bottle half full of amber liquid, and two fired clay glasses—one in front of the one-legged man. Richard had already splashed the other glass full, and was emptying it in long gulps.

"Sakes alive, boy!" their host said. "You must've worked up a powerful thirst somewheres." He gestured at the barkeeper, and the man brought another bottle of the whiskey, and another glass that he set before Melvin. "Folks call me Pegleg Smith. I reckon you boys might just as well do the same." He poured Melvin a drink and refilled the glass Richard had commandeered.

Melvin sipped at the whiskey, wetting his tongue and lips and testing the flavor of the drink. Richard took a long gulp, put down the glass, and belched.

"That's good whiskey right there—tastes mighty fine. Ain't had nothin' but tequila for too long—and I ain't had none of that, these two days."

Pegleg nodded. "Well, son, this here *aguardiente* is good stuff, for certain." He sipped from his glass. "I know that for sure, on account of I make it."

Richard's eyes widened under arched eyebrows. "That right?"

"That it is. Me and ol' Simeon Turley, we been makin' this here Taos whiskey for years. He grows the wheat up north of here a ways." He took another drink. "Good stuff."

Melvin looked on as Richard queried Pegleg. The brothers learned their newfound friend had been a mountain man and fur trapper, had worked for Astor and as a free trapper, and wandered the West with Jim Bridger, Milton Sublette, Kit Carson, Bill Williams, Jim Beckwourth, Joseph Walker, Jedediah Smith, Tom Fitzpatrick, and the like—names largely unknown to the Pates, but mentioned with some reverence by Pegleg.

"But them days is gone, boys," he said as he hoisted his glass in a toast to times past. "Ain't no demand for beaver skins, and there ain't hardly no beavers left besides." Pegleg took a drink and looked to Melvin. "You ain't said a word since plantin' your backside in that there chair. Ain't done nothin' but keep an eye on my stub." He took another drink. "Go on ahead and spit it out, son."

Melvin cleared his throat and stammered some before finding the words. "How'd you come to have but the one leg? If you don't mind my askin'."

Pegleg Smith smiled. "Nah, I don't mind, son. Told the story, must be a hundred times." He swallowed off some more of the *aguardiente*. "Back in '27, it was. We was a bunch of us up in the high Rockies a good ways north of here, place called North Park, when we got us into a scrape with a party of Indian braves. Most of 'em Arapaho, they was. They fell upon us as we was comin' across this little valley. We was ridin' hell for leather to get to somewhere we could find some cover when I took an arrow in the back of this here knee I ain't got no more. I stayed mounted and we got to a stand of trees and fended them off, their arrows bein' no match for our rifles.

"We shaded up there to lick our wounds, mine bein' the worst of the lot. Leg swole up twice its size, it did, and turned black as the heart of whatever Arapaho it was that shot that arrow into it. When it took to stinkin' we knowed it was the leg or me, so we set to cuttin' it off."

Wide-eyed, Melvin leaned forward across the rough table, the story reeling him in, ever closer to Smith. Richard kept at his drinking, but was every bit as enthralled with the story.

The mountain man swallowed off some more of the Taos whiskey and went on. "I liquored m'self up much as I could and still wield a knife, and went to whittlin'."

Melvin's jaw dropped. "You? You cut off your own leg?"

Smith smiled. "Oh, no, boy. Not all of it. By the time I'd sliced through all the meat I was gettin' woozy, what with the whiskey and loss of blood and all. Then I passed out. I don't remember it happenin', but they said Milt Sublette cut through the bone whilst I was out. Then they stuck the barrel of my own rifle in the fire till it was glowin' red and seared off the end of my leg to stop it from bleedin' anymore. They could've warped the barrel of my rifle heatin' it up thataway. I'd a been madder'n hell and took it up with them boys if it had, I'm here to tell you. A good rifle don't come cheap."

Melvin waited while Pegleg emptied and refilled his glass, his own nearly as full as when he sat down. "Then what'd you do?"

"I don't recollect a whole lot of it, what with bein' sick as a gutshot buffalo. Them boys hauled me out of there on a travois. That ride was worse than gettin' shot and losin' your leg. Liked to killed me, bouncin' around on that damn thing over rocks and boulders and near gettin' tipped off the thing and whatnot.

"When finally I got to where I could tell up from down, I was a-layin' on a pile of buffalo robes in a tipi. My pards had left me with a band of Utes who promised to bury me when I died. Only they didn't, on account of I didn't. Did a damn fine job of lookin' after me, howsomever. There was this old woman who tended to my leg. She had some concoction of leaves and roots and who-knows-what all—buffalo dung, I suspect—she'd chew into a pulp and press it onto the stump. Took most all the winter, but it healed up right fine. Spent some of them winter months whittlin' this here peg leg and learnin' to hobble around on it."

Richard kept drinking and Melvin kept wishing he had something to eat as Pegleg told stories of his other adventures. Richard suspected much of it was nonsense, but did not challenge the man for fear of tasting the wooden leg. Among Pegleg's boasts was his prowess as a bar fighter, and the utility of his peg leg when employed as a shillelagh.

74

The whiskey bottle held no more than an inch or two of the Taos whiskey when the trapper ran out of steam. "Well, boys, I reckon I've made enough chin music. Tell me, what is it you-all are doin' here in Taos?"

Richard left out most of the story, but said they had been with a freight outfit on the way back to the States and had left the job after a dispute with the wagon master. "I had my fill of Mexicans already, from when we was in Las Vegas a while back. We was told there was plenty of white men up here in Taos and thought to give the place a try. Me and Mel, we're right handy, and willin' to set our hands to any job of work that comes along."

Pegleg Smith turned his glass slowly around and around on the tabletop as he listened. When Richard finished, Pegleg drained off the last of the whiskey in the glass. "I'll tell you what, boys—I got a situation that might be of interest to you-all. It'll take some time and there'll be a lot of hard ridin'."

"That'd suit us fine," Richard said.

Pegleg stood. "I got other business to attend to just now. What say you boys meet me here tomorrow, along about this time, and we'll talk."

As Pegleg stumped his way out of the cantina, Melvin watched him go. "Did he say ridin'?"

Richard poured the last of the whiskey into his glass. "He did. Hard ridin', he said."

Melvin shook his head. "How do you suppose he rides when he ain't got but one foot to put in a stirrup? Seems like it would upset a man's balance. I guess he could go bareback, but that'd wear out a man's backside pretty soon."

"Beats the hell out of me," Richard said, then gulped down the last of the Taos whiskey. He stood and hitched up his pants. "Let's go see if there's enough food in this here town to fill up that belly of yours."

75

CHAPTER NINE

The cantina door once again hung on two hinges—albeit one of them a strap of leather—when the Pate brothers returned the next day. Pegleg Smith was inside, this time at a table in the far corner. A bottle of Taos whiskey and three glasses sat on the table in front of him.

"Sit yourselves down, boys. Have yourselves a drink," Pegleg said.

Once everyone had sampled the spirits, Melvin asked Pegleg, after a good deal of hemming and hawing, if what he had told them about losing his leg was true. Smith assured them it was, and said that any one of the trappers riding with him at the time would vouch for its authenticity. He even dared the brothers to seek out the Arapaho band and ask them for verification. His answer was every bit as strong in the affirmative when Melvin asked if his using the peg leg as a weapon was a fact. Pegleg allowed that any number of broken arms, bruised ribs, and knotted heads would verify the truth of it.

"Now I got a question for you boys. Richard, yesterday when I seen you tying up at the hitch rail, I seen what looked to be a Kentucky rifle hangin' from the saddle. That so?"

Richard nodded his reply.

"Can you shoot it?"

"Well, hell yes I can shoot it."

"What I mean is, can you hit what you shoot at?"

Richard squirmed some and took a drink before answering.

76

"I don't reckon I could fool you, Mister Smith. Leastways not for long. Fact is, I'm a passable shot at best."

Pegleg nodded. "Appreciate your honesty. I've knowed plenty a pilgrim who claimed he was a deadeye shot, only to get in a shootin' scrape and find out he couldn't hit the ground with a handful of dropped buckshot if he wanted to."

"Well, I ain't that bad a shot. And I ain't ascairt of nothin'."

"And you, Melvin?"

"I can shoot some. Good as Richard, I reckon. Mostly our brother Abel did the huntin'—he can shoot the asshole out of a fruit fly at fifty paces and never flutter a wing, Abel can."

Pegleg laughed. "And where is this brother of yours?"

Melvin shrugged. "Don't know, for sure. Him and Ma and Pa and the others was headin' for Santa Fe when we left 'em back there at Las Vegas."

Smith started with another question, but Richard choked off any talk about their family situation. He said that was all in the past and it had no bearing on the present, or the future for that matter. He prodded Pegleg about the proposition he had hinted at yesterday.

"Boys, what I aim to do is head out north and west of here a good ways. Up to the Ute country. Got some business to attend to there."

Richard sat upright. "You're goin' to do business with Indians? That don't sound none too smart, 'less there's a bunch of you, like them Comancheros."

"Comancheros, eh?" Pegleg laughed. "They ain't nothin' but a bunch of misfits. Decent folks—Indians and white men alike— won't have nothin' to do with 'em. They ain't got an honest bone in 'em. No, son, what I got is legitimate business."

The confusion on Richard's face begged for an explanation.

"You see, boys, there's this friend of mine, name of Wakara, who's a big man among the Utes. Him and me go way back."

Pegleg emptied and refilled his glass. "Couple years back, Wakara gathered a bunch of young men from them bands of Utes up there. Me and Old Bill Williams and Jim Beckwourth and some others joined up with 'em and we went out to California. Been there before, we had, on the same kind of deal. But this time, we made out to do it right."

Melvin said, "What kind of deal? I don't see what you mean."

"Horses. Mules. Jacks. Them California ranchos got better horseflesh than anyplace else—and they got more of 'em."

"So you went out there to buy horses? Is that it?"

Pegleg smiled. "Let's just say we was acquirin' horses, and let it go at that."

Richard nodded in understanding. Melvin looked puzzled.

"Anyways, we gathered, must've been near three thousand head and brought 'em on across the desert to Santa Fe—the ones of 'em that didn't die. Wakara and his Utes sorted out some of their share up on the San Juan River and took 'em on home. But they left a bunch of 'em with us, to sell off in Santa Fe. They're all gone now—have been for some time—and I got silver and gold coin that's owed to Wakara."

The door opened, light brightening the *taberna* and silhouetting the man in the doorway. Richard and Melvin turned to look, squinting in the glare. Pegleg looked down to avoid it, and pulled a pistol from the sash around his waist. The door closed, and the newcomer stood there, his eyes growing accustomed to the dimness.

Pegleg said, "What is it you want, Moreno? I thought I finished with you yesterday."

The man said nothing. He raised his right hand, revealing a Green River knife, its eight-inch blade glinting in the dim lantern light. A low growl rumbled from his throat. He took two steps toward the corner table where Pegleg and the Pates sat, but stopped at the sound of the hammer on Pegleg's pistol clicking to full cock.

"We can do this two ways, Moreno. Either I shoot you where you stand, or I beat the hell out of you with my wood leg, like I did yesterday. Guess I didn't do a good enough job of it—but I'm willin' to have another go."

Moreno stood, shifting his weight from one foot to the other, the knife blade trembling in his hand.

"Come to think of it, Moreno, there's another way. You can slide that pig sticker back into its sheath and walk on out of here, no hard feelin's. Way I see it, that's the onliest way you'll leave here on your feet."

With a snarl, Moreno leapt forward. Richard and Melvin jumped backward from the table, their chairs clattering to the floor.

"Damn," Pegleg said under his breath. He pulled the trigger and blinding white smoke followed the ball out of the pistol barrel.

The fog dissipated, revealing Pegleg Smith still sitting in his chair. The pistol sat on the table before him, still wisping tiny tendrils of smoke. Moreno lay on his back on the floor, the force of the ball having halted his forward motion and tipped him over backward. A dark red stain spread across his chest as blood oozed from a hole in his begrimed buckskin shirt with every beat of his fading heart.

Pegleg pushed back from the table and stood, then stumped his way over and looked down at the dying man. "Damn," he said, again under his breath. The other patrons had to strain to hear him say, "I told you it didn't have to be this way, Moreno." He swiveled on his wooden leg and walked back to the table and sat. He swallowed a mouthful of whiskey. "May as well sit back down, boys. We got business to talk about."

It took the Pate brothers some time to overcome the shock of it all and come to their senses. They righted their chairs and sat down. Richard drained off the whiskey in his glass as fast as he could swallow, and splashed some on the tabletop in his haste to refill. Melvin only stared at their host.

"I didn't want to shoot him. Howsomever, the sonofabitch gave me no choice."

The brothers watched as the bartender and one of his patrons carried the dead Moreno out the door. By the time they returned, conversation once again buzzed, and it was as if nothing untoward had happened.

"What do you think, boys?" Pegleg said.

Richard pondered for a time, staring at the tabletop where Pegleg's pistol still sat. Then the mountain man picked it up and recharged it with powder and ball.

"You know, I seen a new kind of pistol down in Santa Fe a couple years ago, when we come back from California that time. Old Bill, he was holdin' one for security from a freighter lookin' to buy some mules. Called a Colt somethin' or other. Holds five shots in a wheel kind of thing."

Melvin perked up. "Our brother Abel, he's got him a pair of 'em! Colt's Paterson Revolvers, they're called. He got 'em off our uncle Ben, back in Shelby County."

Pegleg slid the pistol back into his sash. "I aim to get me one, when it comes clear they're reliable. Havin' five shots in hand would be right useful at times." He paused for a drink. "Now then, boys, back to business. What do you-all think of ridin' along with me?"

Richard said, "I don't know. How is it you can trust them Indians not to kill us, or worse?"

Pegleg laughed. "Oh, they won't do us any harm. I been dealin' with the Utes longer'n you been breathin' air. Hell, I'm practically one of 'em—got me a Ute wife up there. Woman name of *Wici-ci*. Means Song Bird in Ute. I call her Song, mostly. But that ain't no never mind. What matters is, them

Utes won't do us no harm." Pegleg topped off the glasses all around, emptying the bottle. "Can't say the same for the Navajos, howsomever. We'll be seein' some of their country. They ain't always hospitable to our kind. Paiutes ain't neither, but we ain't likely to encounter any of them—won't be far enough west to run onto a Paiute."

"Would it be just we three?"

"Just you, me, and Mel. We'd be travelin' light. Our mounts and a packhorse. Is them horses of yours fit to travel?"

"Hell, yes. They been a lot of miles and ain't lost a step. They could stand bein' fed up some, but they're game."

"Well, you bring 'em on over to my place and we'll put some corn in 'em for a day or two. Rosa, she'll fix us some supper."

"Rosa?" Melvin said.

"Rosa's my woman. Keeps up the home place. Damn fine cook, too."

"But I thought you said you had that Indian woman for a wife. Song."

Pegleg laughed. "I said it, all right. And I wouldn't of said it if it wasn't so."

"You got *two* women, then?"

That elicited another laugh. "Two, now. I've had a passel more of 'em over the years. Weren't nothin' for a *hivernant* to take up—"

"What's that you're a sayin'?"

"*Hivernant*—such is a fur trapper, a mountain man, who stayed out here of a winter, 'stead of goin' back down to the settlements. Most such men, why, they'd take up with an Indian woman to keep 'em warm over those long, cold nights. There's many a half-breed kid amongst the Crow, the Ute, the Arapaho, the Cheyenne, the Shoshoni, and other Indian tribes to bear witness to it. Hell, I had women amongst most of them tribes myself."

The deep furrows between Melvin's eyebrows and his slowly shaking head brought a smile to Pegleg's face.

"What's the matter, boy?"

"It don't hardly seem right. A man's supposed to marry up with a woman and stick with her. It ain't proper to have more'n one wife, or to lay up with women what you ain't married to."

"Maybe so that's what folks say," Pegleg said. "But that ain't never been the way out here. Besides, I been enough time in the settlements to know that ain't the way it is there, neither. There's men sneakin' in and out of windows and doors ever' night in them towns you come from. They might pretend otherwise, but they ain't bein' honest. Out here, folks just accept the way things is and don't pretend otherwise."

"Still . . ."

Pegleg shrugged. He stood. "Come on along, boys. Rosa's likely got some goat meat on the spit, or a pot of chili goin'. Once you-all pull up a chair at her table, you'll see why a man's smart to have a woman around."

Melvin didn't know whether to agree or disagree. But he was too busy shoveling up beans and chili stew with warm tortillas and chewing roast cabrito to worry overmuch about it. From their seats at a table under a shade tree, the Pates watched their horses, pastured with Pegleg's riding mule, gather corn kernels with slack lips and probing tongues from piles poured onto the ground. With the dried corn consumed, the horses wandered from one stand of bunch grass to another, sampling the tawny strands of cured forage.

By then even Melvin had pushed his plate away, stomach distended with the unaccustomed home-cooked fare. Rosa gathered the dishware, leaving only clay mugs and a jug of wine on the table. Pegleg pushed all that aside, and with a stick of charred wood from the fire, sketched a rough map on the tabletop. Mountain ranges, looking like rows of tents, dominated

82

the drawing. Lines that wandered and wiggled represented rivers.

"This here is the Rio Grande," Pegleg said. "We'll cross that and go on through the Tusas Mountains to the Rio Chama and follow it upstream a ways. Then we'll cut over to the San Juan River, then to the Animas. We'll skirt the San Juan Mountains and the Sawatch Range as we head north. Anywheres in that country we're likely to find sign of one or another band of the Utes. Once we do, they'll tell us where Wakara is to be found."

Richard and Melvin stared at the crude map, suspecting its simplicity did not indicate the hardships likely to be found on the land.

"What do you think, boys?"

The Pate brothers shifted their gaze from the tabletop to Pegleg. Richard shrugged.

Pegleg swept the palm of his hand across the table, smearing the map. "We leave in two days' time."

CHAPTER TEN

Mary, Emma, and Jane sat in the shade of a mesquite tree on
La Placita, the little plaza, in Albuquerque. Completing the
circle was Paloma Ramirez. Paloma, a recent celebrant of her
quinceañera, her entry into womanhood, was near the same age
as Emma. But it was Mary who had befriended her, and
recruited Paloma to teach the Lewis girls Spanish.

"*. . . siete, ocho, nueve, diez, once, doce, trece, catorce, quince, die-
ciseis, diecisiete . . .*" the girls chanted as they practiced numbers.

They named the days of the week: "*Lunes, Martes, Miércoles,
Jueves, Viernes, Sábado, Domingo.*"

And recited names of months: "*. . . Mayo, Junio, Julio, Agosto,
Septiembre, Octubre, Noviembre . . .*"

Paloma's English was effortless. In years past, she had learned
the language in *Tejas*, in San Antonio. Her widowed mother
served as *niñera*, a nursemaid, to the family of a wealthy im-
migrant American merchant, and Paloma had spent her days in
a household with English-speaking children as her playmates
and, in fact, received the same education as her mother's
charges, who learned from a private tutor.

But when her mother died of a fever, Paloma left the Republic
of Texas for Albuquerque, in the charge of her uncle, her
mother's brother, a *hacendado* with vast herds of sheep and
goats roaming the mesa west of the city in winter, and in the
high country of the Sandia mountains in the warmer months.
Tío Enrique, as Paloma called him, lived in the town, with hired

pastores tending the livestock. Paloma ostensibly kept house for *Tio* Enrique as helper to *Tia* Lorena, his wife. But since most of the work was accomplished by a cook and a maid, much of her time was her own, allowing Paloma to stroll the plaza, converse with friends, browse the shops, and, now, help the Lewis girls with their Spanish. The lessons, however, were given as much to laughter and chatter as formal learning.

A wagon drawn by a team of mules drove into the plaza. Emma rose to her feet and brushed the skirt of her dress with both hands. "It is Abel! Abel has come!" She ran toward the wagon, thought better of it, and slowed to a more ladylike walk. But Jane, with no concern for such niceties at her age, passed Emma by and ran to the wagon. She skipped and hopped along beside the wagon, smiling at Abel and spilling a torrent of greetings and welcomes and questions.

The wagon stopped in front of a store, the adobe front above the portico painted to read MERCANTILE. Beneath, in smaller letters, was the Spanish equivalent, LA TIENDA. Beneath that, in smaller letters yet, was LEWIS & PATE, PROP. The building had been occupied by a saddle and harness maker who had grown too old for the work and moved to Durango to live with a daughter. Lee and Sarah stepped out the door just as Emma arrived.

Abel sat on the wagon seat, unsure whose demand for attention to answer. Jane jumped up and down clapping her hands, talking faster than Abel could keep up with. Sarah stood in the shade of the portico, arms folded, and greeted her son while thanking God for his safe arrival. Lee grabbed the sideboards of the wagon, raised himself on his toes, and studied the goods in the wagon, packed tight and deep. Emma stood back, hands clasped behind her back, a smile teasing her lips.

With a smile and nod of his head in her direction, Abel pulled the handle to set the brake and wrapped the lines around it. He stepped down from the offside of the wagon. Jane ran around the wagon and all but upended Abel when she clinched him in a hug. He let her hold on for a bit, then pried her loose to accept a more solemn embrace from his mother. Lee patted him on the back and commented on the state of the load, grateful it had arrived intact and, apparently, without incident.

Abel assured his parents, then walked over to Emma, who had moved into the shade of the portico. He stood before her, unsure of what to say or do.

"You appear to have made it from Santa Fe safely," Emma said. She brushed the sun bonnet from her head and let it dangle down her back by its strings, her honey-colored hair gleaming. She watched the flush climb from under Abel's collar and onto his cheeks.

"Yes. I . . . It . . . I . . ."

Emma smiled, further discombobulating Abel. "Perhaps you should help your father unload the wagon. We will talk later—when you are rested from the journey, and have had a chance to clear your throat of the dust that is making it difficult for you to speak." Emma smiled again, and winked before turning away.

As they worked at the unloading, Abel filled his father in on Daniel Lewis's activities. The men had rented a warehouse in Santa Fe from Manuel Álvarez, but decided to open their first retail venture in Albuquerque, where competition was less severe. Lee and Sarah tended the Albuquerque store, getting it stocked and open for business.

The Lewis girls were there to help, and were living with the Pates, as their father would be traveling a good deal, intercepting freighters on the road from the States to negotiate for goods. He would also be about the countryside establishing contacts with farmers and craftsmen and artisans for the supply of other merchandise, while investigating opportunities for establishing retail outlets in other outlying communities. Abel spent most of his time on the road as well, carrying wares from Santa Fe to stock the Albuquerque shelves. He was not yet familiar with every bump and pothole on the stretch of *El Camino Real* between Santa Fe and Albuquerque, but he was getting to know them.

As Abel and Lee carried the freight into the store, Mary made note of each item and quantity. Bookkeeping and inventory had become her responsibility. Emma and Jane unpacked the crates and boxes and shelved the goods under Sarah's direction. Sarah worked between the store and the living quarters in back, where she finished preparing supper.

With the work done, Sarah called them all to eat. Small talk seasoned the meal, but when Sarah set out a plate of fruit-filled *empanadas*—a local dish she had learned to prepare—Abel cleared his throat to tell of more pressing news from the capital.

"There's trouble brewin' and I don't know what it'll mean. Could cause difficulties for us."

"Well, what is it, Son?" Lee finally said when it appeared Abel would not go on without prompting.

"It's the Texians. Folks say they're fixin' to make war."

"Wait a minute," Lee said. "Why would Texas make war against New Mexico?"

"It don't make much sense to me. But it seems like the Texians think their country runs right up to the river—the Rio Grande. And that means they lay claim to Taos and Santa Fe and Albuquerque, and all them other towns and land east of the river, all the way down to some place called El Paso del Norte."

"And you think the Texians will make trouble for us?"

Abel shook his head. "Not the Texians. The Mexicans. See, them Texians that's stirrin' up trouble used to be Americans, mostly. The Mexicans think they stole Texas, and they ain't never forgive 'em for it. Far as they're concerned, America's behind the whole thing anyway. You know there's already some bad feelin's against Americans what's come here to live—and if the Texians do come and the Mexicans get stirred up, it ain't likely to go well for us."

Lee pondered what Abel said. "What does Daniel say?"

Abel shrugged. "He don't know. He's worried, though."

The ladies looked on as Lee chewed on an *empanada* and sipped coffee.

"I got an idea that might help," Abel said. All eyes turned to him. "Word is, there's Mexican soldiers comin' up from down south to fight the Texians. But Governor Armijo, he don't want to wait. So he's puttin' together volunteers to head east and meet the Texians himself."

Sarah, color draining from her face, asked Abel what, exactly, his idea might be.

"If I join up, things might go better for us. Folks here would see we stand with 'em, and not with the Texians."

"Oh, Abel, how could you even think such a thing?"

"Now, Sarah, the boy's got a point."

"Don't you start with me, Lee Pate! Lord knows your judgment ain't worth beans. I've lost two sons already on account of your foolishness. I'll be damned if you'll deprive me of the only boy I got left."

Lee thought better of saying more and held his tongue. Mary, Emma, and Jane sat, heads bowed.

Sarah took a deep breath. "Abel could be killed, runnin' off to God knows where to fight folks that ain't got one damn thing to do with us."

No one spoke and the silence stretched toward eternity. Then Abel cleared his throat again. "Ma, I knowed you'd be worried. But I can shoot better'n most, and Daniel said he'd see I got a proper rifle and as good a horse as there is to ride. I promise I'll watch myself, Ma. I'll be careful."

Sarah stood and started clearing the table, clattering plates and platters as she stacked them; utensils rattling as they lit in a pan empty of biscuits. Abel raised his bowed head and looked at Emma. She looked back at him with eyes streaming tears.

"Don't you worry neither, Emma. I'll be fine."

She did not answer, leaving the table and rushing into the room where she slept with her sisters. Mary's chair scraped across the wooden floor as she pushed it back. She looked at Abel through narrowed eyes beneath a creased brow, and followed Emma. Jane sat as still as a statue staring at Abel, her expression worried, but worshipful. Abel pushed himself up from his chair and stepped out the back door into the alley behind the store. He found a seat atop an empty barrel. His eyes followed the fog of stars in the Milky Way as it led northward toward Santa Fe and whatever future would be found there.

El Gobernador Manuel Armijo, arrayed in the finery of an officer of the Mexican army—a position no one was sure he held—sat mounted on a white horse in front of the Governor's Palace. Flanking him to either side were the *federales,* Mexican army troops, garrisoned at Santa Fe. Spread before him on La Plaza de la Constitución were hundreds of volunteer troops, their numbers overflowing onto the streets leading into the plaza. They were a motley lot, dressed in everything from fine clothing to tattered workwear, mounted on horses of every description, as well as mules and burros. Many were afoot. Armaments were just as varied. Some carried flintlock muskets, others caplock rifles; there were single-shot muzzle-loading pistols and modern revolvers; there were sabers and daggers and machetes; some were armed with nothing more than pikestaffs, spears, bows, hatchets, and clubs.

Every time Armijo paused in his blustering oration, the volunteers cheered with exuberance, or howled and hollered in anger, fists and weapons hoisted skyward. Abel understood not a word of it, and the ragtag troop was several miles east of Santa Fe before he happened upon a former muleskinner from the States who spoke both Spanish and English.

The man said Armijo had pontificated at length on the sovereignty and strength of Mexico, the approaching menace of the malicious *Tejanos,* and the slaughter and rapine sure to result should the attackers reach the communities and families of Nuevo Mexico. The governor suggested he knew the location and circumstances of the Texian army, owing to the desertion and arrival in Taos of two of their guides. The invaders, some three hundred strong, the deserters said, had wandered for days, lost and hungry, in the stark expanse of *el Llano Estacado,* the faceless high plains south of the Canadian River and east of the Pecos. Armijo said the Texians were tired, weak, and low on supplies, making them easy pickings for the *valientes protectores* before him. He went so far as to suggest the brave volunteers, with a modicum of assistance from the Mexican troops coming from the south, might even conquer and recapture Tejas for la República Mexicana.

The volunteer legion moved at a leisurely pace; the untrained troops spread for miles along the trail. The march lost its luster for many, and they turned back. The *federales* from Mexico met the volunteers before anyone met the Texians, and when the opposing forces did meet, the invaders withered at the sight of some 1,500 trained Mexican soldiers and hundreds of volunteers.

Some wanted to escort the Texians out of the country, others wanted to exterminate them. In the end, the *federales* took them in hand and marched southward, deep into Mexico and prison.

In the governor's absence, tensions increased in Santa Fe. Americano merchants demanded protection from unruly and threatening Mexicans. The American consul, Manuel Álvarez, was attacked and nearly killed, saved only by the intervention of Guadalupe Miranda, second-in-command to the *gobernadora.*

That intervention put Miranda in danger. He feared for his family, and loaded his wife and children into a light carriage and urged them to make haste to Albuquerque and find refuge until tensions eased. Somewhere along the way, not far from the village of Algodones, Lee Pate pulled his wagon off the road to allow the fast-moving buggy and the crazy woman with lines in hand and an angry shout in her mouth to pass by.

But he would travel only a mile or two before meeting the carriage a second time.

CHAPTER ELEVEN

Lee Pate struggled to stay awake after a restless night sleeping on the ground. The mules plodded along the road by rote, having traveled those same miles many a time. With Abel off with Armijo chasing after invading Texians, the job of hauling goods from the Lewis & Pate warehouse in Santa Fe to the store in Albuquerque had fallen to him. As he rolled south, the repetitive squeak of a wagon wheel needing grease lulled him to sleep time and again. He awakened only when his chin hit his chest, or a bump or hole in the road jarred the wagon.

He was not far past the village of Algodones, where he had spent the night under the wagon, when the sound of hurried hoofbeats and the angry shouts of a woman turned him to watch the road behind. The oncoming carriage carried the woman with the loud and demanding voice, dressed in finery, and an assortment of children tucked in among carpetbags and cases and boxes and baskets. He eased the mules to the roadside and stopped to watch as the buggy bounced past, its driver paying him no mind and the children craning their necks to study him wide eyed.

A mile or two down the road a cloud of dust in the distance caught his eye. The dust had settled by the time he arrived at the wreck. The buggy was off the road lying on its side, the front wheel askew with broken spokes, the rear wheel slowly rotating. The carriage horse, looking no worse for wear, stood a few rods away, cropping at bunchgrass growing among the *chamisa.* A small boy sat crying amidst the spilled baggage, wrapped in the arms of an older sister. Another boy, who looked to be about ten years old, stood next to the woman, her fancy clothes rumpled and torn and smudged with dirt.

Standing before them were three horsemen, dressed in the garb of vaqueros, from the wide-brimmed sombreros on their heads to the heavy-roweled spurs on their heels. Lee sensed trouble and reached under the seat for the double-barreled shotgun there. As he approached, he kept one eye on the horsemen and the other on the tracks on the road. From the look of it, the woman had attempted to outrace the horsemen, veered off the road, hit a boulder, and upset the buggy.

The riders turned their mounts toward Lee's wagon as he drew close, and stopped three abreast across the road.

"*¿Que pasa?*" the man in the center said.

Lee ignored him, studying the scene, then looked to the woman, whose fright shone through emerald eyes. "Looks like you-all have had a spot of trouble."

The woman started spilling out rapid-fire Spanish that Lee could not begin to understand, even had he spoke the language.

"*¡Silencio!*" the rider said to the woman, then turned back to Lee. "What is it you want, my friend?"

"Don't want a thing. Just on my way down the road."

"What is your interest in this woman?"

"None at all. Only that she looks to need some help."

The horseman smiled. "I think you should drive on, my friend."

Lee studied the scene again, looking from one rider to the other, then to the woman, then the children. He leaned over and spat off the side of the wagon. His eyes locked with those of the spokesman. "I don't believe I will."

Again, the rider in the center smiled. "Ah, my friend, I fear you misread the situation. You see, that scatter gun you hold has but two barrels—and there are three of us."

Lee nodded. "That's so."

The horseman shrugged. "The arithmetic is simple."

"That it is—my friend. But the thing is, you-all can't know which two of you will die before you can kill me." Lee smiled and shifted his aim a few inches to cover the rider on the right. "How about you, Señor? You ready to die?" He swung the barrel toward the rider on the left. "Or will it be you?"

Then he turned the gun on the man in the middle and hoisted the barrel slightly so he could see down the twin bores. "One thing's for certain sure, *mi amigo*. You'll be the first to go." Lee spat again and watched the riders squirm. The man on the left leaned over and whispered something to the man in the middle.

The spokesman touched the brim of his sombrero. "We have business elsewhere, my friend." He looked at the family, now huddled together near the spilled carriage, then back to Lee. "We would like to lend assistance, but I fear it is up to you to help these unfortunate travelers." He backed his horse out of the line, his eyes never leaving Lee's, and reined his mount around and rode off into the brush toward the river. The other riders followed.

Lee and the woman and children watched them until they were out of sight. The woman let out a long-held breath and dropped to the ground in tears. The older boy looked on with nothing to offer but a worried expression. The girl knelt beside her mother and enfolded her in a hug. The young boy sniffled and wiped his cheeks, the tears smearing dust into mud. Lee set the wagon brake and stepped down to study the broken buggy. In no way could it be made roadworthy without expertise and replacement parts. He checked the horse and found it scraped and sore in places, but free of serious injury.

Kneeling before the woman, he reached out and touched a

hand to her shoulder. She raised her head, sniffed, and blinked away tears. He said, "Are you all right, ma'am?"

Her reply came in a rushing stream of words that escaped Lee. "Albuquerque" flowed past, and he raised a hand to stop her.

"Albuquerque," he said, tapping a finger to his chest. "Me. Albuquerque." He pointed at the wagon.

The woman smiled and leaned into Lee, wrapping both arms around his neck and squeezing, dislodging his hat and knocking it to the ground. The older boy picked it up and swept the dust from the crown where it landed, and handed it back to Lee when his mother turned him loose.

Lee stood and studied the scattered baggage. He picked up a carpetbag and a hatbox and carried them to the wagon, finding space for them in the load. Fortunately, the freight this trip did not make for a large load. The woman scurried about, gathering spilled clothing and other items and stuffing them into boxes and baskets. The older boy and the girl carried trappings to the wagon and handed them up to Lee, who arranged them among the merchandise.

With the wagon loaded, Lee tied the carriage horse to the end gate. He hoisted the little boy to the wagon seat, then offered a hand to the woman to help her up. The older boy and the girl clambered up the sideboards, using a rear wheel as a ladder, and found a place to huddle into the load.

Before taking his seat, Lee got the attention of his passengers and swept the horizon in all directions with his hand, then pointed to his eyes. "Watch. *Hombrés . . . caballos.* Watch." All nodded their understanding. He sat and took up the lines, released the brake, then clucked his tongue and fluffed the lines to wake up the team. The mules leaned into the harness and started the wagon rolling down *El Camino Royale* toward Albuquerque.

Lee helped the woman down from the wagon after stopping in front of the store. He lowered the little boy to the ground. Mary came out and looked at Lee with a question in her eyes, but he said nothing, instead helping the girl down from the back of the wagon, then turning to the mother.

"Hola, Señora," Mary said, with a curtsy and a smile.

The woman sagged with a sigh, and grasped Mary's hands in her own. And even though Mary's command of Spanish was growing, the hurried torrent of words drowned her in confusion.

Mary shook her head rapidly, asking her to slow down. "¡Por favor, Señora—*habla despacio, por favor!*"

By this time, Sarah, Emma, and Jane had joined them on the portico. The woman tried again, speaking more slowly this time, but it was still too much for Mary, and the others could offer no assistance. Lee placed a hand on the woman's shoulder and held up a finger, signaling her to stop.

"Mary, maybe you could fetch your friend Paloma."

Sarah escorted the family inside, through the store, and to the kitchen. She pulled back a chair from the table and gestured for the woman to sit. She ushered the children into other chairs. She poured the woman a cup of English tea from a pot already steeping atop the stove, and offered the same to the children, who asked, instead for *"agua."* Sarah filled glasses from the kitchen bucket and the young boy gulped thirstily; the other children less so, owing to table manners, but drink was clearly needed.

Paloma swished in, pulled up a chair to sit next to the woman, and introduced herself. She asked the woman to tell her story, then listened, nodding in sympathy from time to time, eyes widening at other turns of the tale, and even tearing up toward the end.

Through it all, Sarah bustled around the kitchen, calling on the girls to help with this and that as she assembled a makeshift supper for Lee and the visitors. As they ate, Paloma told what she had learned.

"This is the family of Señor Guadalupe Miranda."

Lee interrupted. "I have heard that name before. Let me see . . ."

"Hush," Sarah said. "Let the girl talk!"

"Señor Miranda is an official of the government. He is *secretario* to Gobernador Armijo—a very important man. *Tio* Enrique speaks of him often. Señor Miranda, it seems, has worked to protect the Americanos in Santa Fe from violence associated with the difficulties with the *Tejanos*. With *el gobernador* away with the fighting, Señor Miranda is left in charge, you see." Paloma paused in thought for a time.

"Some citizens of Santa Fe, partisans supporting Armijo, conclude—wrongly, the Señora says—that the Americans are aiding the *Tejanos*, and so have threatened violence against them. Going so far as to attack the American representative, Señor Alvarez. When the Mirandas gave him shelter, it angered the partisans even more. And so, Señor Miranda has sent the Señora and the children to Albuquerque to seek refuge until it becomes safe to once again return to Santa Fe."

"And what about them fellows who attacked them on the road? Were they these 'partisans' you talk about?"

Paloma asked the question. Señora Miranda shook her head, and talked for a time. "She says 'no.' Those men were only bandidos, and meant them harm only because of the chance encounter on the road. The Señora expresses her gratitude for your rescue."

"Rescue? What the hell is she talkin' about, Lee?"

"Sarah, please," Lee said with a wave of his hand. "Mind your tongue. I needn't remind you there's children present."

"But—"

Lee stopped his wife with another wave of his hand. "It weren't nothin'. Just doin' my Christian duty, is all."

Paloma smiled. "Nevertheless, the Señora is grateful for your intervention. And she expresses her belief that Señor Miranda will look upon you with kindness and find a way to express his appreciation for your actions."

Sarah cleared the dishes from the table, refilled Señora Miranda's teacup and the children's water glasses, and set a plate of ginger snaps on the table. She untied her apron and placed it on its hook on the door. "Now what?"

Lee looked at her with a wrinkled brow.

"Don't be such an ignoramus, Lee. What are we goin' to do with Missus Miranda and these children? They sure can't stay here—much as I would like them to. But we just plain ain't got no place to put them."

Lee kneaded his chin and pursed his lips, watching the children eat their cookies as he thought it over, berating himself for not having realized the problem.

Paloma stood. "Do not worry. I will speak at once to *Tio* Enrique and *Tia* Lorena. There is much room in our home, and the presence of the Mirandas will be no imposition, I think."

"Are you sure?"

"Do not concern yourself, Mister Pate," Paloma said with a smile. "It is very possible that *Tio* Enrique is acquainted with Señor Miranda, as I have said. He would not be averse, in any event, to extending a kindness to such an important official of the government. Even so, *Tia* Lorena will welcome the visitors. She has a kind heart and could not deny them the hospitality."

Paloma spoke to Señora Miranda for a time, then hurried away to make arrangements with her aunt and uncle. The woman watched her go, took a deep breath and let it out slowly and sagged in her chair, worn out body and soul.

CHAPTER TWELVE

The whiskey carried out of Taos on the pack mule was long since gone. Pegleg did not seem to notice the lack, and Melvin did not care much, but Richard had been surly and cantankerous for many a day. Pegleg led the way along the trail as usual, followed by Richard, then Melvin with the pack mule in tow. Richard huddled in the saddle, paying little attention to their surroundings. Melvin, however, overworked his neck shifting his view from the plains rolling out to the west, to the mountains rising in the east.

The mountains. Melvin had never seen the like of them. Blue-gray in color, with brilliant white snowfields on the high slopes, the peaks and upper ridges ending sharp and hard, looking jagged enough to slice the sky. They came onto a creek flowing out of the foothills and followed its path until it joined a larger river.

"El Rio de Nuestra Señora de Dolores," Pegleg said. "River of Our Lady of Sorrows, them Spaniards called it. Fur men mostly just calls it the Dolores." He slid his wooden leg out of the shallow leather sheath that served as a stirrup, and stepped down from the saddle. He stood for a moment, one hand grasping the saddle horn while finding his balance on the ground after hours horseback. "We'll make camp here."

Richard mumbled and grumbled as he dismounted and unsaddled his horse. Melvin unsaddled his mount, then unloaded the mule. He emptied the necessary camp equipment from the panniers, then carried the axe into a grove of aspen trees and set to chopping deadfall for firewood. Pegleg scooped ashes out of a fire ring of river rocks and scratched the hole deeper with a stick of wood.

"Looks like we ain't the first ones been here," Richard said.

"No," Pegleg said. "Trappers been campin' hereabouts since I don't know when. Indians, too. Arapaho, some. Mostly Ute."

"How come we ain't seen none of these Utes of yours? We been riding through their country for days and days—if what you said has any truth in it."

Pegleg exhaled but did not draw another breath as he glared at Richard. "Son, you don't never doubt my word. I have rid over ever' inch of this here land, and have done so since your mama dandled you on her knee. We'll find us some Utes—or they will find us—soon enough. Meantime, you take care what comes out of that mouth of yours, or you'll be spittin' out teeth."

With a harrumph, Richard carried the coffeepot down to the stream and filled it. Coffee was a damn poor substitute for whiskey, he thought, but it was better than nothing. The men sat around the fire, boulders or stumps of log serving as stools. Richard swallowed some coffee to wash down a mouthful of rice and raisins. Another sip followed. Richard screwed up his face at the bitterness of the brew. "Wish to hell we had some whiskey."

Melvin looked up from his eating, shook his head, then bowed again over his plate, shoveling up rice as fast as he could chew and swallow.

Pegleg studied the older brother. "We left Taos with plenty *aguardiente*. You drunk up your share and most all of your brother's and a good bit of mine."

Richard shrugged. "I'd drink a hell of a lot more of it, had we any."

"How come is it you drink so much whiskey?"

Richard thought for a minute, head hung low. He looked up at Pegleg. "Don't know for certain. Feels a hell of a lot better to have some whiskey in me than not. Sets my mind at ease, I suppose. Makes it so I don't think about things so much."

Pegleg sipped at his coffee as he mulled that over. Then, "What is it that troubles you? If you don't mind my askin'."

Richard said nothing. Melvin said, "I reckon what bothers him is family stuff. Leavin' Ma and Pa, and all. I sure do miss 'em—I reckon Richard does too."

"Like hell I do," Richard scoffed.

"Again, if you don't mind my askin'," Pegleg said, "what caused you to leave? Whatever it was, it seems to weigh on you. Somethin' sure as hell is."

After a time, Richard said, "It ain't only just one thing. See, Pa, he's got some strange notions. Left behind a good life back in Tennessee without even knowin' where he was goin'. Me and him don't see eye to eye on much of anything. Then there's Abel, our little brother. Pa favors him over me and Mel both. Abel can't do no wrong in his eyes. Little bastard."

"Oh, Abel ain't so bad," Melvin said.

"You can't say Pa never preferred him over me! By rights, I'm the oldest and Pa ought to've relied on me."

Melvin shrugged. "I reckon so. But you never did nothin' Pa asked 'thout raisin' a fuss and arguin' about it. Abel, he just done it."

Richard said nothing more.

"Come to that, Abel not only done what Pa wanted, he done good at it." Melvin scraped up the last of his food and swallowed it down, then mopped up the juice on his plate with the side of his finger and licked it off. "Abel, he's right handy at most anything."

With that, the men fell into silence. After a while, Pegleg leaned toward the fire and poured himself another cup of coffee. He sat back on the rock he was using for a stool and took a sip. "Rest easy, boys," he said over the rim in little more than a whisper. "We got company."

The brothers sat upright and looked around, but saw nothing. Richard reached around for the rifle propped against the rock beside him.

"Leave it," Pegleg said. "You two just sit tight. Don't do anything foolish."

The unseen Indians became visible when they rode out of a clump of fir and spruce trees. They rode at a walk, single file, the leader circling the campsite until the men were surrounded, then reined their horses around to face the campfire. Melvin counted nine of them. They said nothing.

After what seemed an eternity to Richard and Melvin, whose glances at one another revealed wide eyes, blanched faces, and tight lips, Pegleg spoke.

"That is one damn ugly horse you are ridin' there, Nooch. It was ugly when you stole it out in California, and it don't look to me like it's got any better lookin'."

A young Indian laughed. He swung his leg across the neck of his horse and hopped to the ground. He walked around the fire and extended a hand to Pegleg who gave it a vigorous shake, then used it for leverage to hoist himself to his feet.

"Boys, this here is Nooch. He may not have got all his growth yet, but he'll do." Pegleg slapped the young man on the back and exchanged greetings with several of the mounted Indians, some in English and some in some indecipherable chatter the boys took to be Ute—or the lingo of whatever kind of Indians these were.

The Indians dismounted and staked their horses in the grass along the stream bank. They built their own fire a short distance away, but did no cooking. Instead, they opened parfleches and passed around slabs of dried meat and what looked to be some kind of flat bread. Nooch and a handful of other men huddled with Pegleg, talking well into the night.

Melvin pulled off his boots and shirt and stretched full length in his bedroll, staring at the stars until he dozed off and snored softly through the night. Richard slept little, if at all, fully clothed, lying atop his blankets, wrapped around his rifle.

Pegleg was up at first light and had coffee boiling and corn pone in the skillet when he awakened the Pate brothers. "Best be pryin' them eyelids apart, boys. Daytime ain't goin' to wait on you-all."

Richard sat up, so haggard he could hardly keep his jaws together. Melvin scrubbed the sleep from his face with the palms of his hands, then stretched and yawned. He stood and stretched some more, the bones in his back popping like burning pine knots.

"I'm plumb empty clear down past my knees, Mister Pegleg. I surely hope you got plenty of grub goin' there."

"There's enough and then some for a man of reg'lar appetites. When it comes to feedin' you till you're filled up, Mel, I don't know as there's food enough in the whole world to do it."

Melvin smiled, plopped down on his blankets, pulled on his boots, then walked off into the trees to tend to his morning business.

Richard, shoulders sagged and head bowed, mumbled, "Wish to hell I had me a drink of whiskey."

"All you get this mornin' is coffee, son. That, or creek water. One'll freeze your gullet and t'other will scorch your stomach." Pegleg slid the skillet off the fire, tapped the edge of the coffeepot to test its temperature, then poured his tin cup full of coffee and lowered himself to his stone seat. "You don't look like you slept much, young Richard."

"Not any, 'less I dozed off and missed it."

"Slept like a wintertime bear, myself. Melvin, too, from the sounds of it. What's the matter of you?"

"Them Indians. Kept thinkin' one of 'em would slip up on me and slit my throat."

Pegleg chuckled. "It is wise to keep your powder dry, for certain. Howsomever, when a man's amongst friends he ought not worry so."

"I guess I don't trust nobody I don't know—'specially Indians."

Pegleg sipped his coffee. "Well, I know these Indians. Know them a hell of a lot better than I know you, for a fact. Trust them more, too."

With a snort, Richard said, "You'd trust an Indian more'n a white man? Well, then, I won't shed no tears should one of 'em stick a knife in you. Meantime, I'll be sleepin' with one of my eyes open."

The fire sizzled when Pegleg tossed the dregs of his coffee into the flames. "Here's the thing, Richard. Had one of them Utes wanted to slit your throat, or lift your hair, or even relieve you of your manhood, he'd of done it. And he would not have cared if you was awake or asleep, 'cause you wouldn't know a thing about it till it was too late to do anything about it. So, you might just as well sleep at night. That way, your powder will be dry should someone who wishes us ill come along."

When Melvin returned and fell to eating every corn dodger he could lay hands on, Pegleg said the Utes had told him that Wakara was less than a day's ride southwest, at Sleeping Ute Mountain. Nooch and those with him were on the way to join up with Wakara. The three of them would ride along.

The caravan took its time and located Wakara's camp late in the afternoon. There looked to be about two dozen Indians there. Richard and Melvin stayed in the saddle, watching Pegleg stump around exchanging fervent greetings with several of the Utes. Once acquaintances that had been dormant for a time were renewed, Pegleg directed the brothers to set up housekeeping in a cove among a clump of cedar trees at the edge of the Ute camp.

"You notice anything strange about these Indians?" Melvin said as he laid out a fire ring.

Richard stopped unpacking panniers and watched the camp. "What do you mean? Look like any bunch of Indians to me."

"There ain't no women. No little ones, neither. They're all men or near-growed boys—every one of 'em."

"Beats the hell out of me. Guess you'll have to ask the old man, once he gets done howdyin' with them."

The sun was down but it was yet a long way from dark when Pegleg led his horse over and unsaddled. Melvin offered to stake the horse out near the others and led it away through the gnarly trees. Pegleg bent over his saddle, untied the flaps on the saddlebags, and rummaged around. He stood, two bottles of Taos whiskey in hand.

"Why, you sonofabitch," Richard said. "You been holdin' out on me!"

"Mind your tongue, boy."

"Like hell!" Richard started toward Pegleg.

"You had best stop right there. I would not want to bust your head with one of these bottles. It'd be a waste of good whiskey, if nothin' else."

Richard stopped, shoulders and chin drooping. "C'mon, Pegleg. Give me a drink."

"Not a chance. I brung this whiskey for Wakara, and that's who's goin' to get it."

"Just one drink . . ."

Pegleg turned and hobbled back to the Utes, where his appearance with the whiskey prompted a series of whoops and hollers. Melvin came back to camp to find Richard slumped on the ground against his saddle, watching the Indians. One bottle was already empty, flung out into the brush. The other was still passing from hand to hand, but would not last long.

Melvin put a pot of leftover beans on the fire to warm, boiled coffee, and stirred up a batch of corn pone. Richard showed no interest in the food and Pegleg stayed with the Utes. Melvin ate as much as he could and set the rest aside.

Come morning, he stirred up the fire and sat drinking coffee, grown bitter overnight, and gnawing on corn dodgers gone as hard as the sandstone rocks and boulders covering the ground everywhere. He watched his brother and Pegleg sleep and awaited the sunrise.

Richard was more surly than usual when awakened. But Pegleg was persistent, prodding him with his wooden leg.

"Wake up, son. We'll be pullin' out soon."

Richard groaned and grumbled and sat up in his tousled blankets. He wiped the sleep off his face and watched the Utes moving lazily around their camp. "I thought you come here to give Wakara money that you owed him."

"I took care of it."

"I never saw it."

"You nor nobody else. It was business 'tween me and him."

"I guess you did it when them Indians was drinkin' that whiskey." Richard rubbed his face again. "What'd he do with that money? Pass it around to the others?"

"That's his business. Ain't none of mine. Sure as hell ain't none of yours."

Richard stretched and yawned. "I don't suppose you got another bottle tucked away somewheres."

"You suppose right."

"Say, Mister Pegleg," Melvin said. "I see there ain't no women nor kids with these Indians. How's that?"

Pegleg sat and poured a cup of coffee, tasted it, screwed up his face, and tossed it into the fire. "Most times, when Indians is movin' about from place to place, they all go together—the women takes care of movin' the camp and such. But these Utes are goin' on a raid, so they ain't brought their families along. Left 'em behind, where'd they'd be safe."

"Raid? Raidin' what?"

"They're goin' down into Navajo country. Southwest of here."

Melvin stood and worked the kinks out of his back. "Well, then. Since you already done your business and the Utes is leavin', I reckon we'll be headin' on back home."

"No," Pegleg said. "We'll be goin' with them."

CHAPTER THIRTEEN

Abel entered the store, taking care to close the door behind him without making a sound. But Emma, standing on a step stool swishing a feather duster over the goods on the highest shelves, felt the change.

"I will be right with you," she said without turning around.

"No hurry, miss. I don't mind waitin'."

Emma stood as still as a stone statue. "Abel?" she said, not daring to tempt fate and look.

"Emma."

Abel crossed to the counter and leapt over, not bothering to lift the hinged hatch. Emma stepped down and Abel picked her up and swung her around in the narrow space between the counter and shelves, then set her feet back on the floor. He pushed her away to arm's length. A grin stretched his face; Emma's eyes glistened. She threw her arms around his neck. He wrapped his around her waist. They held one another tightly, Abel's face buried in her hair.

"Land sakes, you two!" Sarah said, coming into the store from the living quarters in the back to see what all the commotion was about. "A body would think you hadn't seen each other in years."

Abel looked up and smiled at his mother. "Sure seems like it, Ma." He grasped Emma's shoulders and pushed her back again to see her face. "However long it's been, it's been too long."

"Come here. Give your mother a hug!"

Abel was locked in an embrace with his mother when Lee came in. "Abel! Son! It is good to see you!" Lee joined the clinch, rocking all three of them back and forth. They were nearly upended when Jane thrust herself into Abel's back at a run. The boy reddened at all the tears and laughter at his return.

"Supper is ready," Sarah said, worming her way out of the clutch. "Leastways it was when I left the kitchen. Could all be burnt to a crisp by now." She tucked a stray lock of hair behind an ear and smoothed the front of her apron. "You-all come on and eat now. Abel—we'll be wantin' to hear all about it."

"What about the store?" Emma said.

"Don't fret about it," Lee said with a wave of his hand. "If'n someone happens in, they'll pull the string." Little things pleased Lee, like the bell he'd hung on the wall at the end of the counter with a pull string to ring it, should they be back among the shelves or in the house when a customer needed assistance.

Abel's report had to wait, what with his jaws working double time on the meal put on the table by Sarah and Jane. "I swear, Ma, this is the first food worth eatin' I've had since I don't know when."

"Oh, pshaw, Son. It ain't nothin' special. Had we knowed you was comin' we'd've fixed up somethin' nice."

"I stirred up the biscuits all by myself!" Jane said. "Baked them in the oven, too!"

Abel smiled. "I do declare, miss Jane, these biscuits right here is the finest I have ever et. By the bye, where at is Mary?"

Sarah said, "She is over there at her friend Paloma's uncle's house. She and Paloma can't hardly be pulled apart. And she likes the company of that Miranda woman down from Santa Fe—that's another story, Son. You remind me to tell you all about it sometime."

For a time, conversation stopped, and they all concentrated

on the meal. Emma ate little. She sat, poking at her food and moving it around the plate, eyes locked on Abel, the faintest hint of a smile teasing her lips.

"Well, Abel," Lee said when the eating slowed, "now that you've taken a bite out of your hunger, how 'bout you tell us of your adventures off fighting the Texians?"

Abel swallowed a last bite of biscuit slathered with preserves and washed it down with the milk that remained in his glass. "Not much to tell. Mostly just ridin' and ridin' and ridin' some more. Once we got out there on the plains, we went into camp whilst scouts went out huntin' the Texians. We lazed around wishin' we had more to eat. There was some of us what could talk. Most everyone only talked Mexican—but I did learn a lot of that lingo, tryin' to talk with them soldiers and others.

"Some of the boys got up horse races to pass the time. Saw some pretty good horses, I'll tell you that. And some of them Mexican boys ride like they're spots on the back of a pinto horse. There was some shootin' contests, too. Handguns and long guns, both."

"You've always been a fair shot, Son. Did you get in on any of that?"

"Sure. I didn't have no money to get in on it at first. But some of the boys backed me—"

"You mean there was wagering?"

Abel smiled. "Sure thing, Pa. None of them folks seemed to think anything bad about bettin'. Why, some would wager on how long it would take a stink beetle to walk across a bare spot, or put money on who'd be the first to break a tooth from bitin' down on a pebble in his beans."

"You know I don't hold with gambling."

Sarah huffed. "Hush up, Lee. Save your preaching for later and let the boy tell his story."

"Ain't much more to tell. Once I got the idea how that rifle

110

Mister Lewis got for me shot, I hit ever'thing I aimed at. I know you disapprove, Pa, but I pocketed a fair amount of silver and gold coins—them that bet on me made them some money, too."

Lee could only shake his head. Sarah reached across the table and grasped Abel's hand and smiled.

"One thing that shootin' did was, it got me the notice of Governor Armijo. Shook my hand, and all."

"I reckon that could come in handy, should he remember you in a time of need. Not all men will, you know."

Abel shrugged. "I don't expect nothin' of it. But it sure made some of the boys take notice."

"Well, I wouldn't forget it, Son. Sometimes who a man knows can make all the difference. Havin' an important man like the governor for an acquaintance may come in handy one day."

Jane said, "But what about the Texians? Did you have to shoot anybody?"

With a laugh, Abel told how, when the Texian force was finally located, the men in it were tired and hungry. They had misjudged the distance to Santa Fe and were ill supplied for the journey, and had lost their way for a time. Once they saw the size and strength of Mexican resistance, they gave up without ever starting a fight.

"Whatever happened to them? The Texians, I mean."

"Well, Jane, I reckon they all just wanted to go on back to Texas and forget they ever left there. But them Mexican soldiers—the ones in the real army, not us volunteers—took 'em all, every one, a prisoner and marched 'em off down into Mexico somewhere. Don't know what'll become of 'em. Could be they'll lock 'em up, maybe put some on trial. Whatever happens, I don't think any more Texians will be invadin' us anymore."

Sarah stood and gathered plates from the table, Emma and Jane helped. Sarah said, "What matters is that you're home safe. It's good to have you back. We missed you, all of us, and we're tickled pink you're back to stay."

Abel said nothing for a minute as he squirmed in his chair. He cleared his throat, took in a deep breath, and let it out again. "Thing is, Ma, I ain't back to stay."

A pile of dishes crashed to the table. All eyes turned to Emma, who stood, propped up by both palms on the tabletop, the color drained from her face, eyes riveted on Abel. Emma sat down hard in her chair. Everyone looked to Abel, awaiting an explanation.

"There was this man with us. Name of Rodrìguez. He's got a rancho not far from here. Near a place called Isleta down on the river south of here."

"What's that got to do with you, Son?"

"He wants me to come work for him on his place."

Emma left the room in a rush, ducking through the doorway and into the hallway that led up front to the store.

"Doin' what?"

"Seems like Mister Rodrìguez owns a lot of sheep. Got 'em spread out down in that country in a bunch of bands to graze. Now and then when his herders brings the sheep down to the river to water 'em, there'll be some bad men—what he calls ladróns—come along and stampede the sheep. Then they gather some of 'em up and drive 'em off. Those boys he's got herdin' for him, they're too scairt to do anything—afraid they'll get killed if they do."

Lee thought on that. Then, "So, what's that to do with you, Son?"

"Well, Mister Rodrìguez, I guess he thinks I can scare off them ladróns, or leastways keep 'em from stealin' the sheep."

Again, Lee thought, then, with a downturned face, said, "What is it, then? You've become a hired gun?"

"Oh, no, Pa! It ain't that! Could be I won't never have to fire a shot. Just standin' up to them thieves might be enough. Leastways that's what Mister Rodrìguez thinks. Just let 'em know their thievin' won't be tolerated no more."

Lee shook his head. "I don't know, Son. Could turn to trouble just as easy."

Abel shrugged. "Maybe so. But I ain't countin' on it." He took a deep breath and let it out slowly. "Thing is, there's pretty good money in it. And I could sure use it."

Sarah laughed, without humor. "Land sakes, Abel! What would you do with money? Don't we provide well enough for you?"

Abel's face reddened and he shifted in his chair. "Sure you do. But it can't be that way always." He paused, and swallowed hard. "See, there's Emma. Someday, if she'll have me, we'll want to start a life together. And that'll take money."

Sarah scoffed. "Oh, Abel, you're just a boy still."

"Maybe so. But I feel like I'm near growed up. Another year or so . . ."

"And Emma? I know the girl's sweet on you, but what does she say? Could be you're just a passing fancy, far as she's concerned."

Abel shook his head. "Don't know. Haven't said nothin' much about it to her. But I got my hopes . . ."

"Lee! Don't sit there like a damn bump on a log! Talk some sense into the boy!"

"Now, Sarah, Abel's got a point. I ain't sure this job of work of his is to my liking, but the boy's wantin' to make his own way, and we ought not hinder him. We weren't much older than him and the girl when we set up housekeepin' back in Shelby County. Besides, it ain't like he'll be gone for long. Long as Emma's here, he ain't likely to stray too far."

"But he only just got back here . . ."

Lee stood and wrapped an arm around Sarah, and pulled her

close. Abel left to find Emma. He found her in the store, standing at the front window, looking out onto the plaza.

"Emma?"

She turned, and looked at him with eyes red and swollen and brimming with tears. He walked over and enfolded her in a hug. "Emma, don't take on like that. Please. I can't hardly bear to see you cry."

"Oh, Abel," she said with a whimper. "You have only just come back to me, and now you are to leave again."

"I know, Emma. I know. But I'm doin' it for you. For us."

"For us? I do not understand."

Abel said nothing for a moment. Emma could feel him squirm in her arms. He could feel his heart pound.

"You know how I feel about you, Emma."

"I guess—I think so."

He pushed Emma away to arm's length. "I only want to make some money. We ain't kids no more. Some of these days, Emma, we'll be wantin' to have a place of our own. Maybe a piece of land. Start a family . . ."

"I don't understand, Abel—are you asking me to be your wife?"

"Yes—kind of—someday—I'll have to speak to your Pa . . ."

"Oh, Abel!" Emma pulled him close and kissed him, long and hard.

Abel still felt the effects of the kiss as he rode out of Albuquerque the next morning.

CHAPTER FOURTEEN

Melvin snugged up the cinch and slid the stirrup leather off the saddle seat and let it fall into place, then swept it aside and checked the tautness of the latigo once again.

"You sure you want to do this, Mel?" Richard said.

Melvin looked at his brother with a crease between his eyebrows and shook his head slowly. "We talked about this already. I guess I'm the one ought to be askin' if *you* want to do what you're settin' out to do."

Richard heaved a big sigh. "Dammit, Mel, don't go actin' like Pa."

"You ever think he might be right? At least sometimes?"

"Maybe so. But this ain't the same."

"It ain't? Why not? Seems like sellin' people is sellin' people. It ain't right."

Trembling and tongue tied, Richard stammered, looking for the right words. "They're Indians, Mel! *Indians!* Hell, they ain't hardly people at all!"

"That's what folks back home said about darkies. They're different, all right, but they're people. So's Indians, seems to me. Ain't right to be sellin' 'em like they was hogs or steer calves or such. Pa never held with it, and I reckon it rubbed off on me some. I don't want no part of it."

Fists clenched at his sides and trembling all over, Richard said, "It's other Indians what'll be catchin' 'em and doin' the sellin'! I'm just goin' along for the ride. Besides, what the hell else is there to do?"

"Don't ask me, Richard. Like I said, I don't want no part of it."

Richard gritted his teeth and hissed, "Then what the hell are you goin' to do?"

Melvin stepped into the stirrup and swung aboard the horse, finding the other stirrup and squirming to find a comfortable seat. "I'm goin' to ride. Just ride."

"Where to?"

Melvin pointed loosely off to the southeast. "Out thataway. Go back the way we come, more or less. That's where there's other folks, down there."

Still atremble, Richard spat, shook his head, and turned and hurried away. Melvin watched him go, then reined his mount around and rode off, with only the vaguest sense of where he was going.

"Dumb bastard!" Richard said when he reached Pegleg, standing at the fringe of the camp. "He ain't got the sense God give a soda cracker."

The old mountain man watched Melvin's horse grow small then disappear down a gentle rise. "Man's got to follow his heart. If he don't, he ain't no kind of a man."

"I don't think he even knows where his heart is. Ask me, our Pa filled his head with fool notions. I never thought Mel cared about such things."

Pegleg shrugged. "I don't think that brother of yours is as dumb as you make him out to be."

Richard stiffened. "What do you mean? You think he's right?"

"About what?"

"About these slaves we're goin' huntin' for. You think what we're goin' to do is wrong?"

Again, Pegleg shrugged. "Can't say for certain. It's the way of things out here. Wakara and his bunch ain't the first Utes to be capturing Paiutes and Navajos and sellin' 'em to the Mexicans, or the Spanish 'fore that. Been goin' on a long time. Long as it's goin' to happen anyway, it don't unease me none to make a dollar off it if I can."

Richard turned and looked off in the direction Melvin had taken, but saw no trace of his brother. Still, he kept looking.

"Better come along, son," Pegleg said. "Looks like we're about ready to ride."

"Wait. When we left Taos, you said you wanted to give Wakara his money and go and see your Indian wife. Was that a lie? Did you mean to go after catchin' slaves all along?"

Pegleg grabbed a handful of Richard's shirtfront and twisted, then lifted until the younger man's toes scratched at the ground looking for purchase. "Listen here, you little sonofabitch. I never told you no lies. Never. Say so again, and I'll put you under." He shoved Richard away and watched him scramble to keep his feet. "I come here to do just what I said. Wakara got his money. I never expected to find him here at this place, but that is as it may be. I aim to go with him and make me some money. As for Song, well, I'll see the woman when I see her. Just when I do, that ain't none of your affair."

Pegleg pivoted on his wooden leg and hobbled off to where the horses were tied. Richard watched him go, then squeezed his eyes tight shut, wishing his head would stop pounding and the quivering would cease. He pinched the bridge of his nose and rubbed his eyes, then looked off in the direction Melvin had taken. For a moment, he thought of following, but gave it up as a foolish notion. He walked to his horse, checked the cinch, and climbed aboard. Nooch handed him the packhorse's lead rope.

Richard eyed the young Ute. "You talk English, boy?"

Nooch swelled with a deep intake of breath, raised to his full height and nodded once. "Some."

"How old are you?"

"Seventeen winters."

"You remind me of my baby brother, Abel. I sure as hell hope you ain't a know-it-all like he is."

Nooch smiled at him and walked away. The look told Richard the boy knew more than he was letting on. *That one bears watching,* he thought. He looked around the soon-to-be abandoned campsite. Sunlight reflecting off a broken whiskey bottle not only caught his eye but caused his mouth to water. He shook his head and touched his heels to the horse's belly, tugged the lead rope to put the packhorse into motion and fell into the line of riders behind Pegleg. Most of the Utes led a pack animal or spare horse. Wakara led the parade, with Nooch riding beside him. Soon, Nooch heeled his horse into an easy lope and set off ahead of the procession.

Although accustomed to long hours in the saddle, Richard grew tired and sore from the pace set by the Utes. As often as not they moved at a rough, but mile-eating, trot. The Indians rode easily for the most part, as if they were an extension of the horse. But Richard felt a jolt with every footfall of his mount. There were no rest stops for man or animal. The men ate or drank only what they carried on their person, which, in Richard's case, was only a canteen of musty warm water. The Utes did not even stop to relieve themselves. Should the need arise, they raised one knee to the horse's back and knelt at a cockeyed angle and let fly on the move.

The landscape grew more forbidding as they traveled. Piñon and cedar trees and thick brush gave way to bunch grass and stone outcrops. In the distance, the flat tops of expansive mesas rose and fell abruptly from the wasteland below. They rode around and up and down defiles and gorges that cut the desert floor, the bottoms of many lined with rivers of sand laid down by water long since gone.

When finally Nooch appeared, skylined in the dusk on the edge of a low mesa, Wakara rode that way, and the riders dismounted at the base of the uplift where a seep filled a shallow tank with clear water before it trickled away and soaked into the sand.

"I don't suppose you got any more of that whiskey stashed away," Richard said as he pulled the panniers from the packhorse.

"Nary a drop," Pegleg said.

Richard huffed, and set to unwinding the latigo from the cinch ring on his saddle horse. "Well, leastways there's coffee to come."

"The hell you say," Pegleg said with a laugh. "This'll be a cold camp. Won't be no fires lit tonight."

Richard pulled his saddle and let it drop to the ground. He spun around to face Pegleg. "Why the hell not? A man ought to at least have some coffee."

"Navajos."

"Navajos? Here? A rattlesnake can't live in this godforsaken place. There sure as hell can't be any Indians out there."

Again, Pegleg laughed. "Oh, they're out there, son. And they know you're out here, too."

"Well, then, if they already know we're here why not light a fire?"

"What, and fix it so's they can see to light into us? No—it's best to keep a dark camp. That way, they can't see us no more'n we can see them."

Richard snorted and sat down on his saddle. He watched the Utes take turns drinking at the spring and filling canteens, and shuffled over to take a turn ahead of the Indians leading their horses to drink. The Utes opened rawhide parfleches and passed around pieces of some kind of flat bread. He tore off a bite and chewed it slowly. It tasted nothing like any bread he had ever eaten before. It was both chewy and crumbly, and when ground down there was a grit to it. Slabs of jerky came around. The dried meat's flavor was unusual—he wondered if it might be buffalo. Nooch brought him a slice of pemmican to round out the meal. Like the jerky, its flavor was unfamiliar, unlike the pemmican his family had purchased in Indian Territory and eaten on the trail out from Tennessee. But it was all food, and filled a stomach empty of all but tepid water since the night before. He rolled out his bed and lay down on his side atop it, curled in a ball with his head pillowed on his saddle.

He was asleep before drawing a third breath, and before drawing a fourth—or so he thought—he was awakened by the prodding of Pegleg's wooden limb. He opened his eyes and sat up in an instant.

"What?" He looked around in the darkness, scrubbed his eyes with his knuckles and looked around again. "What is it?"

"Saddle your horse, son."

"Now? I only just got to sleep."

Pegleg laughed. "Some hours back, you got to sleep. Look yonder over east. The dawn, she's a-breakin'."

Richard looked, and, sure enough, the eastern horizon carried the thinnest ribbon of gray, albeit barely discernable in shade from the rest of the sky. He flexed his back and listened to the bones crackle. He stood and put on his hat. "I don't suppose there's time for a man to take a leak."

"Be quick about it. You've got that packhorse to see to."

"Why me?"

"Why the hell not? You're young and fit. Get to be my age, you'll appreciate havin' a young man about to tend to such things."

Richard came back to camp hitching up his britches to find the packsaddle on the horse and Nooch lifting the panniers onto the sawbuck tree. Richard quickly rolled his bed, and placed it and Pegleg's between the forks of the packsaddle. Nooch elbowed him out of the way and unfurled the canvas sheet over the load. Before Richard could intervene, he uncoiled the lash rope and threw a hitch to secure the cover.

"What you doin' that for? I can take care of it myself."

Nooch tied off the hitch. "You are slow. Wakara will not wait."

Richard drew a breath to voice a reply, but Nooch turned and walked away. Richard saddled his horse, dreading another day in the saddle.

A few hours into the day, with the sun still low in the eastern sky, Richard followed the procession into an alien world. The desert was barren, with but a few spindly plants clustered in nooks and alcoves that offered some protection from the sun. Where the floor wasn't peeling layers of sandstone, it was weathered sand.

And from the floor, scattered as far as the horizon, rose stone pinnacles, spires, towers, monoliths, and buttes. The rock formations reached hundreds of feet into the sky, some nearly a thousand feet, rising from steep talus slopes, ringed by scree skirts.

Richard's breathing turned shallow and he turned from side to side, watching as they rode, sometimes through long shadows stretching from the buttes to paint the desert floor. He wondered how—or if—anyone could live in such a forbidding, foreboding place. He rode up beside Pegleg with a mouthful of questions, but the old mountain man's face displayed dread as deep as his own. He hurried ahead until reaching Nooch, who rode second in line behind Wakara.

"What the hell is this place?"

Nooch studied Richard for a time as they rode, ignoring the curious landscape around them. "The Navajo call it Tsé Bii´Ndzisgaii. In their language, it means the clearing among the rocks, or valley of the rocks. To them, it is all a *hogan*."

"A what?"

"You will see, when we find the Navajo. A *hogan* is a dwelling they live in. It does not go with them, as the Ute lodge does, but stays in one place, like the white man's house. Here is where their gods taught them to build the *hogan.*"

"Can't see why anybody would want to live in this place. Starve to death, if you didn't die of thirst."

"Not many live here." Nooch said that a few families lived on the fringes of the valley, where scarce water could be found. They planted enough squash and corn and beans to survive, and kept as many sheep as they could graze on the sparse vegetation. "The Navajo believe gods and spirits are here. Do you see there, what looks to be two mittens, made of stone?" Nooch said, pointing out a pair of towering buttes. "Those are the hands of a god."

He told of a Navajo story of a goddess called Changing Woman, who had feared huge monsters were about and would harm her twin babies. So, she hid them away underground, here in the *hogan.* But the babies met Spider Woman, who gave them medicine to protect against the monsters. Changing Woman and the twins used the medicine to cast a spell on the monsters, turning them to stone, turning them into the giant buttes and monoliths scattered across the valley.

Richard scoffed at the stories. "How is it you know these things? You been here before?"

"No. I have not. But once an old man of the Navajo came to our country—a medicine man who wandered about following his spirits. He told us stories of his people and his land. I remember."

Richard fell back along the line and took his place at the end. As the sun climbed and the shadows of the buttes receded, disappeared, then crept out in the opposite direction, his eyes were never still. Somewhere, deep in the pit of his fear, roiled a hope that the haunting, imposing red rock monoliths were strong enough to contain their monsters.

CHAPTER FIFTEEN

Abel rode away from the watering place on the river, following a game trail into the willows. He found a place of concealment from where he could see the stream and the approach, then dismounted. A few minutes later, the herd reached the river. Pedro, Manuel, and Esteban pushed the sheep slowly to the water and spread them along the shore to drink. The animals took their turns in bunches, while the boys kept the herd loosely gathered, allowing the watered sheep to wander away from the bank to crop the grass carpeting the river bottom.

From his position, Abel could see the riders before the herders could. The four men reined up on the shallow bluff above the river, smoking and watching the sheep. When the last of the herd turned away from the water, the boys tightened the bunch and started the herd moving away from the stream.

Powder smoke veiled the riders on the bluff as they fired into the air. With devilish screams they laid their big-roweled Mexican spurs to their horses' bellies and stormed off the rise. Manuel, Esteban, and Pedro struggled to keep the panicked sheep from bolting as the herd milled, the *ovejas* bleating and baaing in fear and fright.

In a single motion, Abel grabbed the saddle horn and leapt onto the horse's back, finding the stirrups as his mount crashed through the brush and willows. He let the horse race until reaching the space between the nervous herd and the approaching riders, further upsetting the sheep. Abel hauled in the reins, the horse sliding to a stop and spinning to face the oncoming threat. He settled the horse and drew his Paterson revolvers from holsters on the forks of his saddle. He let his left hand and the pistol in it rest atop the saddle horn. With his right thumb he pulled back the hammer on the other Colt and felt the trigger reach out to find his finger. He stretched his arm and leveled his aim toward the onrushing riders as time ticked by, slowing almost to a stop.

When Abel first rode into the rancho belonging to Señor Rodrìguez near the place called Isleta, the hacienda was all astir. Rodrìguez looked to be berating a boy standing before him. Abel could only capture a word or two of the rapid-fire Spanish coming from the *hacendado*'s mouth, accompanied by angry gesticulation and livid histrionics. The boy stood, head down, offering the occasional answer in a voice too soft to carry. Two other boys sat horseback behind him, one holding a third horse's bridle reins. They, too, looked only at the ground, never raising their heads to meet the eyes of Rodrìguez as they flashed fire.

Rodrìguez threw his hands in the air and sent the boys away. The one on the ground retrieved his reins and climbed onto his horse and the three rode away, slouched in the saddle with heads bowed.

The ranchero still smoldered when Abel approached. He stood quietly by and waited. Rodrìguez watched the boys ride away and then turned to Abel.

"You have come too late, Señor Pate."

"*Lo siento*, Mister Rodrìguez," Abel said. "I came soon as I could. What happened?"

"Those muchachos, *los pastores*—herders of the sheep—they have allowed the bandidos to take away more of my sheep!"

"When?"

"Only today—they have only just reported the theft to me."

"How'd it happen?"

"When the sheep go to the river to drink, the bandidos charge into the flock, then cut off a group and chase them away. It is the same every time they come. Then they run the stolen sheep too fast and too far. Many dead and dying are left on their trail."

"How many of these bandits is there?"

Rodrìguez shrugged. "Sometimes three, sometimes four. Sometimes only two."

"Same ones? Same men?"

"*Si.*"

"Where do they go?"

"The trail leads to the east, toward the mountains over there."

"Your boys follow them?"

Rodrìguez attempted a smile and shook his head. "They have tried. But when the *ladrones* fire their pistols, they retreat." The ranchero sighed. "I expect too much of them. They are *jóvenes*— they are youngsters. Those muchachos know nothing of guns and of fighting."

"What would you like me to do, Mister Rodrìguez?"

"Put a stop to this thievery."

"I know that. Any particular way you'd like me to go about it?"

"No, Señor Pate. That is your decision."

Abel stood for a time studying his employer. He looked around the hacienda. He mounted his horse and eased into the saddle seat. "I reckon I'll go talk to them herders of yours. Where'll I find 'em?"

The *hacendado* flung a hand in a vague direction, then turned and walked toward what Abel took to be the main ranch house. He watched until Rodrìguez closed the heavy wooden door, then rode off the way the man indicated. Abel soon found the track of the band of sheep and the herders and followed it through a gap in the low hills and found the herd scattered across a shallow valley, nibbling at the scarce scrub there. The three boys he had seen at the house squatted in a circle atop a low rise, their horses tethered to brush nearby. They stood and eyed him as he rode toward them, paying particular attention to the pistols in their sheaths on his saddle fork, and the rifle in its scabbard alongside.

"*¿Habla usted Inglés?*"

The tallest of the boys stepped forward. "*Un poco.* A little."

"How old are you?"

"Fourteen."

"Fourteen, huh? *¿Catorce?*"

"*Sí.*"

"And them two?"

The boy pointed at his partners in turn, saying one was twelve and the other fourteen, as he was, but younger by seven months. He learned their names were Pedro, Manuel, and Esteban.

Abel stepped down and dropped the reins, ground-tying his horse. He squatted, and the boys followed suit, forming a circle as they had before. He and the oldest boy talked, Abel in his broken Spanish and Pedro in his even-more-broken English. Between them, and with interjections from the other boys, they managed to communicate.

Abel asked them about the bandits, about how they stole the sheep, how often they came, and where they took the sheep. The story they told was much the same as that related by Rodrìguez. The boys were embarrassed at the repeated loss of livestock, and felt it reflected badly on their *bravura,* their bravery. But they had no firearms, and despite their responsibility to the sheep and to Rodrìguez and the rancho, did not wish to die over the loss of a few *ovejas.*

Abel stood. The boys did likewise. Abel picked up the bridle reins. "Come the mornin', I want one of you-all to come with me. Take me down to the river where you water them sheep and show me where the *ladrones* got at 'em, and which way they went. *¿Comprende?*"

"*Si,*" Pablo said. "And then?"

Abel stepped into the stirrup and swung into the saddle. "And then I aim to find them outlaws and get back them sheep if I can." The eyes of all three boys widened. Abel turned his horse away and started back toward the hacienda.

The sun had yet to rise when Abel and Pablo stopped atop the low bluff above the river bottom. One had to study the dark water in the Rio Grande to detect any flow or movement. The lay of the land was clear to Abel, and he had no trouble envisioning the ease with which the bandidos could attack and stir the watering herd, then separate and drive away the sheep they stole. He asked Pablo questions, and the boy added detail to the account.

They rode down to the river and let their horses drink, then Abel followed the riverbank upstream and down, rode through the brush and willows that enveloped the watering place, looking for a place of concealment that offered a clear view of the area.

Pablo showed Abel the way the *ladrones* went following the attack. Abel sent the boy back to the rancho and his duties with the sheep, then set out along the trail of the stolen animals. After a few miles, over which the tracks showed the sheep and the thieves moving at a rapid pace, Abel encountered dead and dying sheep. Some of those still living lay flat on their sides, panting and gasping for breath, their legs already creeping skyward in approaching death. Others, on their feet, limped and hobbled, moaning and crying with weak bleats. He doubted that many—if any—of the woolies still drawing breath would be alive come sunset.

The trail led into the foothills skirting the higher mountains. Abel rode slowly, stopping from time to time to look and listen, to smell the air. The sun was falling ever nearer to the plain and mesas and low black cinder cones to the west. His caution was rewarded with a whiff of wood smoke. He rode deeper into the hills, following what he believed to be the direction of the scent, and saw a wisp of smoke above a low ridge ahead.

Abel dismounted and dropped the reins, trusting the horse not to wander. He pulled one of his pistols from its saddle holster and climbed the few rods to the crest of the ridge. Peeking over the top, he saw the fire. Two men sat on a log near the fire; a third man stood over a pannier, rummaging around inside it in search of something. Abel studied the area around the camp. Tucked as it was near the top of a shallow draw, the only easy access was from below. But, that would be the direction from which the men would expect trouble, should trouble come. So, Abel returned to his horse and led the animal farther uphill until, he guessed, he would be above the campsite.

He checked the loads in the pistol he carried, then tucked it into his waistband. He checked the other pistol and carried it with him. Carefully, he scaled the low ridge, steeper here than where he had climbed it below, and skirted around a clump of *piñon* trees on the crest to reach the top of the draw above the camp. He darted from one tree to another, concealing himself as best he could before stepping out into the base of the ravine, where nothing grew save *chamisa* and other low brush.

When he went, he went without hesitation, walking into the camp upright and with intention. The men must not have expected company, for they did not see Abel until he was but a few yards from the campfire. One of the men looked up, saw him, and dropped the tin cup from his hand. The other two, startled at the noise, looked to their *compañero,* then followed his eyes to the intruder standing all but amongst them, with a revolver in hand, pointing their direction.

One of the men leapt to his feet and reached for a rifle leaning against a boulder. He froze at the sound of the hammer on Abel's pistol ratcheting to full cock.

"Get up," Abel said, gesturing toward the other two men with his pistol. *"Manos arriba."*

With all three men standing, hands in the air, Abel sidled around and picked up the rifle. He tossed it out of the way, then pulled a single-shot caplock pistol from a sash around the waist of one of the bandits.

"¿Mas armas?"

One of the men tipped his chin toward a jumble of blankets and saddles stashed between two boulders. There, Abel found two more pistols.

"¿Mas?"

All three men shook their heads.

"¿Habla usted Inglés?"

Again, the men shook their heads.

Abel shrugged. "Oh, well. I guess you-all can die just as dead in Spanish. How do you say dead? *¿Muerto?*"

The eyes of one of the men widened, and Abel shifted the barrel of the revolver in his direction. "Well. Looks to me like you do understand what I'm sayin' and know what I'm talkin' about." He gestured with the pistol and the man stepped forward. "Now, here's what I want you to do. Take that pig sticker I know you got in your boot and cut into that lash line yonder and tie them two up. Hands behind them."

The bandit did as ordered. Abel sat them all down on the log near the fire, the unbound man in the middle, the backsides of the men on either side hanging half off the narrow seat. Abel bound the man's hands, then threaded a length of rope to bind the three of them together.

Abel walked around the fire and sat on a flat-topped boulder placed there as a seat. He said, "Where are the sheep? *¿Las ovejas?*"

The men looked at each other, but none spoke. Abel pointed the pistol at them. They talked back and forth in fast-paced Spanish Abel could not keep up with, then the man in the middle said, "We do not know." He shrugged. "Albuquerque . . . Santa Fe . . . Las Vegas . . . El Paso del Norte . . . Chihuahua . . . who can say?"

It took time and repetition and many questions, but Abel learned there was a fourth man involved, and he took care of the business end of the enterprise. These men only rustled livestock. Their partner took orders, arranged buyers, and saw to the delivery of the animals they stole. Some were driven away for sale at the markets, others taken to butchers to slaughter and sell as meat, still others to stock the ranges and replenish the herds of unscrupulous rancheros.

Abel fetched the rifle and battered the stock against a boulder until it shattered and splintered, rendering the firearm useless. Two of the pistols were loaded, and he discharged them into the dusky sky, then hammered all three pistols against a rock, bending and twisting the firing mechanisms. The men looked on, despondent.

"Now, *mis amigos*," Abel said. "Here's what's goin' to happen. When that partner of yours comes back, you-all tell him your thievin' days is over. If ever you-all come to steal sheep from Señor Rodrìguez—or if I hear tell of you-all rustlin' stock anywhere in this country—I will kill you. Dead. *¿Comprendé?*"

Abel untied the rope binding the men together. With his knife, he sliced through the lashing around the wrists of one. As the man flexed his cramped arms and rubbed his wrists, Abel hit him over the head with the barrel of his revolver. The man slumped off his tenuous seat on the log and lay on the ground.

"When he wakes up, he can untie you two. Then you-all had best climb on them sorry horses of yours and get out of this country—and stay out."

Abel rode slowly through the night, his horse picking its way back to the ranch. Rodrìguez praised his work, but did not believe they had seen the last of the *ladrones* and asked Abel to stay on.

For weeks to come, Abel stayed around the ranch, pitching in to help wherever he could, but with few duties other than accompanying the boys to the river when they took the sheep to water. He spent many a day in the company of the herders, developing a friendship with Pablo as they helped each other improve their ability to speak the other's language.

And then one morning as he sat horseback among the riverside brush and willows, the thieves came. As they stormed toward the river, yelling and shooting to frighten the sheep, Abel rode out to meet them. Too late, the men realized their pistols—useless until reloaded—would not serve them well in the face of the revolvers in Abel's hands. Only the bandido whose head Abel had smashed carried a load, and in his excitement, and shooting from horseback, he wasted his shot.

Abel stood firm as the riders came on fast, fanning out as they came. One of the men was unfamiliar, and Abel took him as their leader. He pointed the pistol in his direction and fired. The bullet found its mark, whistling over the horse's head to smash the center of the rider's chest, tipping him backward out of the saddle to somersault to the ground where he bounced once, then moved no more. One by one, deliberately but quickly, Abel fired at the other three, missing once but putting a bullet in each of the bandits before any of them reached him. He rode to where each had fallen. One was still alive, gut-shot and suffering. Abel dispatched him with a bullet to the head. Another still breathed, frothy blood bubbling from a chest wound, but drew his last breath before Abel could put a bullet in his head.

Watching the blood leak from his victims, Abel's mind flooded with the torment of the first blood he had drawn.

It had been what now seemed a lifetime ago, back in Tennessee. After the family fled, father sent his boys back home to Shelby County to retrieve from his brother, Ben, family records rightfully his by birthright. Uncle Ben refused, and gave Melvin a beating. He refused again when offered money, and threatened to kill the boys if they persisted. Richard declared the mission a failure and readied their return to the trail. Abel, however, determined to carry out their father's wishes, made another attempt. It ended in the dark of night and a fight the boy did not want, a fight that left Uncle Ben lying in the street, his throat slit with his own knife, and blood on Abel's hands.

And he thought of the Comanchero who stole Jane during their sojourn along the Canadian River, his evil intent snuffed out by bullets fired from Abel's gun.

Abel shook his bowed head and heaved a long sigh as he watched the soaking blood stain his latest victim's shirtfront even as it sullied his soul.

Meantime, the boys had settled the frightened sheep, just as frightened themselves by what they had seen. Pablo helped Abel catch the outlaw horses and drape the bodies over the saddles, tying hands and feet together under the horses' bellies. He tied bridle reins to saddle strings, towing the nervous horses with their bloody loads back to the rancho. He handed the reins of the horse he led to Rodriguez.

Abel told the ranchero where to send his pay, then rode off toward Albuquerque.

CHAPTER SIXTEEN

Daniel Lewis took to the mercantile business like a coyote to a gut pile. The easy manner that drew people to him masked his ambitious approach to negotiation. Favorable contracts with freighters and packers were on the books—for importing and exporting goods to and from the States, California, and Chihuahua—as well as profitable relationships with local growers and craftsmen. He also had an agent in Las Vegas to ride out and make early connections with wagon masters on the road from Independence.

The Lewis & Pate Mercantile sign hung above doors in Albuquerque, Las Vegas, Bernalillo, Abiquiu, and other outlying communities and pueblos. In many cases, those stores and trading posts gave residents easy access to goods not readily available before Lewis set up shop there.

Daniel had established an office in the Santa Fe Warehouse. Mary left Albuquerque to take up the reins there, and she tended to day-to-day operations, keeping the books and seeing to business during her father's frequent absences to make deals for the sale and purchase of merchandise, and to seek out locations for Lewis & Pate stores.

While he helped out whenever and wherever he could, more and more often Lee Pate felt like an unnecessary appendage to the business. The ins and outs of buying and selling and finances and merchandising were beyond his ken and outside his interest. More than anything, he wanted to get back to the land.

His hopes to do so hung on a conversation with Guadalupe Miranda.

Miranda had come one day to Albuquerque to see to the safety of his family. He offered Enrique Ramirez funds for their care and keep, which were refused out of the obligation of hospitality. Miranda then entered the Lewis & Pate Mercantile, asking for Lee Pate. Invited into the living quarters in the rear, Miranda accepted coffee. Sarah set out cornbread left over from breakfast.

"It is with humble heart I come to you, Señor Pate. It is to you I owe the safety—the very lives—of my family. It is a debt that cannot be repaid."

Lee waved him off. "Think nothing of it, Mister Miranda. I did no more than what any man would do."

"I do not believe this to be so, *mi amigo*. Many would have passed by, thinking it none of their affair. But you, Señor Pate, you risked your own safety, your very life, to protect strangers. As it happens, those who were strangers to you that fateful day were *mi familia, mi alma y corazón*. I am thus forever in your debt."

Again, Lee waved him off.

Miranda sipped his coffee, drizzled honey on a square of cornbread, and studied his host as he ate. "At the risk of vanity, Señor Pate, I will ask if you know who I am."

"Why sure, Mister Miranda. Well, not exactly, maybe. I know you're some kind of official in the government up in Santa Fe. The governor's right-hand man, or some such."

Miranda nodded. "You have the gist of it. I am, officially, secretary of affairs for Nuevo Mexico, as well as personal secretary to Gobernador Armijo. But, in all modesty, my influence reaches beyond my official duties." He paused and asked for more coffee, which Sarah poured, after which she stepped back and pretended to busy herself at the stove.

Miranda said, "What occasions your presence in Nuevo Mexico, if I may be so bold as to ask?"

Lee related at length his dissatisfaction with conditions in the States, particularly the practice of slavery. He told of the family's exit from Tennessee to distance themselves from what he deemed a corrupt and sinful society. He told something of their travels, and their winter in Fort Smith to earn money to complete the journey. He told of their meeting with the Lewis family in Fort Smith—refugees of a sort themselves from conditions in the States, having fled violence against Mormons in Missouri, where the Lewises had settled after emigrating from England to join their fellow Saints. And he told of the journey of the combined families across Indian Territory to reach Mexico.

"And how do you find conditions here, Señor?"

Lee shrugged. "Can't complain, I suppose. This storekeeping business is doin' good—but that's all due to Daniel. It's a living, but I can't say it's to my liking."

"What would you prefer?"

Lee considered his reply. He knew what he wanted to say, but thought about how best to say it. He stirred his coffee, then took a long, slow sip. "Back in Tennessee, I grew crops. Raised livestock. Cattle, hogs, some sheep. I can't see as how what I know about growin' crops would matter in this country, bein' dry as it is. But cows is cows, I reckon." He paused for another sip of coffee. "What'd please me, judgin' from what I've seen of the land hereabouts, would be a piece of property where I could run some cows. Sell off the calves for beef after they get some growth on 'em. But we been told land will be hard to come by, us bein' foreigners in this land and all."

Miranda let Lee's dreams lie for a time. Then, "It could be, *mi amigo,* that arrangements could be made."

Lee dared not reply, but he looked intently at Miranda. He

cast a glance at Sarah, then back to their guest.

"You see," Miranda said, "there is land, much land, that is unassigned. Grants of land are the province of Gobernador Armijo, but I am not without influence in such decisions." Again, he paused to reflect and sip his coffee. "There is one location in particular that comes to mind. You see, when the people of Mexico cast off the rule of Spain, there were those who resisted independence. Even here, in Nuevo Mexico, there were loyalists who maintained allegiance to Spain. Those who refused, after much encouragement, to declare fealty to the revolutionary government, were expelled and their lands appropriated. Some of these holdings were extensive. And, I am sorry to say, some have lain idle for years."

Sarah, anticipating the need, carried the coffeepot to the table and refilled Miranda's mug and poured more for Lee, as well. His mug, however, stood mostly full as he rotated it in trembling fingers.

Miranda helped himself to another piece of cornbread, the anticipation in the room as thick as the honey he drenched it with. "There is one such abandoned *estancia*, rancho, that comes to mind that might suit your purpose. It lies a day's ride west of Santa Fe, and a little north, on the Pajarito Plateau. It is both a rugged country, and a paradise. The high mesas, covered with heavy forest and broad *prados*, are an enchanted land for *las vacas* and *las ovejas*. Both cattle and sheep thrive there. And yet, it is a hard land, as the mesas are interrupted by *barrancas, cañones profundos*—how do you say?—deep canyons, gorges, and defiles."

Another pause, another bite of cornbread and another sip of coffee. "Would such a property be of interest to you, Señor Pate?"

Lee swallowed hard. "Sounds like just the thing, Mister Miranda. But, much as I might want to, I ain't got the means to pay for a place such as that."

This time, it was Miranda who waved off Lee. "Such accommodations could be worked out. Certainly, there would be the matter of tribute to Gobernador Armijo for exercising his authority in arranging the conveyance of the property. As for myself, it would be impolite for me to accept any token of your appreciation, as it is I who am indebted to you."

Lee could hardly speak. "Then . . . then . . . you think it might be possible?"

"Possible, for certain. Probable, perhaps." Miranda stood and extended his hand across the table. As he shook hands with Lee, he said, "Allow me some time to consult with *el gobernador*. I am confident he will be persuaded when apprised of your valiant rescue of *mi familia* in their time of need."

Lee, his nerves nearly getting the best of him, mentioned to his guest Abel's service against the Texians, and the notice Armijo had taken of the boy. He did not see his guest out, leaving that courtesy to Sarah. He sat, and did not leave the chair for the remainder of the day.

Within a week, a messenger from the capital city summoned Lee to Palacio de los Gobernadores. He shuttered the store and loaded Sarah, Emma, and Jane in the wagon and took the road to Santa Fe. Unlike his first visit to the Palace of the Governors fronting the Plaza, Lee was immediately escorted to Miranda's office. There, he was told that Governor Armijo had approved the grant of the *estancia* on the Pajarito Plateau. Lee could hardly contain himself as Miranda outlined the details of the transfer. He swallowed hard at the sum Armijo demanded—off the books—for the transfer, but was confident Daniel would front him the money for his share of the mercantile business, or lend him funds enough to satisfy the governor's immediate demands. Lee would set his signature to paper to covenant paying Armijo the balance over time.

No sooner was the ink dry on the documents than Lee loaded the wagon, fluffed the lines, and set the team of mules on the road to the plateau to examine his new holdings. Sarah and Emma shared the wagon seat with him; provisions and camp equipment filled the wagon bed. Jane had protested, but stayed behind in Santa Fe with Mary.

As the wagon rolled along, visions of paradise, dreams of a promised land, filled Lee's head. Sarah did not share his joy. Her uncertainty grew as the road turned to overgrown ruts, cluttered with deadfall and fallen rocks as it climbed the mesa, the road often little more than a narrow shelf scratched into the side of precipitous, nearly vertical, slopes. Lee reined up the team often, setting the brake and chocking the wagon wheels so he could clear the trail.

"I swear to God, Lee Pate, that you have again let your damn dreams get the best of you. Of us," Sarah said, tucking a stray lock of hair back under her bonnet.

"But is it not beautiful?" Emma said. "So many trees. So different from the desert."

Sarah sniffed. "A body can't eat scenery."

"Now, Sarah, this is the best chance we've had. Better, even, than back in Shelby County. We've been handed an opportunity here, and I ain't one to look a gift horse in the mouth. And you needn't fret about keepin' your belly full. Ain't you took note of all these cattle? Them's ours for the takin'."

"I seen 'em all right. They don't act like any cows I ever seen. Wild as deer, they are. Hidin' in the damn bushes like they ain't never seen a human bein'."

Lee smiled. "Not to worry, dear. They'll calm down once we get a brand on them."

Sarah scoffed. "That's if you can catch them."

"Abel can do it," Emma said. "You know how handy he is.

139

Once he sets his hand to a task, he will not cease until it is finished."

Lee smiled again. "The girl's right. Me and Abel, we can get it done. We'll hire some of these Mexican boys to help us. Some of them rides like they was born horseback, and they's mighty handy with a rope. We can learn to handle cattle like they do in this country."

Sarah said nothing more. She rode along with her jaw set, sweeping her hair out of the way.

"If I am reading this map properly, the road will soon end at what is labeled 'la hacienda,' " Emma said.

"Yes, and look at that map," Sarah said. "There ain't another blessed thing on it for miles around, but empty space."

"Ain't that grand!" Lee said. "A world of our own."

"More like our own little corner of hell."

"Now, Sarah. You could at least give it a chance."

"I'm about all out of chances, Lee Pate." Sarah wiped away a tear before it could fall. "You and your damn dreams."

They rode on for a time in silence broken only by the calls and chirring and clicking and chirping of birds and insects, and the occasional sound of cattle crashing through the brush as they approached. The road passed through a stand of aspen and evergreen trees. The woods opened up to reveal a broad, grassy meadow ringed by trees.

Emma's rapid intake of breath held for a moment, then she exhaled slowly, a low moan, a sigh, escaping with the breath. Lee stopped the wagon and stood, one boot propped on the foot board as he studied the scene. Sarah lifted the skirt of her apron and wiped her face.

"Would you look at that," Lee said, barely above a whisper.

Across the expanse, perhaps a quarter or half mile away, tucked into the verge of the forest, stood several buildings. The tallest, a two-story affair, had walls of cut stone and looked to be the main house. Around it were other structures, some glowing white in the sun, the others the color of mud. A few looked to be small houses, the others outbuildings. A large, low-slung building appeared to be a barn of sorts. Low adobe walls fenced off the homes, and a network of pole corrals lay among the outbuildings.

Lee removed his hat and mopped his head with a soiled handkerchief from his pocket. "What do you think, Sarah?"

"Looks mighty lonesome, I'd say."

"It is beautiful," Emma whispered. "I cannot wait for Abel to see it."

The closer the wagon took them to the hacienda, the more the picture faded. The yard was overgrown with low scrub. Small, scattered saplings sprouted where trees had taken root. Sheets and slabs of mud plaster were missing from walls. Pole fences were broken down, posts rotted and drooping. The roof of the barn sagged, and looked to be spotted with holes. Swallow nests pimpled the upper walls of the stone house, and the birds flitted in and out of empty windows.

"What do you think of your paradise now, Lee Pate?"

"Now, Sarah. There ain't nothin' wrong that can't be fixed with a little work."

Emma sighed. "I cannot wait for Abel to see it."

CHAPTER SEVENTEEN

Melvin sat cross legged atop a low outcrop, his face glowing in the golden light of a falling sun. He studied the land roundabout, looking for something, anything, that might be edible. For days he had lined his stomach with nothing more than leaves and grass. His attempts to catch fish by hand from the river below had been unsuccessful. The dried meat and pemmican the Utes furnished him—at Pegleg's request, demand, even—weeks before when he abandoned the party bound to capture slaves among the Navajo, was long since gone.

Unsure of where he was or where he should be, Melvin had wandered, weak and tired and confused. He believed the stream to be the Rio Chama, the river he had followed with Pegleg and Richard on their way north, but could not be certain. As he sat and watched and watched and sat, lacking the will or strength to do more, he detected a wisp, a slender trace of what he took to be dust, wafting in the still air upstream above a ridge opposite the river. The dust continued to rise in thin strands, then formed into a faint cloud which thickened as time passed.

Melvin, entranced by the rising haze, soon imagined he heard voices, then the thrum of falling hooves, the ring and jingle of spur rowels, the creak of leather. And then, in silhouette, there appeared, rising over the crest of the ridge, a rider. Hard on the heels of his mount came a laden mule, then another, and another, until half a dozen topped the ridge, followed by another rider with a similar string in tow, and then another.

Rising from his seat, Melvin hollered and waved his arms overhead, then jumped off the outcrop to scuttle down the slope toward the river. But his feet failed to keep pace with his intention, and he fell, tumbling down the hillside. When he came to a halt in the mud at the edge of the river, Melvin stood and waded into the stream, arms still flailing. The riders across the way watched as they passed, looks of wonder in eyes staring out of dusty faces.

Reversing course, Melvin left the water and clambered back upslope to where his horse stood, head up, neck outstretched, eyes and ears pinned on the passing pack strings. Gathering the reins and grasping the saddle horn, it took Melvin three tries to find the stirrup with his probing foot. As soon as his seat hit the saddle, his heels pounded the horse's flanks. He rode headlong into the stream, drumming the horse's belly and lashing its rump as he whipped the reins from side to side. The horse clawed its way out of the water and up the steep bank. Melvin kept pushing the animal up the slope, angling toward the horses and mules on the ridgetop.

The pack strings had passed when Melvin reached the crest, but he found himself in a mob of loose mules and horses, following the trail in twos and threes and fours. He let his horse move along with them as he craned his neck this way and that, and when he saw a rider through the dust behind, he reined out of the herd and stopped beside the trail.

When the last of the loose stock passed, he saw there were two riders, both mounted on mules, bringing up the rear. Dust coated the men and their mules, sifting in small dribbles from wrinkles in their clothes, from hat brims, and from creases and crevices on their saddles and blankets where it settled. The dusty drovers were young, Melvin saw, or thought he did, studying their soiled faces. He fell in next to one of them.

"Where you-all goin'?"

The rider only looked at him, the red-traced whites of his eyes staring out of his dusty face.

"Well, then, where are we? Is there any town hereabouts? You-all got anything to eat?"

The young man smiled, white teeth gleaming out of the dust. He shrugged. *"No entiendo. No hablo inglés."*

Melvin thought for a moment, then pantomimed eating. The young man smiled again, then reached behind and untied the laces on a saddlebag. He reached in and pulled out a small cloth bundle, which he set on his oversized saddle horn and opened. He handed Melvin a thin slice of *carne seca*, jerked meat, and a tortilla wrapped around a paste of mashed beans. Melvin hardly bothered to chew, and the tortilla and its stuffing were gone in a few bites. The jerky required him to work his jaws to moisten and soften and chew the stringy meat. As he did, he looked at the Mexican and rubbed his stomach.

The boy shrugged. *"No mas."*

Melvin swallowed the wad of meat and followed it down with a long draught of water from his canteen. Somewhat revived, he peppered the two young riders with questions as they moved along the trail, none of which resulted in any response other than curious stares, shrugs, wagging heads, and the repeated, *"No entiendo."*

As the sun dropped below the horizon, the pack train dropped off the trail along the sidehills and ridgetops to a grassy meadow along the river. The *mozos* pulled the packs from their mule strings and turned the animals loose to graze. Melvin surmised this place was a regular camping spot for there were rings of stones, blackened by the smoke of many fires, on a patch of ground where little grass grew, the dirt packed to hardpan from much use.

Melvin sat horseback as his newfound companions watched their herd drink at the river and move onto the grass. They rode to the fires, already lit and heating pots and *comals* pulled from the packs. Melvin watched the men tending to the fires, and although the smells of cooking food had yet to fill the air, his stomach rumbled and his mouth watered. He unsaddled his horse and staked it out in a grassy spot rather than allowing it to mix with the mules and horses of the pack train.

"Ven conmigo," the young man he had been riding with said. His face, now scrubbed clean of dust and dirt, showed a smile. *"Ven,"* he said, with a wave of his hand signaling Melvin to follow.

Melvin followed the boy across the campsite and stopped near a circle of men, squatting on the ground and talking. The boy touched one of the men on the shoulder and said something to him in a soft voice Melvin did not hear, nor would have understood had he heard. The man left the group and stepped to where Melvin stood.

"You are Americano."

Melvin could only nod, surprised at the sound of the first few English words he had heard outside his own head or mouth for many days.

"You are hungry?"

Again, Melvin nodded. The man smiled and said to be patient, as food would be ready soon. He said the fare would be simple, as their stores were low as they were near the end of their journey.

Melvin said, "Where you-all been? Where you-all goin'?"

The man told him they were traders returning from *Alta California*. And that soon, in a matter of a few days, they would reach Abiquiu, the place of their departure nearly half a year before. There, the train would disband, save enough of the *mozos* and drovers to move the bulk of the goods and livestock on to Santa Fe and the stockyards and warehouses and merchants there.

145

"And you?"

Melvin pondered the unexpected question. Then, "Can't rightly say. Don't know of any place where I should go, or where I ought to be."

"You are on your own?"

"I reckon so. I was with my brother, but we parted ways up north of here somewheres, up where them Ute Indians are. Only place I knew to go where there was people was down this way. 'Fore that, I was in Taos, and Las Vegas. Last seen my Ma and Pa in Las Vegas, long time back. Me and my brother left 'em there and set off on our own." He shrugged. "Guess it's just me, now."

He talked with the man through supper and well into the night, telling the tale of his family's journey from Tennessee and his travels with his brother Richard. He queried the man about where work might be found, and how a man on his own might find a place in this strange—at least to him—country.

The last words Melvin remembered hearing before falling asleep in his deep fatigue, said something about a woman and a place called *El Potrero de Chimayó*.

The journey through the "Valley of the Rocks" yielded little. *Hogans* were few and far between, and most of those the slavers came across were temporarily abandoned. Wilting corn, squash, and bean plants revealed their keepers had slipped away days ago. Sheep were scattered, and pens where horses and burros were kept sat empty. A few *hogans* were still occupied by wizened old people, struggling to keep the crops watered in the absence of younger family members. Only two captives had accompanied the travelers since leaving the valley—a young mother and her child. The woman was ill, and the grandmother who cared for her was left dead, killed by a Ute determined to take the mother and child despite the old woman's feeble defense and the young woman's sickness.

Mother and child clung desperately to the bare back of a mule, the woman's feet hobbled beneath the animal's belly, for two long days across folded and fractured desert stretching southeastward from the valley where the tall rocks rose into the sky. A meager water source quenched the thirst of the riders and their mounts at the end of the first day's ride. The trail skirted Black Mesa, which loomed to the southwest, until reaching Chinle Valley. They followed the valley and the wash to the south, then turned east along the watercourse toward the mouth of a canyon cut into a range of mountains, and stopped for the night.

The Utes tied up the woman, back against a tree. As the others readied the camp, Nooch squatted next to the captive and gave her water from the small, sluggish stream wandering through its sandy bed. He talked to the woman as she cradled her little girl in her lap. The conversation was halting, owing to Nooch's limited ability with Navajo speech and her ignorance of the Ute language. The talk mixed Navajo and Spanish words, along with signs, in an attempt to communicate.

Richard watched them. He asked Pegleg what the questioning was all about.

"Can't say," Pegleg said, sitting in the sand massaging the stump of his missing leg. "Most likely Nooch wants to know what we'll find once we follow this stream into that canyon. Won't be nothin' good, if you wonder what I'm thinkin'. When he's done with her, ask Nooch what he knows. He'll tell you—if he thinks it any of your affair."

After a time, Nooch offered the Navajo woman more to drink, then left her bound to the tree. He passed along to Wakara what the woman told him, and they talked for a time. After the camp had eaten, Richard beckoned Nooch.

"Say, Nooch, what's that there girl got to say?"

Nooch sat with the two white men. "Many things. She is angry at being taken. She fears she will lose her child. She believes her man will come for her, and kill us all."

Pegleg asked if she had said anything about the canyon they would enter come morning.

"Some. She says it is a sacred place to her people; to the *Diné.*"

Richard interrupted. "*Diné?* I thought she was a Navajo."

Nooch shrugged. "Navajo is the name given them by the Spaniards. To my people, they are *Pahgow'witch.* They say they are *Diné*—The People."

"To hell with all that," Pegleg said. "What'd she have to say about this place?"

Nooch thought for a time. "This is the home of her man. His family is here, and this is where he lived until joining her clan when they married. It is called *Tséyi'*, 'The Place Deep in the Rock.' Others call it *Cañon de Chelly* in the language of the Spaniards and the Mexicans. She says there are many other canyons and *barrancas* inside. They are narrow, with high walls, and the grass grows in there always, and there are trees that grow fruit, and gardens, and sheep. The Navajo have lived here longer than anyone can remember. But others—the *Anasazi*, the Ancient Enemies—lived here before. Their homes, where the Navajo do not go, are still there, hidden in the cliffs."

Pegleg chewed on what he had said. Then, "Wakara, he's bound to go in there?"

"He says he is. He believes we will capture many people to sell."

Richard said, "He don't seem none too concerned about them knowin' we're here."

Nooch smiled. "They know already. They have watched us."

"He must not think they'll put up much of a fight."

"They will fight. But the *Pahgow'witch* are no match for the Ute."

Pegleg laughed. "I reckon them Navajos have a different idea about that."

"The woman thinks so."

Richard asked what he meant.

"She says if we go in there, we will die."

CHAPTER EIGHTEEN

Richard marveled yet again at the world he found himself in as they entered the canyon. The walls grew higher around him as he rode, sandstone cliffs in every shade of dun and red, rising until reaching a thousand feet. The Ute party rode quietly, watching the narrow canyon ahead and the walls above for signs of danger.

After a mile or two in the *barranca*, Wakara signaled a stop. The canyon split: one gorge continuing eastward; the other angling off to the northeast. The Ute leader sent for Nooch and the Navajo woman. Pegleg rode ahead to listen. He returned and told Richard they would continue into *Cañon de Chelly* proper. Then he told what the woman said about the other defile.

"Years back, 'fore her man was born, in the time of his father and grandfather, she says the Spanish soldiers came here and lit into the Navajos. Killed a bunch of 'em. More'n a hundred, she says her man's people told her. That's why they call it *Cañon del Muerto*—Canyon of the Dead."

"Well, hell," Richard said. "I'm glad we ain't goin' in there."

Pegleg chuckled. Don't you worry, son. Once we clean out this other canyon, we'll come back here and ride on into *Cañon del Muerto*."

Richard swallowed hard, and without thinking about it, pulled his father's rifle from its saddle scabbard and checked the load and priming.

The party rode slowly, every eye alert. Here and there on the sheer cliffs, in places that looked insurmountable, Richard saw what looked like brick structures. Some were small and others sizeable; some plastered with mud, others bare; some crumbling with decay, others firm and strong. Cliff faces along the trail were pecked and scratched with drawings. The clustered pictures showed fantastical animals, human-like figures, and geometric designs. They passed peach trees, corn patches, sprawling squash plants, and green, growing crops Richard did not recognize. There were *hogans* built of upright posts mortared with mud, roofs covered with brush and dirt around a smoke hole, with a doorway always on the east-facing angle of the octagonal houses.

But no people.

They saw no smoke, no fires, no signs of life. The only sounds were bird calls and the chatter of insects, and even those faded as they passed.

Still, Richard could feel eyes on him. The behavior of the others, scanning the canyon walls, the alcoves in the cliffs, the slot canyons branching off the main gorge, showed that they, too, knew they were not alone. Even the horses—those they rode, and those on leads brought along to carry captives— snorted and tossed their heads, ears pinned back and eyes showing white, pawing at the ground and prancing, occasionally rearing or kicking out, forcing the riders to keep a tight rein and to squirm into a deeper seat.

The riders rounded a bend in the canyon and on a low hill to the right, a narrow sandstone pinnacle rose out of the ground. A short way up its face, the rock split, forming two narrow spires rising skyward, one reaching much higher than the other, rising almost to the height of the thousand-foot canyon walls.

Every rider reined up his horse to stare at the rock. The Navajo woman laughed without humor. Wakara hissed, his eyes riveted on the young mother, his look intimidating her to silence. He said something to Nooch, and the young man rode to the woman, snatched the lead rope from the man who held it, and led the woman to Wakara. They talked, again with Nooch interpreting what the woman said.

Her report angered Wakara. He shouted at the woman in Ute, the words meaning nothing to her, but their delivery making the point. Her child whimpered, then started crying. Wakara lashed out with his quirt, striking the woman on the shoulder, then the head, and said something more to her, this time in a quiet voice even more ominous than the yelling. The woman cupped a hand over the child's mouth, stifling the crying, whispering calming words to the child, even as her eyes, flashing fire, locked on the Ute leader.

Richard turned to Pegleg. "You get any of that? What she said?"

"Some. Leastways, what Nooch said she said." He nodded toward the tall, thin spire. "That there's what the Navajos call Spider Rock. The woman said she ain't never seen it, but her man told her about it. Says Spider Woman lives up there. She's kind of a goddess or some such to them. Helps them and protects them from monsters and such like." He pointed to the top of the pinnacle. "Says Spider Woman keeps the bones of her victims up there." He dropped his gaze and leveled it at Richard. "Says that's where our bones will be soon enough, and even our spirits won't never get out of this place."

Richard stared at the spire, and shuddered. Without a word, Wakara heeled his horse into motion and all the horses followed as if strung together by a strand of Spider Woman's web. Just beyond the Spider Rock, another deep canyon branched off to the south, but Wakara ignored it and rode on into the main canyon. The gorge cut ever deeper into the plateau, but, here, they encountered fewer signs of life. The sandy canyon floor showed signs of wildlife, but no tracks of humans or their kept animals.

Wakara called a halt and talked things over with Nooch and some of the other men. After the talk, they reversed course and rode back down the canyon. Burning eyes, weary from a long day of intense sunlight reflected off canyon walls, continued to scrutinize every nook and cranny in the canyon, looking for an enemy as yet unseen. The party passed out of the canyon's mouth and halted at the campsite they had left that morning. Wakara did not want to spend the night within the confines of the canyon's high walls.

And no one of the Utes, nor either white man, would dispute his decision.

Wakara had them on the move at first light, and by the time the sun showed itself over the canyon walls, they were within the confines of the Canyon of the Dead. Here, despite the daunting name of the place, were more signs of habitation—*hogans,* crops, orchards, and wandering sheep, burros, and horses. Clear water flowed in a narrow stream that meandered along a broad, sandy bed. Cottonwood trees, some green and growing, others gray skeletons, stood along the way.

Still, they saw no one. And, still, they felt they were being watched. More ruins, homes of the Ancient Enemies, clung to the cliffsides. It was unlikely danger would come from among the adobe cliff dwellings, as the Navajo avoided them. But there were plenty of places where menace might lurk, both above them and from the many smaller *barrancas* branching off the main stem of the canyon.

The attack came at once, without warning, despite their watchfulness. With hissing and whooshing, a blizzard of arrows stormed off canyon walls where no one of the Utes had seen any sign of an attacker. Horses, pierced by the darts, panicked, rearing and spinning. Lead ropes, stretched to the limit of the arms of their holders, jerked loose. Freed horses and mules darted and dodged, looking for refuge. Utes fell, some dead and some wounded.

Richard followed Pegleg as he spurred his frightened mount out of the middle of the canyon toward the cliff wall on the left. He saw the Utes doing the same, seeking refuge against both walls. This provided shelter from attackers above, but, at the same time, offered those on the opposite cliffs a better angle at an exposed target.

Pegleg dismounted, stumbling on his wooden leg in the sand, but managing to maneuver his way between the canyon wall and his skittering horse. Richard followed suit, his control of his mount made difficult by the long rifle in his hand. By the time Richard found what concealment the horse offered, Pegleg had his rifle out of its scabbard and trained on the opposite cliffs, seeking a target. Again, Richard followed the old mountain man's lead and propped his elbow on the saddle seat, training the gun barrel on the sandstone wall. He detected a narrow ledge several yards up the sheer wall and his eyes followed it to where it held a cluster of fallen boulders.

A head appeared, peeking out around the edge of a rock, then the man leaned out to unleash an arrow. Before Richard could draw a bead, Pegleg's rifle belched fire and smoke and Richard watched the Navajo fall backward. When two of his companions showed themselves to pull him—or his body—to safety, Richard fired and one of the men collapsed, falling atop the first victim.

A few other guns fired from here and there among the Utes, fired by those who carried firearms. As Richard recharged his rifle, he looked up the canyon and saw Nooch fire, and, across the canyon, a Navajo fall and bounce once off the cliff before landing on the canyon floor.

The gunfire slowed the rain of arrows and the fighters on the cliff walls scampered to safety, some falling to rifle fire, others to arrows from Ute bows. No gunfire came from above. Richard felled another Navajo as he dodged between boulders. Pegleg had fired twice more, his skill at reloading far surpassing Richard's, and each shot found a victim.

A stream of pebbles fell from above, and Pegleg hissed at the Ute fighter across the way, pointing upward. The Ute watched and unleashed an arrow, and a Navajo with an arrow through his throat scraped his way down the sandstone wall, leaving a smear of blood, then fell between Richard and Pegleg.

Richard's horse spooked and spun away, tossing its head and prancing and snorting. Richard rushed toward the frightened animal, and it backed away as he approached, his haste causing more fear. He slowed, reached out a hand, and spoke softly. He took another step toward the horse, but stopped when an arrow from a Navajo bow pierced his shoulder just below the collar bone and tore its way through his body, stopping only when it slammed against the inside of his shoulder blade bone.

Dropping to his knees, he looked for the man who shot him. Crouched on a ledge on the cliff across the canyon, lower than where he and Pegleg had shot the other attackers, knelt what looked to be a boy no more than twelve or fourteen years old, bow in hand and still upright. He stared at Richard wide eyed, as if in disbelief that his arrow had found its mark. Richard, panting shallow breaths and weaving in an attempt not to fall over, stared back at the boy. Then, a red hole drilled through the boy's head and a clot of blood, brain, bone, and hair spattered the cliff wall behind him. He tipped forward and fell, rebounding off the sandstone wall a number of times before thudding into the sand at the end of his fall.

Smoke still feathered out of the barrel of Pegleg's rifle when he reached Richard. He looped an arm under Richard's and hefted him to his feet, struggling with his wooden peg in the sand as he helped the wounded and woozy victim back to the relative safety against the cliff.

Richard watched through a fog, sitting legs spraddled, back against the slickrock wall. The fighting soon wound down and the Utes fetched frightened horses, and gathered under Wakara's orders. They collected their injured to tend to their wounds, and draped the dead over the backs of horses. A few of the Utes checked the fallen Navajos, dispatching those who still breathed by slitting their throats or smashing skulls with war clubs. They left the Navajo to lie in the bloody sand, absent scalps that now hung from Ute belts and rifle barrels.

Richard was barely awake when Pegleg and Nooch and a Ute whose name he did not know gathered around to check his wound. They laid him flat and the Ute sliced through his shirtfront with a heavy knife. In his haze, Richard feared the blade would soon pierce his heart, and used the little strength he could muster to struggle upright. Pegleg pressed him back down and said something Richard could not fathom, but the mountain man's steady voice calmed him.

The Ute he did not know probed the flesh around the wound and talked to Pegleg and Nooch with words Richard did not understand.

"Can you hear me, son?"

Richard forced his eyes open to see Pegleg's face inches away. He nodded.

"We got to get that arrow out of you. It struck bone and didn't come out. If we don't get it out, it's likely to fester. Kill you, it could. You savvy?"

Again, he answered with a weak nod.

"This is goin' to hurt some. Just so's you know." Then, "Here, drink this."

The Taos whiskey burned its way down his throat. Richard

coughed and sputtered. "You sonofabitch! You been holdin' out on me!"

Pegleg smiled. "No, son. Kept this back for medicinal use. You ought to be damn glad I did."

He gave Richard another drink, then another. Then he splashed whiskey on the wound, the fire of it reversing the sedative effect of what Richard had swallowed.

"Dammit!" Richard said, struggling again to sit up.

"Calm yourself, boy. It's for your own good."

"To hell with that. Don't be wastin' good whiskey thataway. It'll do more good inside of me than out."

Pegleg fed him more of the whiskey and waited for him to relax. "Nooch, you grab aholt of his head and that other arm." He told the other man who had experience treating wounds, to hold Richard's legs. Grinding his foot into the sand to find a steady base, Pegleg propped his wooden appendage on Richard's chest next to the arrow shaft. He grasped the arrow with both hands, fidgeting to find a secure grip. Pegleg leaned his weight onto the wooden leg and onto Richard. "Steady now, son," he said, and lifted on the arrow.

Richard writhed and squirmed in the sand. The two men holding him bore down with their strength. Pegleg kept pulling on the arrow. With a snap, it popped loose and burst out of the hole, followed by a stream of blood. Pegleg studied the shaft, minus its point. He swore, and tossed the arrow aside.

Richard closed his eyes and drifted away.

CHAPTER NINETEEN

Abel crashed downhill through the timber, his mount clawing to keep its footing on the steep slope, with Ignacio hard on his heels. The cow they chased ducked under and through thick brush men and horses were forced to skirt, losing ground with every stride. The timber thinned and then gave way to a grassy vale at the bottom of the slope. With reata swinging, Abel drew a bead on the running cow and his loop settled around her wide horns. He jerked the slack out of the rope and dallied around the saddle horn, then angled away to slow and turn the cow. Ignacio's loop flew under the cow's belly and around her heels as she hopped, fighting the rope at her head. After taking his dallies, Ignacio slowed, then stopped. Abel kept moving, stretching both ropes in the process, then the cow. The animal tipped to her side and lay there, panting between bellers and bawls.

Abel, also short of breath, double-half-hitched his rope to the saddle horn, dismounted, fetched a tie rope from his saddlebag, and walked to the cow. The cow, angered at her helplessness, tossed her head as Abel took a wrap around her neck and knotted the rope, avoiding the menacing horns as he did. He pulled Ignacio's loop off her hind legs, then hurried back to his horse before the cow could regain her feet and attack. Ignacio recoiled his rope, and when the cow stood, landed a loop over the horns. Then the two of them rode closer to the mad cow, taking new dallies as they approached, always keeping the reatas taut to prevent the cow from charging either horse. With cow in tow, they rode to the verge of the timber and Ignacio guided the way to a stout aspen tree. He threw off his dallies and, stepping off the offside of his horse, took a wrap around the trunk of the tree. With Abel helping from horseback, they pulled the bawling cow to the tree until her head snugged up against the trunk. Ignacio found the tie rope around the animal's neck and knotted it around the tree, then loosened both reatas and pulled them from the cow's horns.

The men rode away coiling their ropes, leaving the cow to snort and beller and paw, but helpless to get away from the tree that held her fast.

"Your roping is much improved, muchacho," Ignacio said. "You may yet make a vaquero—someday."

"To hell with you, *el viejo*. Only thing I'm worried about is whether you can keep up with me. Don't know if that was tree branches I heard rattlin' and snappin' back there, or if it was your old bones."

Ignacio threw his head back and laughed.

Abel looked around the small meadow and saw several cattle necked to trees. He watched a pair of vaqueros ride out of the trees across the way, hard on the heels of a fleeing cow, much as he and Ignacio had done. Another pair of vaqueros had just finished necking a young bull to a tree. Abel whistled to catch their attention and signaled them to come to him. Then the four riders crossed the narrow valley tucked between the steep slopes, arriving just as the other two hands secured the yearling heifer they had captured to a tree. The men—some little more than boys—sat horseback in a circle as Abel spoke.

"Buen trabajo hoy. Muchas vacas," he said in his halting, but improving, Spanish, congratulating the men for their work capturing the cattle. "If them others is doin' as good, we'll have a good herd put together *muy pronto*. Let's go home and eat and get some sleep."

The crew with Abel, along with six other hands he had hired had, for many weeks now, been gathering feral cattle off the land granted to his father. The animals, left to run wild for years since the former owner had been forced into exile, were no more domesticated than the deer and elk and antelope that shared the land. The men would leave the cattle necked to trees for a day or two, then come for them. Tamed somewhat by hunger and thirst and futility, the cattle were gathered into herds and held, often for weeks until they became accustomed to the presence of men, then driven to ranch headquarters. There, the hands would brand them, and turn the majority of the young bulls into steers. The cattle they wished to keep were thrown back onto the range, and those cut from the herd driven to market in Santa Fe.

Abel's new life and work had started when he came home to Albuquerque after finishing his work on the *estancia* near Isleta—despite the *hacendado*'s entreaties for him to stay on there. But he found the Lewis & Pate Mercantile in Albuquerque under the care of a Mexican man and his wife. They handed him a letter in his mother's hand.

He could almost hear his mother's frustration in the words she wrote. She wrote that his father had been given land as a reward for the rescue of a government official's family, and they had taken up residence there to start yet another new life in an unfamiliar place. The Lewis girls were in Santa Fe with their father. Emma, and later Jane, had been at the "rancho" in the mountains to help get the house in order, but had returned home. Lee had taken on hands to get the outbuildings and pens repaired, clean the well, and do whatever other work needed doing to get the place in shape. She wrote that Lee wanted Abel to recruit men experienced at working with cattle and come to the ranch. And to stop in Santa Fe to see if his father had left further instructions for him with Daniel Lewis. A map to reach the ranch filled the final page of the papers.

Abel knew something of vaqueros, as he had often sat with them and other ranch hands evenings in the adobe bunkhouse at the Isleta hacienda, playing card games with dried beans for stakes. The Mexicans teased his attempts at their language, but helped him learn words and phrases along the way.

The ranch on the plateau took possession of Abel's heart and soul the moment the road left the woods and into the big meadow and he saw the hacienda across the way. The place had come a long way since Lee and Sarah settled in, bringing with them workers to see to repairs.

The workers were mostly single men, but one family besides the Pates lived at ranch headquarters. The woman cooked for the hands in the bunkhouse with help from her two teenage daughters, who also took care of the cleaning at the big house, while her man supervised work on the buildings and structures and tended to the milk cows, pigs, chickens, and sheep in the pastures and pens.

As much as he loved life at the ranch atop the Pajarito Plateau, Abel looked forward to every opportunity to trail cattle to market at Santa Fe, as the drives afforded an opportunity to see Emma. Both found their time apart increasingly intolerable, and talked more and more of marriage. Daniel did not object to the idea, save only his concern for the ages of the young couple—Emma was but sixteen going on seventeen; Abel only a year or two older. The Pate parents were less sanguine, despite their affection for Emma.

Lee said, "Son, there's a heap of work to be done, and you well know it. If you was to bring that girl up here, you wouldn't hardly see her no how."

"It's all right, Pa. Emma and me, we don't mind. Besides, she could help out around here."

"You'd have that girl work herself to a frazzle out here in this godforsaken place? You'll make her an old woman 'fore her time," Sarah said. "When young'uns come, it'll be even worse. This ain't no place to be startin' a family."

"Emma don't see it that way, Ma. She thinks this place is right fine—and she ain't scared of work."

"Still—"

"That's enough said, Sarah. If Abel and Emma's minds is made up, they ain't no use tryin' to talk 'em out of it," Lee said. "I only wish they'll wait on it for a time, till we get this place built up some."

Abel sighed. "Nothin' ain't goin' to change—place like this, there'll always be work to do. But that's what me and Emma like about it. We can make it into a home to suit us—and kids, when they come along. And there's two other houses here already. They don't need much done to make 'em ready for livin' in."

Sarah scoffed. "Oh, Abel, them ain't much more'n mud huts! All right for the hired help, but not fit for white folks. Hold off, at least, till we can put up a stone house like this one."

Another sigh from Abel, this one heavier than before. He said nothing more, but grabbed his hat from the peg by the kitchen door and walked to the bunkhouse.

Over the days and weeks to come, Lee and Sarah talked and argued and disagreed about the prospect of a new Pate family taking root on the rancho. Despite his wife's objections, Lee realized Abel was determined. He sat the boy down when next he brought a herd to headquarters. After the bulls, cows, heifer calves, and newly minted steers were branded, and those for sale cut out and readied for the trail, Lee explained the financial situation to Abel as well as he could.

The tribute to Gobernador Armijo for the grant had been paid by Daniel from Lewis & Pate Mercantile funds, the greatest share of which belonged to Daniel. So, too, were the expenditures for the hired help, supplies, and equipment necessary for renovation and repairs. In a sense, Lee explained, Daniel Lewis owned the biggest share of the ranch.

But, Daniel had no more interest in being a rancher than Lee had in being a storekeeper. So it was agreed between them that income from the ranch, with Lee's shares in the Mercantile business and cut of the profits, would repay Daniel's investment. Then, the men would part company as friends.

"Don't know how it'll all work out, or when this will become Pate land free and clear," Lee said. "Can't see that it makes much difference one way or another, far as you and Emma are concerned. But it's somethin' you need to know."

"I figured as much—or somethin' like it," Abel said with a shrug. Then a smile spread across his face, twinkling his eyes. He reached out and clapped his father on the shoulder. "Come to think of it, Pa, from what you're tellin' me, Emma already owns a piece of this place, in a way. Hell, she could be the one givin' orders around here if we ain't careful!"

Lee laughed at the thought. "Could be, at that—by the bye, you had best watch your language, boy. You still ain't so growed up that I won't take you over my knee."

When Abel and the vaqueros put the market cattle on the trail off the plateau bound for Santa Fe, Lee came along, driving a wagon that would return to the ranch filled with supplies. But when the wagon left Santa Fe, a second followed. Daniel Lewis sat next to Lee on the supply wagon. Abel held the lines of the other, with Emma beside him and Mary beside her, with Jane kneeling behind, her elbows on the back of the seat, a smile beaming out from between Abel and Emma. Abel had left his saddle horse with the vaqueros in Santa Fe. They would return to the ranch after another night on the town.

"I have misgivings about this marriage," Daniel said to Lee

as they rode along. "Not so far as the union is concerned, you understand—I cannot imagine a finer young man than Abel. And my Emma, well, she is glowing, and I have every confidence she will make your son a fine wife."

"Well, what is it then?"

"As we have discussed, it has to do with the . . . the . . . legality of the union. Well, not so much the legality, as the . . . the . . . I cannot find the words for it, but I cannot help but wonder how our Father in Heaven will view it."

"Surely you don't think he'd object?"

The wheels turned, both those carrying the wagon, and those in Daniel's head. "Not that he would object, *per se*—but that there will be no clergy officiating. Will the marriage be solemnized in the eyes of the Lord?"

Now it was Lee's turn to ruminate. "Well, Daniel, we've talked this out, and there ain't no other way."

There was no religious authority in Santa Fe, or anywhere in New Mexico—or elsewhere in Mexico, for that matter—other than la Iglesia Católica Romana, the Roman Catholic Church. Neither the Pate nor Lewis families held with its teachings or traditions—the Pates loosely bound to Methodist beliefs, the Lewises with ties to the far-distant Mormons of the Church of Jesus Christ of Latter Day Saints.

"The kids have asked you to say words over them, Daniel. What with you bein' an Elder of your Mormon faith and all, that ought to be solemn enough, oughten it?"

Daniel shook his head. "It does not work that way among the Saints. I am an ordained Elder, certain enough. But that ordination alone does not bring with it the authority to sanctify wedding vows."

"Well, it'll have to do. We're lucky we ain't been made to become Papists as it is. It's the law, you know. I think Guadalupe Miranda overlooked that out of kindness when he got us this land grant. I sure don't want to stir that pot."

"Nor I, Lee. Nor I. I suppose all will be well in the end. Surely the Lord God knows our circumstances, and He will bless the union."

"I reckon so."

The ceremony was a simple one. The morning after reaching the ranch, the families gathered in the front room of the stone house. Abel and Emma held hands, and stood before Daniel. He opened the Bible in his hands.

"The Lord tells us, in the tenth chapter of The Gospel According to Mark: '. . . from the beginning of the creation God made them male and female. For this cause shall a man leave his father and mother, and cleave to his wife; And they twain shall be one flesh: so then they are no more twain, but one flesh. What therefore God hath joined together, let not man put asunder.' Abel Pate and Emma Lewis, you have chosen to join together in matrimony according to God's will. Emma, do you vow to cleave to Abel, and no other?"

"I do."

"Abel, do you vow to cleave to Emma and no other?"

"I do."

Daniel closed the Bible, took a handkerchief from his pocket and dabbed his forehead, then put it back in his pocket. "From this day forward, Abel and Emma, you should consider yourselves man and wife in the eyes of God, and enjoy the blessings and responsibilities associated with the state of matrimony. Abel, you may kiss Emma, your wife."

The families applauded the show of affection, and Daniel spoke again. "This union has the blessing of your parents and families, and, we trust, the blessing of our Heavenly Father. In his name, Amen."

The "amen" echoed among the family members gathered there.

Rachel, Mary, and Jane took turns embracing Emma and wiping away tears. Daniel shook hands with Abel. Lee left the room and came back with a broom.

"One more thing," Lee said, tapping the broom handle to the floor for attention. All eyes turned to him. "Back in Tennessee, them poor unfortunate souls held in slavery weren't given the right to be married, in a legal way of speaking. So, they had a sign of they own to signify their bein' wed. 'Jumpin' the broom,' they called it. I think you-all ought to do the same." He dropped the broomstick to the floor. "Abel, take Emma by the hand and you-all jump on across."

Another round of laughter and applause followed the couple taking the leap.

Abel grabbed his bride around the waist, lifted her off the floor and spun her around. "We done it, Emma! We done it!" He kissed her again and again. "Now, let's celebrate! Let's have a party!"

Silence fell over the room like a blanket. Sarah looked at Lee. Lee looked at Daniel. Faces paled.

Lee spoke. "I'm sorry, Son. We never thought to arrange anything."

"It all came on so sudden-like," Sarah said. "I never had time to bake a cake nor a pie."

Daniel said, "The girls and I must return to Santa Fe." He clapped his hands together. "We shall arrange festivities at a later date. What do you say?"

"That will be wonderful, Father!" Emma said. "Don't you agree, Abel?"

Abel nodded. "I suppose so. I just thought . . ."

"Well," Lee said, "there is work to be done. But don't you worry none about it, Abel. I'll see to it today. You and Emma go on over to the little house and rest up. I imagine you-all are tuckered from the travel and all."

"I sent the girls that keeps house over to tidy up," Sarah said. "Emma, I trust you'll find it suitable. We can see about furnishing it proper later on, when there's time."

"I'm sure it will all be wonderful, Missus Pate—or should I call you Mother?" Not waiting for an answer, she took Abel by the hand and walked across the yard to the adobe house. She closed the door and leaned back against it, smiling at her husband. "What is the matter, Abel?"

He looked at her and shrugged. "I don't know. Nothin', I guess. I just thought—"

Emma stilled the reply when she threw her arms around Abel's neck and pressed her lips to his.

CHAPTER TWENTY

Richard sat in the saddle, both hands gripping the horn, barely able to stay atop the standing horse. He knew not how long he had been unconscious. Nor, for that matter, how long he had been awake. He only knew that his head threatened to float off his shoulders at any moment, or, if not that, tumble off his neck and fall to the ground. His shoulder throbbed and burned, and he felt blood trickling down his ribs despite the wadded fabric and buckskin binding someone had wrapped the wound with.

And now he sat, watching the chaos and mayhem in the box canyon.

Had Richard been awake at the time, he, like most of the others in the raiding party, would have expected Wakara to turn back and leave *Cañon del Muerto*. They had, after all, lost several men—some dead, others, like Richard, alive but no longer fit to fight. But Wakara was adamant. The Ute leader pointed out that it was not happenstance that the attack happened where it happened. The *Pahgow'witch* fighters were protecting something, he said. And since the Utes had seen no women or children, they must be concealed somewhere in the canyon beyond the place of the fight.

The best Ute trackers rode farther into the canyon slowly, trying to make sense of the smeared, jumbled tracks in the soft sand. The rest of the riders followed behind, led by Wakara, who warned them to be alert, as the Navajo warriors who had scattered after the fight could reassemble and attack again, at any time and from any place.

The trackers found the trail of the women and children and old people leading into a slot canyon whose entrance, tucked into a recess in the wall, was barely visible. The men rode carefully into the narrow *rincón*, which allowed no more than two horses abreast. Riding quietly, with only the snorting of horses, footfalls in the sand, and the squeak and rattle of saddles and bridles to betray their presence. All eyes looked upward, fearing every shadow in the cliff walls, every crevice, every alcove, concealed sudden death.

The walls parted, opening into a bay. The refugee Navajos the Utes sought were huddled against the far fringes of the pocket. Ute raiders dismounted, and the Navajos sprung to life. Some attempted to bypass the attackers and escape the canyon. Others clawed and clambered up the scree that bordered the sheer cliffs in places. Some fought, rushing the Utes with knives and clubs and rocks, but most who attacked were dispatched before inflicting serious damage. An old man sat cross legged in the sand, chanting a song no one paid attention to, even, apparently, the gods to whom it was directed.

The Utes chose their captives, primarily young women, and children old enough to ride. Their hands were bound and they were thrown onto horses and mules, most to ride double. Those who dismounted were beaten and put back onto the horses, some more than once before accepting their fate.

Retracing their steps through the narrow passage at a trot, the Utes followed Wakara as he regained the main stem of *Cañon del Muerto* and, to the surprise of many, turned upstream to ride deeper into the gorge.

As the last of the party reached the canyon, Navajo fighters on foot came running after them, unleashing a storm of arrows. Wakara detailed Pegleg and the best riflemen from among the Utes to stand and fight. Almost every one of their first shots felled an onrushing Navajo, the rest of the attackers scattering to find protection along the canyon walls. Pegleg told the men to reload, then mount up and move farther up the canyon. Nooch concurred, and, despite the orders coming from a white man and a Ute barely beyond boyhood, every fighter followed. The running fight continued for a time as they retreated in stages up the canyon until the Navajos, disheartened and diminished in number from wounds and death, gave up the chase.

The riflemen hurried up the canyon to catch up with the main party and the captives. Along the way, they passed two dead Navajos: one a young woman with her head caved in, probably from a blow from a war club, the other a boy who looked to be barely into his teens, a stab wound in his chest and a slit throat. Both had been scalped.

"*Estúpido*," Nooch said with a shake of his head. "That boy did not need to die. Or that woman. They should have behaved."

With a wry laugh, Pegleg pointed out that to some, death was preferable to what they knew was to come—suffering, torture, a life of servitude in a strange land. "It ain't no easy thing to decide, one way or t'other. How 'bout you, Nooch? Was you to be captured by an enemy, would you give up, or fight?"

"They would not capture me."

"We all like to think not. Howsomever, it happens. Suppose it did? What if them Californios had caught you on that horse raid we went on? What would you have done?"

Nooch rode on in silence for a time, contemplating an answer less abrupt and more thoughtful. Then, "As you said, it is not easy to say. But I believe I would resist. Perhaps that boy back there who lost his hair was not so stupid after all. I would be brave and fight to the death, like that boy." He shrugged. "At least that is what I hope I would do."

"Not me," Pegleg said. "I been captured. I bided my time,

kept a clear head and a sharp eye. It took time, and that time weren't pleasant, but when I saw a chance to get away, I got away."

"Did they come for you?"

"Can't say. Never caught up with me if they did." He laughed. "Could be they figured I was more trouble than I was worth and just let me go."

Nooch thought it over, and Pegleg said no more, until, "Thing to remember, boy, is that you can't do one damn thing if you're dead."

When they reached the main party, Nooch rode ahead to report to Wakara. Pegleg stayed at the rear, where Richard rode, still barely able to stay in the saddle.

"How you holdin' up, son?"

Richard turned his sagging head toward the voice, bleary eyes showing little recognition or care.

Pegleg reached back into a saddlebag and pulled out a bottle of whiskey. "Here. Try a little taste of this medicine."

He uncorked the bottle and held it out to Richard. The wounded man grabbed the bottle, its weight causing his arm to droop. He rested the bottle for a moment on the saddle horn, then lifted it to his lips. He shuddered as the whiskey settled into his stomach, again balancing the bottle on his saddle horn.

"You old bastard. I knowed you was holdin' out on me. How much more of this stuff you got stashed?"

"That be the end of it. Have another snort, but that's all for now. You can't hardly stay astride and upright as it is."

The sheer walls of the canyon fell away as they rode uphill, becoming nothing more than steep slopes, then low bluffs. Finally, they broke out of the canyon altogether, finding themselves atop a broad mesa that looked out on an eternity stretching away to the east. Santa Fe was out there, somewhere.

★ ★ ★ ★ ★

For two long days, Richard slumped in the saddle, his mind fogbound and his shoulder throbbing. Despite the parched desert air, his skin, rendered by fever, was as dank and clammy as it had been on muggy, humid summer days back home in Shelby County, Tennessee. Wakara led the party across barren wastelands into the Chuska Mountains. Although forested with piñon and juniper, the scrub trees offered little shade or respite from the sun.

The Navajo captives went hungry, and the Utes gave them only enough water to keep them alive. Should any complain, or a child cry or whimper, they were silenced by blows from hands or quirts, even pulled from their mounts to be beaten and kicked, then flung back aboard the horse to ride some more.

Mountains gave way to barren, broken mesas. Riding into the sun following another fitful night of weeping and whimpering, punctuated by beatings, the party dropped off a mesa into a broad arroyo following the course of a dry stream bed. Prairie dogs chattered atop their warrens as they watched the passing parade.

Through filmy eyes, Richard saw clusters of ruined buildings, complexes of rectangular walls interspersed with circular enclosures. Built from blocks of hewn sandstone, the thick walls of the abandoned cities bore record of the past presence of thousands of people. But Richard did not know if what he saw was real, or a phantasm of a fevered mind.

Days later, whether two or ten Richard could not say, they reached the Rio Puerco, tumbling down from the Sierra Nacimiento, and the village of Nacimiento, tucked along the banks of the stream and the mountain foothills. The Utes, captives in tow, rode through the village, unseen eyes watching them from the shadows of doorways and windows.

Just outside the town proper, Pegleg rode up beside Richard

and reached across and took up his bridle reins, unwrapping them from the saddle horn where he had secured them earlier. He led Richard's horse into the yard of an adobe hut shaded by cottonwood trees. A dog rose from its slumber beside the door and barked at the intruders. After a time, a woman came to the doorway, wiping her hands on the bib of her apron.

Pegleg said, "Reinard here?"

The woman offered no reply, only turned back into the house.

In a moment, a man appeared, a cloth tucked in his shirtfront like a bib, chewing food and holding some kind of bone with a few shreds of meat clinging to its otherwise slick surface. He watched the mounted men, pulling the remaining meat from the bone with his teeth, then tossing the bone to the cur dog.

"I'll be damned if it ain't Pegleg Smith," the man said, between licking his fingers.

"I see your eyes ain't failed you yet."

"Not any of it." He turned aside and looked off into the distance. "If you'll look on that ridgeline yonder, there's a whitish-colored rock just down a ways and to the right of a lone cedar tree. Look close at that rock, and you'll see there's a blue-tail fly sittin' atop it, washin' his hands. Leastways that's what I see. Don't know if you can see it or not."

Pegleg smiled. "I see you're still full of bullshit, as well."

The man laughed. "What brings you to my door, you old reprobate? Ain't seen you for what? Must be seven year."

"Sounds right. Six, maybe." Pegleg raised himself in the stirrups, and rolled his shoulders, spine cracking and saddle leather creaking, then lowered himself back into the seat. "Here's the thing, Reinard. This child here, he's packin' a Navajo arrowhead inside him. It ain't settin' too well—got him a mite under the weather."

Reinard had been watching Richard, slumped in the saddle, head bowed. "He don't look none too smart, I can see that. We had best get him off from that nag and into the house."

Pegleg swung out of the saddle, planting his peg leg and stepping out of the stirrup, holding the saddle horn for a moment to steady himself. He looped the reins of his horse around the top rail of the low pole fence that fronted the house, then hobbled around to stand beside Richard's horse.

"C'mon, son. Let's get you off that horse 'fore you fall off."

Richard raised his head and looked around. "Where are we?"

"See that feller there? That's Henry Reinard. Times past, me and him shared many a campfire. Reinard and his woman, they're goin' to take a look at that shoulder of yourn. Maybe so, you can hole up here for a while till you get healed up."

Pegleg wrapped an arm around Richard's waist and slid him out of the saddle. Buckling at the knees when his feet hit the ground, Richard leaned into Pegleg as he took him by the arm, slung it around his neck, and lifted him. Reinard mirrored the hold on the other side, and between them they carried Richard into the house, his toes dragging.

Inside, they ducked through a low doorway leading to a back room, turned around and backed up to a bed. They lowered Richard and sat him on the bed, but he sagged and tipped to the side, his head on the wool-stuffed tick and his feet on the floor.

"Don't leave me here, Pegleg," he mumbled.

"Ain't got no choice, son. Only chance you got to keep drawin' breath is to let Reinard and his woman look after you."

"Nooo . . ." Richard said, the word trailing off as he lost consciousness.

Outside, Pegleg passed Reinard a pouch of coins to cover the cost of caring for Richard. Reinard refused the purse, but his dissent lacked sincerity.

"Go on, now. Take it," Pegleg said. "If nothin' else, see that the boy gets planted proper."

174

CHAPTER TWENTY-ONE

Melvin shoveled out a gap in the ditch bank and watched water from the *acequia* spill out and creep down the rows of the bean-field. When the streams reached the bottom of the field, he filled the gap, moved downstream and opened another, and would repeat the process until all the beans were watered. Then, he would do the same for the corn rows and the pepper patch.

Through the morning, he sat on the ditch bank, warming in the sun as its light glinted and glistened and sparkled off the flowing water. His eyes wandered across the pastures, the green meadows, the cultivated fields tucked among the gentle hills and ridges of this place called Chimayo. He felt at home here.

After the mule train, homebound from California trading, disbanded in Abiquiu, the man he had met among the packers brought him here. They had ridden into the tumbledown yard of a small *granja*, the farmstead suffering visible neglect.

"This was the home of *mi hermano*, my brother. He was a bad man."

Melvin studied the small house, adobe brick showing through peeled-off mud plaster. A low-slung barn, another decrepit adobe structure, stood behind. The lean-tos and pens attached to the barn walls showed gaps and voids in the upright wooden posts of which they were made. Crumbling adobe walls, and tree-limb stakes woven together with twigs, formed fences and small pens confining a few sheep, a flock of chickens scratching in the dust, two nanny goats with milk-filled udders, a shaggy

175

burro watching him with alert ears, and three spotted shoats snuffling around in the dirt and muck of their enclosure.

"Looks like somebody still lives here," Melvin said.

"*Si*. Lupe Zaragoza—the widow of my brother."

"What happened to him?"

"He died. Of a fever. Now she is on her own here, with two children."

"She ain't married again?"

The man shook his head. "No. *La gente de Chimayo evitaa Lupe*. How do you say it? People of the town avoid Lupe."

"Why's that?"

With a shrug, he said, "Some believe she is a witch, *una bruja, una hechicera,* and that she gave my brother poison, or cursed him with *elmal de ojo,* the evil eye. But it is not so. My brother mistreated her, abused her. Had she killed him I would not fault her for it. But she did not. As I have said, he was taken by a fever."

Melvin sat for a time, saying nothing, thinking of what the man said, and wondering. Then, "So why are we here?"

Again, the man shrugged. "It is a thought I have. You tell me you have no place to go. And Lupe, she is alone here. And as you can see, this place needs attention she cannot give it. She and her two little children, *una niña y un niño*, are getting by, but only just. And so, my thought is that perhaps you will stay here, and help Lupe. Tend to *los cultivos y los animals,* the crops and the stock." He paused for a moment to allow Melvin to ponder. "She could not pay you, of course. But you would be fed, and have a roof over your head," he said, with a nod toward the barn. "And perhaps you would find other work in the town. What do you think, *mi amigo*?"

Melvin sat silent, looking around. Just when the man lost hope that his scheme would play out, Melvin spoke.

"Wouldn't folks talk?"

"Perhaps. But Lupe, as I have said, has no *reputación* to lose. Besides, it is no strange thing for a man and a woman to be together, if it comes to that, even in Chimayo. *¿No es así?*"

Melvin thought some more. "What if she—Lupe—won't have me?"

The man laughed. "It is not a marriage that I am proposing—merely a working relationship, where one helps the other."

"That ain't what I mean. What if she don't go along with this plan of yours?"

"We shall ask her," the man said with a nod toward the rise beyond the barn.

Melvin looked that way, and saw a barefoot woman walking along a path bordering the community *acequia* as it traced the bottom of the hill. She was thin, and wore a dress that left the bottom half of her calves exposed—a length Melvin knew would be considered indecent back home in Shelby County, Tennessee. Her hair was long, wrapped in a braid draped over her shoulder and dangling over a breast and down to her waist. She carried a wicker basket in the crook of her elbow. Trailing behind were the children—a girl who Melvin guessed, in his limited experience, to be about four years old, and behind her a boy of perhaps two years. He walked with his eyes down, stopping now and then to examine some curiosity on the path, or in the grass and brush along its edge, then running to catch up at his mother's commands.

The woman did not break stride when she saw the two horsemen, but turned and said something to the children. They hurried to walk close behind Lupe, the girl holding on to her mother's skirt, the boy watching the men wide eyed as he trotted along.

"Hola, Lupe," the man said when she stopped before them.

Lupe nodded in greeting, her eyes shifting from her brother-in-law to Melvin, then back again, and then again. The man asked Lupe what Melvin took to be a series of questions, which she answered in few words. Their words were all in Spanish, and Melvin understood none of them.

With the niceties out of the way, the man launched into a long explanation of his purpose there. Again, Melvin did not comprehend the rapid-fire Spanish, but thought he heard his name mentioned once or twice.

The woman stood, grasping her basket, her eyes wandering about the place as the man talked. Sometimes she dropped her gaze, watching her bare toes as they traced lines in the dust. When the man finished, she peppered him with a series of questions, some of which he answered promptly, others after some consideration.

Then the conversation continued give-and-take, the man and woman exchanging what Melvin took to be, at various times, ideas and suggestions and challenges and disagreements and concurrence. His hollow stomach and shallow breaths led him to believe that a big part of his future was being decided here—with him having no part of it, nor having the slightest idea of what that future might hold.

But his future had been decided that day, and on mornings like this, wrapped in the warm blanket of the sun, serenaded by riffling water and songbirds, Melvin could not contemplate a more satisfying future. There had been—and still was—much work on the farmstead. No sooner had he unsaddled his horse and stowed his bedroll and few belongings in the barn, Melvin found tools in a lean-to and went to patching holes in the animal pens where stakes had broken and fallen away, and posts sagged and tipped.

Over the days and weeks, he cleared encroaching brush from the yard, hoed weeds from the fields, and thinned overgrowth from the vegetable garden. He learned to milk the goats. With gestures and demonstrations from Lupe, learned when and how to take the water from the *acequia* to feed the crops in this arid country. He visited the town and watched men building with adobe, learning the art of patching peeling stucco—mixing straw and gravel with the clay and sand for the first coats, and smoothing and blending the outer layer to shed the little rain that fell.

The children found him a curiosity, and followed him in his work, and tugged at his clothing, encouraging him to play. From them, he learned the rudiments of their language, and taught them English words and phrases, everyone delighting in the newfound knowledge.

His relationship with Lupe followed a slow and winding path, wending its way through shyness, awkwardness, and the language barrier. But she kept his clothing patched and laundered, and fed his abundant appetite, amazed at his capacity to put away food. She watched from the corner of her eye as he sat quietly in the evenings in the light of candles and the fire, playing with the children or just holding them on his lap while she washed dishes, sewed or mended, carded wool, spun thread, sat at her loom, or saw to preparations for the coming day. She knew not how to respond when, one day, he put coins in her hand as she set out for town to buy staples.

And then one quiet evening, as Melvin settled into his corner of the barn, squirming his bedroll into the heap of corn shucks that cushioned it, the doorway darkened. He looked up to see Lupe's silhouette, framed against the darkness beyond, creating a void in the stars. She stood there for a time, as if as uncertain as Melvin about what was happening. And then she walked to Melvin, knelt beside him, found his hand and, with gentle but insistent pressure, led him out of the barn and into her house and her bed.

The next day, Melvin rolled his bed and blankets and stowed them atop a *viga* in the barn, and moved what few belongings he owned into the house.

Early one morning, before the dawn, Lupe awakened Melvin and told him to hitch the burro to the cart. This day, the family would set out on the two-day journey to Santa Fe, where Lupe would bargain for the best price on her woven goods, and get pocket money for baskets of corn and peppers and squash and beans and melons she heaped onto the cart.

As Lupe went about her business in Santa Fe, Melvin wandered the plaza and the streets beyond, fascinated with the hustle and bustle of the city. He rounded a corner and all but collided with a woman. He pulled off his hat to apologize, and recognized the woman as Mary Lewis.

"Melvin? Melvin Pate? Is it really you?"

"Y-y-yes, M-Mary. It's me, all right."

"Well, glory be! What brings you to Santa Fe? Where have you come from? Where have you been? Is Richard with you?"

The storm of questions addled Melvin, rendering him tongue tied and red faced.

"Never mind. Have you anywhere to be at the moment? Follow me—I have a bit of business, then we shall talk."

Melvin watched her walk away, then put his hat back on and hurried to follow. He struggled to keep up as Mary wove through the foot traffic and dodged wheeled vehicles. At the entrance to a nondescript building, she told Melvin to wait, and ducked through the door. Melvin leaned against the wall, watching people come and go. Before long, Mary came back out, fastening her reticule.

"Have you time to talk, Melvin? Come with me. We shall go to my office."

Melvin said nothing, lost in wonderment, and followed the determined woman through the streets of Santa Fe. He followed her through the doorway of a building with a small sign affixed to the wall beside the door. It read, LEWIS & PATE / COMERCIANTES, and, in smaller letters, MERCHANTS AND TRADERS.

Inside, Mary bustled past a clerk seated at a desk, tossing off a greeting as she passed, and led Melvin through another doorway into another room. He removed his hat and looked around. A desk, faced by two rail-backed wooden chairs with upholstered seats, filled most of the room. Bookcases lined the wall behind the desk, one shelf holding a few books, but most occupied by tidy stacks of files and papers and ledgers.

"Please, sit," Mary said, removing her shawl and bonnet and hanging them on a coat tree. Melvin sat, as directed. "Now, do tell," Mary said as she sat down, leaning forward and folding her arms atop the desk, smiling.

Melvin swallowed hard. "Don't know where to start. I seen my name—Pate, Pa's name, I suppose—on that sign by the door. What's that all about?"

Mary launched into an extended, but efficient, telling of the families' arrival in Santa Fe, their establishment of a store, and the expansion into a profitable network of retail outlets in surrounding communities. She told of Lee Pate's acquisition of a land grant and the thriving ranch there.

Melvin's mind reeled as he tried to keep up. "This ranch— whereabouts is it?"

Mary explained its location atop the Pajarito Plateau to the west. Melvin asked about his parents, and learned that both his mother and father were well, and living at the ranch.

"What about Abel?"

Mary smiled. "He and Emma are wed, and Emma is with child. I am to be an aunt! They, too, are at the ranch. Abel all but runs the place—under your father's direction, of course." She smiled again. "But, as you might imagine, Abel has things well in hand and requires little direction. Now, about you—is Richard with you? You did not say."

Stumbling through a rambling account of their travels since leaving Las Vegas, Melvin admitted he did not know what had become of Richard after he had left him with the slave-hunting Utes. He had heard nothing from, or of, him. Sometimes, Melvin said he pondered taking a trip north to Taos to see if Pegleg Smith, the old trapper they had thrown in with, was there, and if he knew of Richard's whereabouts. But he had not made the trip.

Mary shook her head, slowly, and sighed. "He was a troubled soul, our Richard. I hope he is well, wherever he is." She asked Melvin to say more about his situation, to tell about Lupe and the children.

The mention made him sit upright. "Tarnation! I best be getting' back to 'em." He stood and put on his hat. "Sorry, Mary, but I better go."

She stood. "I shall come with you. I would like to meet your Lupe."

They found the family in the shade under the portico of the Governor's Palace. The children nibbled at cold tamales from the clay pot Lupe had filled before setting out from home. Lupe looked suspicious, even fearful, when she saw Melvin walking toward them with a lovely white woman.

Melvin stood before Lupe and took off his hat, hands grasping opposite sides of the brim and pressing it to his chest. In halting Spanish, missing some words and mispronouncing others, he attempted an introduction.

Mary let him struggle for a time before coming to the rescue. She greeted Lupe in near-flawless Spanish, introducing herself and learning the names of the children. Then, she tucked her skirts and knelt on the edge of the blanket and engaged in a lengthy conversation with Lupe. Melvin stood by, helpless, still grasping his hat and rocking slowly back and forth as he shifted his weight from one foot to the other. He wondered, as he had once before, if the course of his life was being decided without him.

The women kept talking, laughing and seeming to enjoy the conversation. Then Mary leaned forward and embraced Lupe, then sat back and grasped both her hands. They exchanged another hug, and Mary stood, smoothing her skirts.

"Melvin, your new family is a delight! Now, promise me you will at least send a letter to your mother and father, if not visit them at the ranch. I know they will be pleased to know that you are well situated and happy." She embraced Melvin, and before he could muster the courage to return the hug, turned and walked away, disappearing into the crowd on the plaza.

CHAPTER TWENTY-TWO

The spider clung to the web in the corner of the window frame, silk strands shimmering in the streaming sunlight. Richard swiped at an itch on his nose and brushed off a housefly. It buzzed upward, flitting back and forth, and darted toward the light. The threads of the web quivered when they captured the insect and the spider skittered across the fibers, hugged the thrashing fly, then sunk its fangs into the fly's thorax and pumped venom until the fly ceased struggling. Richard watched the spider step back from the dying fly, perhaps to rest. Soon, it would cloak the fly in a bundle of web thread and leave it as its innards liquefied, ready to eat at the spider's leisure.

Richard threw off his blanket, kicking away the tangle around his legs, and sat up in bed. His head objected to the move, and his stomach lurched. When the room ceased swaying, he reached for the bottle on the bedside table and held it up to the light to check its contents. Seeing but a tiny puddle in the bottom, he sighed, then lifted the bottle and let the few drops dribble onto his tongue, shaking the bottle for good measure. He stood, his hand reaching out to steady the wall in the heaving room.

Richard shuffled into the living area of the house and found Reinard and the woman gone. He poked around on a kitchen shelf and found a half-full bottle of whiskey and put it on the table. The enamel coffeepot on the little stove was still warm so he poured a clay mug half full of the dark, bitter brew and carried it to the table, sat, and topped off the mug with whiskey.

His shoulder wound itched, and he reached inside the dressing to scratch, studied the bloody pus on his fingers, and wiped it on his pantleg. He did not know how long he had been with Reinard—several weeks, surely; many months, perhaps—most of that time spent in a fevered fog, unconscious for long periods. Still, despite the passing days, the hole the arrow had cut through his flesh would not heal. Reinard told him he had probed the hole in an attempt to extract the arrowhead embedded in bone, but without success. And Richard knew it was still there, feeling it disturb meat and muscle when he moved his arm or shoulder a certain way. The woman washed the wound every day or so, dressed it with a poultice of unknown origins and bandaged it, the cloth soon discolored from seepage.

Other than a greasy skillet on the stove and a couple of stale tortillas on a plate on the shelf, Richard saw no sign of food. He folded one of the stiffened tortillas and scraped it through the congealed fat in the frying pan and ate. He had little appetite, and his already slender frame had wasted away until his ribcage looked like the knurls on a washboard, and his knees were the thickest part of his legs. He chewed the greasy tortilla into a doughy wad and washed it down with the whiskey-stiffened coffee, shuddering at the taste of the tepid potation. He pushed it aside, drinking, instead, unadulterated *aguardiente* directly from the bottle.

Back in the bedroom, he pulled on his rumpled, musty, and stained shirt. He bent down to pick up his boots, and once again his equilibrium went into disarray. His hand shot out and he caught himself on the edge of the bed. He twisted around and sat, grabbing his head with both hands in an attempt to steady the world. When the dizziness passed, he pulled on his boots, found his hat, and walked out of the house, the soles of his feet seldom losing contact with earth.

Richard stopped for a moment to breathe the fresh air. He

looked at his horse in the small corral behind the house, and the saddle perched on a rail in a low, open shed. He thought of saddling the horse, but accomplishing that, then managing to mount the animal, seemed insurmountable. So, he hitched up his sagging pants and shuffled out of the yard and onto the road toward Nacimiento.

After stopping to rest atop a fallen cottonwood log on the banks of the gurgling stream, Richard made it into the village. The town offered only one commercial enterprise. Inside, the low-ceilinged room featured a bar on one side where drink and whatever cooked food available that day were served; a store counter on the other side fronted shelves stocked with food staples and dry goods. In between, a few rough tables and chairs sat around a smoky fireplace.

"I see you are out and about once again, *mi amigo*," the proprietor said. He propped the broom he had been scratching the floor with against the wall and stepped behind the bar, knowing from Richard's few other visits that he would patronize that half of the business. "You do not look well, Señor Ricardo."

"A mite shaky today, Angel. Can't seem to steady myself. I believe some of that coffin varnish you pass off as whiskey might help. Can you fix me up with a bottle?"

"*Si*, Señor Ricardo. So long as you have dinero, I will have the whiskey. But I think maybe it is not so good for you, *mi amigo*. Would you not like something to eat? *Mi mujer* made today a pot of *posole*. It is *muy bueno, muy sabroso*. I will get you some, no?"

"Thanks all the same. Food ain't settin' so well these days. I'll just take the whiskey. Have a drink here, rest up some, then take the bottle and go on back home—back to Reinard's place, anyway."

"As you wish," Angel said.

Reinard found Richard passed out and slumped in a kitchen chair, his head cradled on arms folded atop the table, when he and the woman came home. He washed up and sat opposite him. The woman stoked the fire and threw in stove wood to heat the skillet as she beat a dozen eggs in a bowl. Reinard picked up Richard's bottle and examined its contents. Something less than a third of the whiskey remained. The woman patted out tortillas and dolloped chorizo into the frying pan. Reinard reached across the table, grasped Richard's forearm, and gave him a shake.

Richard jerked awake. He looked around the room through rheumy eyes, attempting to get his bearings. Then he sat, chin on chest, eyes closed. taking deep breaths. He yawned, wagged his head slowly back and forth, strained to lift his eyelids, then raised his head some and looked at Reinard through half-open eyes.

"Boy, your eyes look like two piss holes in the snow."

"Feel 'bout the same, I reckon," Richard mumbled. "Though I don't know much about snow." He sat as still as he could, head bowed and taking deep breaths. Reinard said no more.

The woman slid a plate of food in front of each man. Reinard spooned salsa from a clay jar onto the sausage and eggs, rolled a tortilla, and ate. "You had best get some food in that belly of yours," he said as he poured out more of the hot sauce.

"I can't see how that pepper sauce ain't burned a hole in your stomach by now."

Reinard laughed. "Less likely to do so than that whiskey you drink. You could use that stuff Angel sells to de-hair a hog, or scorch the pinfeathers off a plucked chicken."

Richard sat and sagged and stared at nothing, dissipated as he was by pain and fever and fatigue. And whiskey.

"You know, son, we don't aim to keep you here forever. Fact

is, the woman is already weary of tendin' to you. But you can't leave in the shape you're in. So you need to get your strength back. And you can't do that if you don't eat."

Richard shrugged. "Don't seem hungry much. When I do eat, it pains my insides."

"That's on account of you've pickled your guts with all that damn whiskey. Now, I ain't opposed to strong drink on general principles—hell, I enjoy a snort now and again as much as the next man. And I've been known to go on a toot m'self from time to time. But, son, there's limits to how much a man can stand of anything—whiskey included. You need to lay off the sauce and eat some food and get some meat back on your bones so's you can be on your way. Like I said, we can't keep you here forever."

Richard did not stop drinking. But he did start eating, forcing himself to fill his stomach even when he did not care to. He even indulged in a meal at Angel's place on some of his visits there to replenish his supply of alcohol. Before long, he could walk to town and back without stopping on the way to rest, and his gait lost the look of an invalid. He took the woman's advice to bind his arm in a sling, and the wound stopped seeping and closed. The pain was still there, but not as intense and the stab of it less frequent. And not so bad that another drink of whiskey could not take the edge off it.

He awoke after another fitful night and morning of tossing and turning. He sat up in bed and swallowed down the dregs from a whiskey bottle. Then, he lay back down, head and shoulders propped against the wall, waiting for the room to stop seesawing and for his clouded eyes to clear. He watched dust motes dancing in a beam of sunlight, and followed the ray up to the window. He noticed right away the absence of spiderwebs in the corners of the casement. Apparently, the woman had swept them away and disposed of the weaver.

Reinard and the woman were pushing back from dinner when he slumped out of the bedroom. He ate a little, then cajoled Reinard into accompanying him to Angel's place for a drink. As they walked to the town, they had to step aside, leaving the road for a detachment of *federales* coming up the road behind them. Hoofbeats drummed as the horses, eight of them, trotted past. The soldiers, most of them young men, wore soiled and frayed uniforms and were coated with dust, but sat their mounts with as much dignity as they could muster.

Richard said, "What the hell do they want?" as the creak and rattle and jingle of the riders faded away as they continued on the road.

"Nothing," Reinard said. "Just out on patrol. They come through here now and then, so's people will think they're bein' protected. All for show, mostly."

Later, they stood at Angel's bar. They shared a bottle—Richard emptying three or four glasses to Reinard's one.

"Y'know, Reinard, I don't say it often enough, but I'm obliged to you-all for takin' care of me all this time. I am surely in your-all's debt."

Reinard chuckled. "Don't thank us, son. It's Pegleg Smith you owe. He gave us money for your keep—or to see to your buryin', whichever."

They drank some more in the quiet room, empty save their presence and that of Angel dancing a broom around a floor that did not need sweeping. The door opened and a man came inside and stepped away from the doorframe while his eyes grew accustomed to the dim room. Richard watched him when he stepped out of the shadows. The man walked across the room so quietly in leather moccasins it seemed his feet did not touch the floor.

Angel smiled and greeted the man in Spanish. Richard got the impression he was well known to Angel, even, perhaps, a friend. Angel propped the broom against the wall and joined the Indian. They talked quietly across the bar, laughing now and then.

The man held an intricately woven wool blanket around his shoulders. A cloth headband wrapped his head, and his hair was tied in a bun at the nape of his neck. Richard looked away after studying the man. He said nothing, turning his attention to the whiskey in his glass, then swallowing it off and pouring more to inspect.

When the bottle neared the bottom, he waved Angel over with a fresh one. "Who the hell is that Indian?" he said, with a nod toward the man standing quietly at the other end of the bar.

"Take it easy, Richard," Reinard warned.

Angel lifted their glasses one by one and wiped the bar. "He is called Atsidi."

"What the hell's he doin' here?"

"He passes this way from time to time. Atsidi is *un platero*. A silversmith. And he works with *el turquesa*, the turquoise. He travels to Santa Fe to sell his wares, and to trade."

"Where's he come from?"

Angel shrugged. "I cannot say for certain. He speaks of a place to the north, a place he calls *Tsé Bit'a'í*, or 'Rock with Wings.' Do you know it?"

Richard shook his head. "He looks like a Navajo."

"*Si.* He is Navajo."

Without a word, Richard took up Angel's broom from where it leaned against the wall. With the longest strides he could muster, he walked over to Atsidi and swung the broom like a club. The Navajo ducked aside, and the broom head struck him on the shoulder, the straw bristles scratching the side of his face.

"Richard!" Reinard said.

190

Angel shouted, *"¡Basta!"*

Richard reversed his hold on the broom and took to beating Atsidi with the end of the handle. Most of the blows were parried by the backpedaling Navajo's forearms, but one vicious swipe split the skin of his forehead and blood poured down his face and into his eyes. Richard kept swinging, the broomstick finding its mark more often as Atsidi tired, and the blows shook him. He fell to his knees. A final sidewise swipe landed on the side of the Navajo's head and the broom handle snapped. The Indian tipped over and crashed to the floor. Richard dropped the remains of the broom. Bent at the waist, his hands grasped his knees and he gasped for air. Through the fog, he heard Reinard call him a damn fool. Angel knelt beside the bleeding man. Reinard asked if Atsidi was still alive.

"*Si.* He breathes still. But he is badly hurt." Angel stood and stared at Richard, then back at the unconscious Atsidi. "I go for the *federales*. I know their *acampar*—where they have camped."

"No," Richard said between ragged breaths.

"You have done a bad thing, Señor Ricardo," Angel said, and hurried out the door.

They watched him go, then Reinard knelt beside Atsidi, the blood pool around his head spreading slowly as it seeped into the floorboards. "He's hurt bad. May well die." He looked up at Richard. "Son, you had best be gone when them *federales* get here."

Richard stood unmoved, as if nothing Reinard had said made sense. Then, with a shake of his head, he realized what he had done and started for the door, stopped, rushed over to the bar for the bottle of whiskey, and left.

CHAPTER TWENTY-THREE

Selling off surplus cattle enriched the Pate family. Even after operating expenses—which were substantial, given the isolation of the ranch—the income was considerable, and soon paid off the tribute owed for transfer of the land grant. Wild cattle still holed up in the *barrancas* slicing into the eastern rim of the plateau and were hunted regularly. But most of the roundup operations had moved westward, through the intervening ridges and valleys and into the broad meadows of *Valles Caldera*. Abel saw to the construction of cabins and pens along the fringe of the grasslands to allow vaqueros to stay out for weeks gathering herds. Lee invested in herds of sheep, as well, sending out herders with bands to graze the natural pastures tucked among the ridges atop the mesas.

Sarah still chafed at being atop the plateau and cut off from society, but had improved the ranch headquarters to better suit her sensibilities. Most all the adobe buildings—"mud huts" to her way of thinking—now sparkled with whitewash. The fences were repaired and refurbished, encroaching plants cut back, gardens blooming despite the short growing season, and domestic workers performing to suit her, including the cook she had taken on. Lee basked in his new life as landed gentry, overseeing ranching operations but leaving most of the management, and all day-to-day operations, in the hands of Abel. Lee and Sarah both looked forward to expanding the Pate family dynasty, with Emma great with child. Winters were harsh and long. Wood cut from the forests throughout summer kept the Pates and the skeleton crew kept on through the season warm, but activity outside four walls was rare.

With springtime well underway down below in the valley of the Rio Grande, Abel braved the road off the mesa one day, where winter still held sway. Under the guise of arranging buyers for cattle to be gathered in pending spring roundups, he—more than anything—had cabin fever and needed to get out and breathe air not tinged by woodsmoke.

But upon reaching the valley, rather than going south to Santa Fe, he rode northeast to Chimayo.

Early one evening Abel reined up and sat horseback at the edge of a well-kept farmyard. He watched a young girl and even younger boy struggle to carry a pail of water toward a chicken run. Water slopped over the rim as the two walked, arms outstretched, and set the bucket down beside the fence. They tipped the pail and let it spill into a trough hollowed out from a small cottonwood log. Then the girl lifted the lid of a bin beside the coop and filled a smaller pail with kernels of grain, which she and the boy tossed by the handful into the run, scattering feed for the scratching, pecking, clucking hens. The girl dropped the container back into the bin and let the lid fall with a bang.

The noise startled the little boy, and seeing Abel gave him another start. He tugged the girl's arm and pointed. When she saw the horseman, she grabbed the boy's hand and led him running to the house. After a time, a young woman stepped through the doorway, the children hugging her skirts. She watched Abel, but said nothing.

Abel watched her for a moment. "Hello."

The woman nodded.

"I'm lookin' for my brother. Melvin—Mel."

The woman thought for a moment. "*¿Él es tu hermano*—Mel?"

"*Si. Mi hermano.*"

She bent and said something to the girl, and she turned and ran through the yard, then disappeared along a path that followed a ditch around the curve of a hillside. The woman went into the house, the little boy clinging to her skirts. A moment later, she returned, grasping a mug in both hands. She walked over to Abel and held the steaming drink toward him. *"Ven, por favor. Café para ti."*

Abel stepped down from his horse, removed his hat, and accepted the drink. *"Gracias."*

"¿Hablas español?"

Abel shook his head. *"No. Solo un poco."*

She nodded. *"Mi inglés*—it is not so much."

Abel smiled. He knelt down and smiled at the little boy. "What is your name?—*¿tu nombre?"*

The boy ducked his head and retreated farther behind his mother. He peeked out from behind. "Miguel."

Abel smiled again and offered a handshake. *"Miguel. Bueno. Yo soy* Abel."

Miguel smiled faintly and took the proffered hand. "Abel."

"No, no, no!" the woman said. *"¡Lláma lo* Señor Abel! *O* Señor Pate."

The boy looked at his mother. *"¿Señor Pate? ¿Como con Papi* Mel?"

Abel said, *"Lláma me Tío* Abel. Uncle Abel."

The boy again looked to his mother. *"¿Tío* Abel?"

The woman nodded, patting the boy on the head.

"The girl, the *niña?"*

"Rosa—Rosita."

"And you?" Abel said. "You must be Lupe."

Lupe blushed and ducked her head. *"Si."*

Abel bowed slightly. "It is a pleasure to make your acquaintance, Lupe." He replaced his hat. "I have read about you-all in a letter from my brother. He claims to like it here."

Melvin rescued Lupe from further attempts at conversation when he came down the path and across the yard, holding hands with the girl. His face showed equal parts restraint and pleasure as he approached. "Abel. I couldn't be no more surprised had Rosita told me that Jesus Christ his own self had come callin'."

Abel smiled. "Now, Mel, you know Pa wouldn't hold with such blasphemous talk."

"Likely not. So don't you go tellin' on me."

The brothers embraced, pounding each other on the back. They stood back, pleased, but a bit embarrassed by the show of affection.

"What brings you here, Brother?"

Abel shrugged. "Got tired of bein' cold. It's still winter up on the ranch. Needed to stretch my legs some."

"Ma didn't send you to fetch me home, then? I worried she might when I sent her that letter."

"No. She don't know I was comin' to see you. If she did, she likely would want me to bring you home."

Melvin ducked his head and studied his feet for a moment. He looked up and shook his head. "No, Brother. This here's my home now."

Abel made a show of looking around. "Looks like a fine place, Mel. You'll have to tell me how you come to be here."

Melvin nodded. "All in good time. Right now, I believe I'm ready for some supper. You'll eat with us, won't you? And stay over?"

"Got no place else to go, so I'm yours if you'll have me."

"C'mon, Rosita," Melvin said to the girl. "Take my brother on into the house and let's get somethin' to eat."

Lupe had already slipped away, and the table was set and supper ready to be served.

"Somethin' smells mighty good," Abel said. "As I recollect, Brother, it takes about a bushel and a half of groceries just to make a dent in your appetite. How does this mite of a girl fix enough food to fill you up?"

Melvin smiled. "Just you wait. You get one taste of Lupe's grub and you'll be eatin' more'n me."

After the meal, the brothers sat at the table, talking and sipping wine Melvin poured from a jug. The boy and girl sat in the corner watching, the presence of a stranger—or any visitor—in their house a novelty. Lupe knelt near the *horno,* spinning wool in the light of its fire with a drop spindle. She drew out the carded fibers with one hand, spinning the spindle with the other, the shaft resting on her thigh and the whorl nestled in a fired-clay bowl on the floor beside her. Across the room sat a loom, a basket of bundles of colored yarn beside it.

Melvin told of his chance meeting of Mary Lewis in Santa Fe, which the Pates already knew of, Mary having passed news of the encounter on to the family. He expressed surprise at the success of the families. "Sounds like Mister Lewis and Pa has made a success of becomin' merchants. Mary says they got stores in lots of places. And you and Pa has got a big ranch."

"That's so. But the tradin' business is mostly Daniel's doin'. Pa did what he could, but his heart wasn't in it. He's lots happier now that we've got that land. It ain't the best setup, bein' so high up on the plateau, but it's workin' out. We got it goin' pretty good, and money's come in like Pa never would have guessed. I ain't never seen him so happy. He's even heard tell of some old gold and silver mines the Spaniards had over on the other side of the mountains from home, and is thinkin' of hirin' some men to look into it. Pa, he can't stop thinkin' of ways to stay busy."

"What about Ma?"

"Oh, you know Ma. She's some contrary by nature. But she's doin' all right. Misses bein' around folks, but I think once Emma and me's kid comes along, she'll have somethin' to take her mind off it."

"A baby, eh? That's good. But I don't guess one baby will be enough to suit you and Emma."

Abel smiled. "No. She's determined to have a passel of 'em. I'm more than happy to do my part." Abel sipped his wine. "You know, Mel, you ought not dismiss the idea of comin' up there with us. There's plenty of work. And plenty of room. Fact is, there's an extra house up there sittin' empty, and if it don't suit you, we can build somethin' that will."

Melvin sipped his wine, then yawned and stretched. "Naw. I like it here with Lupe."

"Bring her and the young'uns with you. I thought you knowed I meant it that way."

"No, it ain't that. Lupe's got a nice little setup here, and I got it in pretty good shape. It's enough work to keep a man busy, but not so much as to be a burden. We grow enough to keep food on the table, and some extra to sell. And Lupe's got her weavin' and that helps. 'Course it don't hurt none that Mary Lewis promised her a ready market for whatever she makes. Gives her a good price, too."

"Well, as long as you're happy, that's what matters. But you had best find a way to come on up there and bring Lupe and the kids for a visit. If not, Ma's likely to come after you—and you don't want that to happen. Now that she knows where you are, she ain't goin' to give up till she sees with her own two eyes that you're all right."

"I reckon we can do that. What would Pa have to say if we was to show up?"

"Oh, you know Pa. He's likely to point out all the things you done wrong and are still doin' wrong with your life. But that's just his nature. Still and all, he'll be glad to see you, and pleased you're makin' out. And there ain't no doubt him and Ma both will take a shine to Lupe and Rosita and Miguel. It's a fine family you've got goin' here."

"I got to tell you, Abel—I've really took to those kids. Couldn't love 'em any better if I'd fathered 'em myself. Smart as a whip, both of 'em. They're pickin' up on English lots quicker than Lupe, or me with Spanish—sometimes Rosita acts as a go-between when we get stuck talkin' about somethin'."

"I reckon there'll be more little ones around here before long."

Melvin only smiled, and sipped his wine.

The brothers talked well into the night and beyond, hardly noticing when Lupe and the children had slipped into the back rooms to sleep. Melvin told what he and Richard had done after leaving the family at Las Vegas, and of his parting company with Richard. He had no idea what had become of their brother since then.

After a few hours' sleep, Melvin showed Abel around the place, his pride bursting at the emerging bean plants and corn stalks in the fields, bragging on the growth of the hogs in the pen, the egg-laying abilities of the hens, the quality of the milk from the nanny goats and the cheese they made, and on and on through every detail of small farm. Then Abel filled up at dinner, saddled his horse, and started for home.

He did detour through Santa Fe to contact buyers and arrange contracts for delivering cattle, so as to accomplish his stated purpose for coming down off the plateau. He spent time with the Lewis family, learning of developments over the winter in business, politics, and elsewhere. When he left to climb the plateau, Jane rode beside him on a sturdy, surefooted mule. Learning of Emma's pending confinement, she would hear of nothing other than being at the ranch to keep house and tend the baby for her sister. While she may not have been more excited at the prospect of a little one than Emma, she was certainly more animated about the blessed event.

Abel sat one evening with his parents at their kitchen table, filling them in about their middle son. Lee smiled at reports of the well-tended farm; Sarah expressed both pleasure and dismay at the thought of his adopted family.

"Tell me, Abel—have they wed? Are they married, Melvin and this Lupe?"

Abel considered the question. "As much as me and Emma, I suppose. There ain't none of us got the blessing of clergy nor any official license."

Sarah sighed. "Well, I suppose there are disadvantages to living at the end of nowhere, where even God can't find you."

"Now, Sarah," Lee said. "It seems to me the boys have done right well in pairing up with a mate. They've done nothing more nor less than what many a patriarch and prophet in the Good Book done."

Abel recounted Melvin's report of the freight outfit he and Richard had hooked up with, with an eye to returning to the States. He told of their time in Taos, and partnering up with the old mountain man, Pegleg Smith, for a trip to Indian country. He told of the meeting with the Ute band, and Melvin's parting ways with Richard after refusing to go along on the raid on the Navajo to take hostages to sell into slavery into Mexico.

Lee's ire rose and he fidgeted and fumed at the thought of a son of his participating in the slave trade, no matter the circumstances. "I took my family out of the United States of America and suffered considerable hardship to escape the evils of slavery! And now a son of mine, my own flesh and blood, is a slave catcher! The thought of it is more than I can bear," he said, his anger collapsing into anguish, his head falling onto his forearms, folded on the table.

"It ain't the same thing, Pa. From what they told Mel, all them Indian tribes have been stealin' people from one another and sellin' 'em off for years."

Lee sat upright, eyes both flaming and awash with tears. "Nonsense! It is contrary to God's law for a man to hold another man in bondage!"

"But Pa, them patriarchs and prophets you talk about in the Good Book, they done it."

Lee shook his head. "If you spent more time with the Good Book, you would come to know it is not so simple. In them days, it was mostly bond servants they spoke of, held in a kind of slavery till their debts was paid. Or, if they were captives taken in war, they were held for a time, but not for always." His enthusiasm built as the sermon continued. "The Apostle Paul condemns 'menstealers' in his first epistle to Timothy. And he wrote to the Galatians, as recorded in the third chapter of that epistle, 'There is neither Jew nor Greek, there is neither bond nor free, there is neither male nor female: for ye are all one in Christ Jesus.' So don't you go thumpin' the Bible to argue for slaveholding until you've spent as much time in its pages as have I. We are all God's children, and every one among us ought to be treated as such—not as merchandise."

Abel sat silent, head bowed. Sarah, too, sat speechless. Then Abel raised his head and turned to his father. "I'm awful sorry, Pa. I didn't mean nothin' by it. I only want to say that from what Mel said, Richard got caught up in it without meanin' to."

"That is as it may be. But he could've walked away from it, like Melvin did."

"Could've done, maybe. But from what Mel said, he wasn't thinkin' right in his head on account of too much drink for too long."

"That I do not doubt. But it does not forgive the sin, and in itself is sinful. In that selfsame Epistle to the Galatians, Paul names 'drunkenness' among the sins that will keep a man from inheriting the kingdom of God." Lee sighed, and a teardrop traced a path through the wrinkles on his face. "I fear Richard is lost. He reminds of the man who has dug himself into a pit with his sinfulness, and ain't got the good sense to stop digging."

CHAPTER TWENTY-FOUR

Richard slid down the side of the dugway on his backside, then ran deeper into the gully, sweeping aside brush and crashing through undergrowth as he went, then ducking down behind an outcropping boulder to wait.

He had quit the road when the sound of hoofbeats and jingling bridle chains warned him of the approaching *federales*. His breath came in gasps he tried to suppress as the troopers approached, the drumming of hooves and rattling of tack growing louder. He peeked around the concealing rock and watched the riders above pass by, going at a trot and looking neither right nor left. Apparently, the soldiers were less than enthusiastic about capturing their prey. As their passing faded into the distance, Richard sat down on a rock to take stock of his situation.

He did not know how much distance he had covered since leaving Angel's place in Nacimiento. Other than the clothes he wore and the whiskey bottle in his hand—its contents diminished by the drinking he had done as he traveled—he had nothing. His horse, his saddle, his father's Kentucky rifle, and his few other belongings were left at Reinard's, and attempting to retrieve them would only invite trouble. Even his hat was gone, lost in the attack on the Navajo in the cantina. He found a single silver peso in the pocket of his vest, and dropped it down the shaft of his boot for safekeeping. After slaking his thirst, if only temporarily, from the whiskey bottle, he climbed out of the ravine and onto the road and continued his way southward.

A few hours down the road he again heard the approach of the *federales*. And again, he left the road and found concealment among the brush and boulders between the road and the river. The passing soldiers, now moving at a walk, made no attempt to survey their surroundings in search of the man they pursued. Richard assumed their hunt for him was a matter of form, and the *federales* had no interest pursing a man accused of nothing more than beating an Indian. Whether the victim was dead or alive, and if that fact affected the intensity of their pursuit, Richard did not know.

When night fell, he made his way down to the banks of the Rio Puerco, drank, washed his face, and found a snug place at the base of a cottonwood tree to curl up for the night. Come morning, the sun was late reaching him, tucked as he was against the base of the Jemez Mountains rising to the east. He did not stir until the sun warmed him and brightened his eyelids. He sat up and knuckled the sleep from his eyes, yawned and stretched, then stood, moving with care to avoid jarring his head, which throbbed from the effects of yesterday's liquor. The pain subsided when he doused it with a few draughts from the bottle. He held the bottle up to the light and wondered if what it held was sufficient to get him to the next settlement—the location of which he did not know.

Kneeling by the river and laving water over his face and head, Richard bowed deeper and sucked water from the stream, swallowed, and sat up. The drink roiled his stomach, more unsettling than the alcohol that preceded it. He walked up to the road, stopped and looked as far along its length in both directions as he could see, then set out southward across the broken landscape. The road followed the foothills skirting the mountains, bound on the other side by the Rio Puerco. When the road and river started to diverge, he went again to its banks for a drink, and filled his stomach. The road ahead looked long and lonely, and he knew not when he would again find water. And, as much as he preferred whiskey, he was well aware the thirst it quenched was of a different kind. Besides, the level in the bottle had dropped noticeably since morning.

Richard saw no other soul on the road through the day. When he huddled at dark among a cluster of sandstone boulders that still held heat from the sun, he wished the river were still at hand. He checked the whiskey bottle to confirm it was empty. Still, he carried it, in the event he found a spring or stream to fill it with water. The yapping of coyotes through the night disturbed his sleep, and he gave up the attempt and started walking at first light. The road climbed onto a shallow red sandstone mesa, which rose higher in another step up to the left of the road. Richard had not traveled far when he saw a cart drawn by a burro approaching from the south. He stopped in the road and waited, believing no one from that direction would have heard of his crime.

Richard sat on a rock and watched the cart draw nearer, creaking its way along the road. Given the time of day, he suspected the man walking beside it had, like him, gotten an early start on his day's journey, and that a settlement of some kind must be nearby. The man eyed Richard as he approached, slowing, then stopping, beside him.

Richard mimed drinking. "*¿Agua?*"

The man nodded. Never taking his eyes off Richard, he reached into the cart, wiggling his hand between the front boards and the canvas that covered the load heaped above the sides. He came up with a *bota*, a stoppered leather bag usually filled with wine. Richard had never seen such a thing, and looked it over with furrowed brow. The man took it back, pulled the plug, and demonstrated how to squeeze out the liquid, squirting a narrow stream into his mouth.

Richard smiled, gave it a try, and handed it back. *"Gracias."* He searched his mind for the proper Spanish words to ask if there was a town nearby, and said, *"¿Hay un pueblo?"*

The man pointed down the road the way he had come, and released a torrent of words Richard could not begin to understand. He waved away the words with his hand and said, *"Dónde?"*

Snapping a twig from a dry brush beside the road, the man showed him where, by scratching a rough map in the dust, showing a bend in the road ahead, leading to an *X*. He poked at the *X*. "San Ysidro." He pointed at the sun and moved his finger across the sky a short way, which Richard understood to mean where the sun might be when one reached San Ysidro from here. He nodded, thanked the man again, and set out on what looked to be a short walk to this place called San Ysidro. He left the whiskey bottle lying beside the road.

Before long, the road curved to the east and rounded the end of the red mesa. Richard followed, and within a few miles he saw the green fields around a little town tucked into a narrow valley, with a stream snaking along its bottom. People in the fields stopped to watch as Richard sauntered along the road, then went back to their work. Like most places he had seen in this country, the buildings in San Ysidro were squat adobe structures, their outer walls punctured from within by log *vigas* that supported the roof. The only noteworthy building was a church, its bell tower reaching heavenward over the town. As the road became the street through the village, inches of dust, sifted fine by trampling feet and hooves, covered its surface. Barking dogs darted out from among the houses, lost interest when he did not react, and slunk back.

Seeing nothing in the way of a commercial enterprise along the street, Richard sat in the shade of a tree in the plaza, across from the church, leaning his back against the trunk. Soon, he was asleep. Some time later, he knew not how long, voices roused him from his slumber. Whispers, laughter, and more whispers penetrated the fog. He opened his eyes to see a handful of children standing in front of him. They quieted when he looked at them, some blushing and backing away.

"Hello."

Some of the children giggled at the greeting, eyes glancing at each other, then at Richard.

He tried again. "Hola."

Again, the youngsters giggled.

"*¿Inglés?*"

A girl, the tallest of the group, stepped forward. "*No Inglés.*" She said something else to the other children, and they talked back and forth for a time, then one of the boys turned and ran away. He returned after a few minutes with a man by the hand, tugging and leading him across the plaza. The man looked to be in his middle years, and his dress suggested he had been brought in from the fields. He removed his battered straw hat.

"Good day, señor."

"Hallelujah," Richard said. "Someone who talks English. Is this San Ysidro where I'm at?"

"*Si.* Yes. San Ysidro."

Richard looked around at the town. "As you can see, mister, I ain't got a thing to my name. Is there any work to be had around here?"

"*¿Trabajo? Si.* There is always much work to do. *En los campos. Con los cultivos.* How do you say? The farm fields? We work always."

"No, what I mean is, would anyone be willin' to hire me on? I can put my hand to most any job of work that needs to be done."

The man scrunched up his face, working pursed lips back and forth. Richard could not tell if he was trying to make sense of what he had said, or thinking of a way to reply.

"Thing is, you see, I've had a run of bad luck. Ain't got a thing but the clothes on my back. I ain't ate for days."

The man shrugged. "*Lo siento,* señor. In San Ysidro, we too are poor. I know of no one here with the means to pay you."

Richard sagged. Then, "Well, supposin' I didn't need no pay? What if I offer to work for bed and board?"

"Bed and board? I do not know what this means."

"Food. And a place to sleep. Hell, I'll sleep anywhere if there's a roof over it. And I'll eat anything that's put in front of me. Like I said, I'm in a bad way."

The man looked around, lost in thought, rocking gently back and forth on his heels. The bell in the church tower started ringing, waking him from his reverie. "Ah! *El mediodía.* Time for *la comida.* To eat. The workers will come now. You come."

Richard followed the man across the plaza and down a side street toward the river, passing field workers as they went. The man hailed one of them. Richard guessed from his appearance—his clothing less tattered and torn than most, his straw hat not so stained with sweat and greasy dust—that he must be among the more prosperous in the town. The two talked for a while, the man from the fields impatient with the delay. After a lengthy exchange, he held up his hands, as if in surrender, and looked at Richard.

Richard looked to the man who spoke English. "Well?"

The man smiled. "This man is Raúl Mendoza. Señor Mendoza has most graciously invited you to share *comida* with his *familia.* After *la comida,* the food, he will show you some work to be done."

The room was dim, lit mostly by light coming through a window covered with what looked to be oiled sheepskin. The only other light sources were a candle stuck with its own drippings onto a clay saucer in the center of the plank table, and a smaller candle flickering in a niche in the wall, standing with *re-tablos* and *santos*, hand-carved and painted statues of saints and angels. Richard recognized the tall girl from the plaza, seated on a bench at the table, next to an older boy, his dust-smudged clothing suggesting field work.

The woman, bustling around the stove and working at the rough cabinets and shelves and countertops against the far wall, pulled a stack of bowls from a shelf and put them on the table. She showed Richard where to sit, and put a bowl at his place. She said something to the girl, who fetched faded cloth napkins and mismatched spoons for each setting. Next, she brought clay mugs and a pitcher, and poured milk, most likely from a goat, into each mug. The girl and her mother danced around and dodged one another as the girl did her work while the woman set out a plate of warm tortillas, then carried a cast-iron kettle around the table, filling each bowl with a stew, the piquant steam of which brought tears to Richard's eyes even as saliva filled his mouth at the prospect of food.

After the meal, the woman and girl cleared the table. The boy left through a doorway into the back of the house, and the girl followed. The woman brought two small drinking glasses to the table and put one in front of each man. Next came a bottle, which she placed before the man, then left the room. With a hint of ceremony, the man pulled the cork from the bottle. He gestured for his guest to pass his glass. Richard handed it over and watched as the man poured a drink—little more than a thimbleful—into the glass, then did the same with his own glass. He corked the bottle and set it aside. He picked up his glass and held it toward Richard.

"Mezcal," he said. "Mezcal Desde San Baltazar Guelavilaen Oaxaca."

Richard recognized the word "mezcal," but nothing else. He held up the glass and sniffed, feeling the tang of alcohol in his nose. He poured down the drink in one quick swallow, shuddering inside as it warmed its way down.

Mendoza sat upright, eyes wide at what Richard had done. Then he relaxed, taking a tiny sip of the mezcal, barely wetting his tongue. He savored it, eyes closed, before swallowing. Richard looked on as he repeated the act, stretching the tiny amount of liquor into several reverential tastes.

When, finally, Mendoza finished the ritual, Richard watched him return the bottle to its place on the shelf. Then he took his straw hat from a peg on the wall, turned to Richard, and said, *"Ven,"* signaling with a hand for him to follow.

Richard followed Mendoza out the door and around the side of the house to the yard behind. Outlining the hollow rectangle of the backyard were a chicken coop and run, a pen holding several nanny goats, a low barn with open lean-to sheds flanking either side, a pigpen, and a granary. Mendoza pushed a wheelbarrow, spade, and pitchfork from under one of the sheds and wheeled it to the pigpen. A sow with seven piglets nearly ready to wean grunted and snuffled at the fence, thinking it feeding time. Mendoza shooed them away with the shovel.

He had only to point at the bog in the bottom of the pen—an odiferous soup of manure and urine mixed with straw and mud—the tools, and the wheelbarrow for Richard to understand what was expected. Then Mendoza led him back along the path beside the house, down the street past two other houses, and to an embankment that fell away to the river. The slope was littered with refuse—clearly a dump for all manner of garbage.

"¿Entender?"

Richard nodded that he understood, and they walked back to the house. At the door, Mendoza called for his son, and they left for the fields. He worked the shovel and fork, favoring his sore shoulder. Minutes later, up to his ankles in pig shit, Richard realized the loathsomeness of the situation. With the wheelbarrow only two-thirds full, he climbed over the fence and out of the pen. He stomped his feet in a vain attempt to shake off the clinging mess, gave it up, and pushed the wheelbarrow to the embankment and tipped out the mess. Most spilled, but thick clumps of the pigpen mess clung to the bottom and sides of the barrow bed. With one hand holding the wheelbarrow upright, he used the other to claw the excrement loose and fling it into the gully.

He stopped and held up his hand and stared at it, then swore a string of oaths seldom heard in polite company. Slamming the wheelbarrow down, he maneuvered it back up the street, around the house, and into the backyard, letting it tip on its side next to the pigpen. With his mostly clean hand, he scooped water out of the trough shared by the goats and chickens and used it to wash the dung off the filthy hand. Wiping his hands dry on his pants legs, he left the backyard.

On the street, he looked both ways, but saw no one about. He eased open the door of Mendoza's house and peeked in. There was no one in the room; the girl and her mother must still be in the rooms at the back. He slipped through the doorway and took the bottle of mezcal from the shelf. As he made his way back to the door, he lifted a straw hat from a peg. Worn and dirty, with the brim broken on one side, it was still better than going bareheaded in the sun.

Richard hurried down the street, and skidded down the embankment to the Jemez River. He followed the narrow watercourse, concealing himself as best he could among the willows and sparse cottonwood trees along its banks. Well past the town and the cultivated fields, he regained the road unseen and continued his journey.

To where, he did not know.

CHAPTER TWENTY-FIVE

Abel Pate rode along the fringe of trees where the pine forests gave way to the broad, grassy meadows of the caldera, hunting for cattle. Spying a distant scattering of the animals, he stopped to study the area for landmarks. He would return with his vaqueros, perhaps tomorrow, to herd this bunch of the wild critters to pens they had put up in the valley. As they had done elsewhere on the plateau, they would brand the animals, then cut out and hold those to drive to market in Santa Fe.

As he sat horseback admiring the land that had become his home, he envisioned the activity that would be going on now at ranch headquarters, some twenty miles across the plateau. He thought of home, and Emma. He thought of Luke, now toddling about and growing into a mind of his own. He smiled at the memory of their going about the naming of their firstborn son. Emma had wanted a biblical name, and Abel did not disagree. She suggested several of the more common names from the book—John, James, Mark, Adam, Daniel, Benjamin, Peter, and the like.

Abel pretended to prefer something more exotic and lobbied for names that made Emma cringe. He feigned disappointment as she refused Meshach, Zacharias, Uriel, Othniel, Esdras, Naphtali, Gomer, Ehud, and other unusual appellations. Their good-natured exchanges ended when Abel made a show of surrender and, affecting disappointment, suggested Luke. Emma agreed, threw her arms around him and peppered him with kisses, thanking him for not insisting on Balthasar or Mordecai or some such. He only grinned, never letting on that Luke had been his preference all along.

He thought of their newborn son, and imagined him even now nestled in the warmth of Emma's breast. James. Jamie. Another name from the pages of the Good Book, this one the mother's choice—although Abel had pretended, briefly, to campaign for Issachar. Emma, not fooled by his lobbying, told him that if he had any objection to James, he could take up residence in the bunkhouse, and she would help him pack his things.

Smiling at the memories, he turned his mount and started back to the cow camp cabin and corrals where the vaqueros were working on cattle gathered earlier. As soon as he started, Abel stopped the horse with a surprised jerk on the reins. Coming toward him from across the Valle Grande were three mounted men, already less than a furlong away. He saw right away they were not any of the men in his employ. And he surmised their intentions as less than friendly, as the rider on the right carried a rifle propped upright on his thigh, while the one on the left had a rifle laid across the forks of his saddle.

Abel saw those two as subordinate to the man in the middle, who rode half a length ahead. He was a small man, his *sombrero* hanging down his back from a thong around his neck. His face had not seen a razor for several days, but it did not appear his custom to wear a beard. He did, however, sport a mustache thick and long. All three wore worn clothing, patched and stitched together with makeshift repairs.

They reined up a few yards shy of where Abel sat his horse waiting for them. The presumed leader asked if he spoke Spanish.

"*Sí, algo. Por favor habla despacio,*" Abel said, asking the man to speak slowly.

"You are the man who is rounding up the cattle?"

Abel nodded agreement.

"You are not to take cattle from here. Here is where I have charge of the cattle."

"By what authority do you make such a claim?"

The man shrugged one shoulder as if the question deserved no answer. Abel said nothing, waiting to see if his silence would unnerve the man, and force a reply.

"I take the cattle because I can. Because we have always done so. They are like the deer. As I said, my friends and I have taken the cattle from here always."

Abel let the answer lie for a while, again letting tension build in the silence. Then, "No more. These cattle belong to me."

Now it was the Mexican's turn to ask what authority lay behind Abel's claim.

Abel said, "My family took over the old ranch on the plateau with the authorization of Governor Armijo."

Again, the man shrugged. "The title from the governor carries no force here. The Valle Grande is beyond the borders of the ranch."

"That is as it may be. Maybe so, maybe no. But these cattle ain't like the deer—they ain't here natural. They're strays. If it weren't for the ranch, they wouldn't be here at all."

The man smiled. "And yet they are wild, like the deer. They have not known the presence of man for many years. They carry no brand. So my friends and I, we take them as we please."

"Not no more, you don't. You leave the cattle be and get the hell out of here."

Again, the man smiled. "I think not, my friend." He turned and nodded at the rider on his right. While Abel and the man had talked, the rider had sheathed his rifle and unstrung his reata from the saddle. In a few beats of Abel's pounding heart, the man built a loop, spun once overhead, and threw. Even before the loop settled, he jerked back his slack, tightening the rope around Abel's chest and pinning his arms. He stacked a pair of dallies around the saddle horn as he wheeled his horse around and put the spurs to him. The horse leaped forward, snatching Abel out of the saddle and onto the ground.

The other rider dismounted and rolled Abel onto his stomach, wrenched his arms behind his back, and tied his wrists together with a length of braided leather rope. He pulled off the loop over Abel's head, grabbed the binding on his wrists and jerked him to his feet, nearly wrenching his shoulders out of their sockets.

Abel grimaced, and sweat beaded his face. "You-all don't want to do this."

The leader, now dismounted as well, grinned. "And why is that, my friend?"

"Because I'll kill you."

The response came when the man's rawhide quirt, strung to his wrist, cut a gash across Abel's cheek. Blood from the wound spread, turning pink as it mixed with the sweat. The other man sunk a fist into Abel's gut, forcing the breath from him and causing him to buckle. He lit on his knees, but refused to fall farther.

The man with the quirt circled him, raining blows with the lash on his head, his arms, his back, and his chest. When Abel finally collapsed, the attackers worked on him with their boots. A blow to his head turned the world dark.

Night had fallen when Abel regained consciousness. He lay still and took stock of his condition. He hurt everywhere, but felt nothing that would indicate a bullet wound, or knife cuts, or broken bones. His wrists still tied behind him, he struggled to sit up. Light from the moon and stars revealed no one nor any thing around him. His mount had spooked and run away when Abel had been so rudely unhorsed. He tried to stand, but between the pain and the loss of the use of his hands and arms, he failed. It took several tries to find his feet, each failure requiring many minutes of suffering and waiting to regain the strength and will to try again.

When he finally got upright, he stood, weaving and heaving, as his throbbing head tried to find equilibrium. Then he turned slowly in a circle, straining through the dark to locate himself, and then shuffled off in the direction—he hoped—of the cow camp.

Stopping frequently to rest and catch his breath, Abel studied the dark landscape. Out on the grassy plain, a tree-covered hill stood like an overturned soup bowl on a tabletop. From time to time, Abel caught a glimpse of a flickering fire. With no other sign of human life, he assumed the fire to be at the camp of the cattle rustlers. He determined to pay them a visit—if he could first find his way to help.

Abel stumbled and staggered on through the tall grass. Now and then he fell. Each time, it proved more and more difficult to rise, the physical challenge of getting up without the aid of hands and arms intensified by the pain and exhaustion from the beating. He sat on his knees, legs tucked under, after a struggle to stand up after a fall. Through gasping breaths, he barely heard the whistle. Holding his breath, he strained to listen. There it was again—the distant, faint whistle of another person. He kept listening and heard it again. It seemed to be nearer. Then, he heard another whistle, farther away.

Struggling to get to his feet, Abel tried to whistle, but only a weak discharge of air left his parched mouth. He worked his jaws and sucked on his cheeks and tongue to work up moisture to whistle, but to no avail. He gave it up and hollered, mustering as much volume as he could, which did not amount to much.

"¡Hola!" he yelled. "Help!"

He heard nothing in response, and repeated his call. He heard a loud whistle, then another, fainter, then the approach of a horse, followed by another. The hoofbeats paused and the rider called out. Abel responded, and soon the rider neared, guided by Abel's voice as he talked.

"Señor Abel!" the *vaquero* said. "We did not know what happened to you—your horse, it came in alone. We have been searching through the night."

"Well, I'm damn glad you-all did. I'm in a bad way."

By now another rider had arrived. He dismounted and freed Abel's hands, forced to cut the leather bindings as they were drawn too tight to untie. "*¿Qué pasó?*"

"*Ladrones*," Abel said, rubbing his chafed wrists and throbbing hands. He told how he had been daydreaming, and taken by surprise by their approach. And about the beating—at least as much of it as he could remember before blacking out. "Take me back to the camp. I'll get some rest. Soon as I'm up to it, I'll be goin' after them."

"We will go with you, Señor Abel. We will tend to these dogs."

"*Gracias.* You and the others can go along and handle the cattle they've gathered—but I will tend to these *hombres* myself."

"But señor—"

"Enough! Get me out of here."

Abel sagged in the saddle, passing in and out of sleep as they rode, staying mounted only because of the *vaquero* riding behind the saddle and keeping him from falling from the horse. Back in the cabin at the cow camp, the two rescuers each slung one of Abel's arms across his shoulders and helped him to bed. Throughout the early hours of the morning, other vaqueros came into camp, returning from their searches, relieved that Abel had been found.

When Abel awakened late in the afternoon, one of his men cleaned his wounds with warm water and a rag. Refreshed by a plate of beans and tortillas, Abel stretched, working out the kinks and stiffness. Then he assembled his men and sketched out a plan for tomorrow.

The sun was yet to rise when they reached the hill rising from the Valle Grande. Riding along its edge, they soon discovered the ashes of the campfire Abel had seen in the night, and grass trampled by the small herd gathered there by the thieves. A faint trail showed the direction the cattle had taken through the tall grass.

Unhindered by recalcitrant cattle, Abel and his vaqueros made good time across the *valle*, heading southwest, where, one of his men told him, a trail followed a canyon out of the mountains and led to Pueblo de Jemez and the village of San Ysidro.

"We'll be onto them long before that," Abel said, nodding toward a faint cloud of dust hanging in the air. He divided his men, sending a trio wide on each side, with instructions to cut off the herd and hold them while he dealt with the thieves.

Spurring his horse into a gallop, Abel was soon within sight of the small bunch of cattle, pushed along by the three *ladrones*. He spotted the leader, flanking the herd on the left side. He veered toward him and urged his horse to lengthen his stride, pulling the leather string on the fork of his saddle as he rode, turning loose his reata. As he rode past, Able saw wide-eyed surprise on the face of the thief trailing the herd. The man shouted, arousing the attention of the leader just as Abel drew near him.

The leader wheeled his horse around and faced the surprise attack, just in time to see Abel swat him full in the face with the coiled reata. The blow knocked him out of the saddle, his foot hanging briefly in the stirrup as his spooked horse skittered and danced away. The ruction stirred the cattle, but Abel's vaqueros arrived in time to mill the frightened animals. The bandit leader found his feet, and tried to calm his horse as it backed away, avoiding him. Abel's mount, just as frightened as the cattle, resisted his sawing on the reins, but he managed to slow the horse and turn it around.

The man riding drag had quit the herd and was coming fast to aid his leader. Abel pulled one of his Paterson revolvers from its holster—hanging, this day, on the forks of his saddle, rather than their usual place in his saddlebags. Abel spurred his horse into motion toward the leader, still trying to get ahold of the reins dragged by his skittish horse.

The other rustler arrived and rode up to the loose horse, leaned down, snatched a rein near the bit, and jerked the horse to a stop. But before he could pass the bridle rein to his boss, a bullet from Abel's pistol hammered his chest. His body went limp with the assault and he dropped from the saddle. Both of the bandits' mounts spooked and ran away.

The bandit leader paled, staring at his friend bleeding on the ground, scarlet foam bubbling out of the bullet hole as his lights went out. The Mexican turned to Abel and tipped the front of his sombrero back, letting the hat fall from his head, captured by the leather thong around his neck to hang at his back. "*¿Y ahora qué?*"

"I'll tell you what happens now," Abel said. "Now I am going to kill you."

The bandit shrugged. "You have me at a disadvantage."

"No more so than what you had me the other day."

"And yet you live."

"No thanks to you."

The *ladrone* pulled a heavy, long-bladed knife from a sheath at his waist. He waggled it in the air before him, sunlight glinting from the polished steel. "Perhaps you will put away your gun, and fight me as a man—*mano a mano.*"

Abel laughed, but there was no mirth in it. "It ain't quite *mano a mano* with you holding that knife in your hand."

The Mexican only smiled. Abel looked around and saw that four of his vaqueros had the cattle under control. The other two were riding after the third bandit in a race across the plain. Abel slid the revolver back into its scabbard and stepped down from the saddle, his only weapon the braided rawhide reata coiled in his hand, and set his sight on the outlaw.

Still smiling, the bandit watched Abel approach. He glided toward Abel as the cowboy walked away from his horse.

Abel flexed his shoulders to relieve the stiffness, turning to follow the circling knife as the man holding it sidled around him. Abel turned his head, seeming to shift his attention to the chase. The Mexican took the opportunity to leap forward and thrust the blade toward Abel's midsection. But Abel stepped aside and swung the reata, the coils knocking his attacker's arm down, and followed up with a backhand swat, the rope hitting the bandit's shoulder, knocking the smaller, lighter man aside.

Unfazed, the outlaw recovered his balance like a cat. As he turned, he swiped the knife in a threatening arc. Once again, Abel slapped the snakelike coils across the *ladrone*'s arm and hand, this time dislodging the knife.

The Mexican dove after the lost blade, but lost the race when the arch of Abel's boot caught him under the chin. He flipped backward with the force of the blow. As the rustler hit the ground, Abel dropped his rope and reached down and picked up the knife. Without ceremony, he stepped across the bandit's body, lifted his head and shoulders off the ground by a hank of hair, and sliced the outlaw's throat cleanly with the blade. He dropped the man, let the knife fall to his chest, and stepped away.

When the vaqueros returned with the *ladrone* who tried to escape, the man stunk of urine. His face was pale, and his chin quivered. "Por favor, señor," he said in a trembling voice. *"No me mate."*

"I ain't goin' to kill you," Abel said. "You go on back to wherever you come from. You tell anyone there who thinks to come up here and steal cattle what happened to your friends. And tell them the same thing will happen to them. *¿Comprendé?*"

CHAPTER TWENTY-SIX

The sun teased the western horizon as Richard hurried along the road from San Ysidro. There was a possibility of pursuit, but he doubted the theft of a half-empty bottle of mezcal and a battered straw hat would launch a posse.

The bottle in question, long since empty and tossed to spin through the air then shatter and scatter in shards among roadside rocks and brush, was of little note to Richard. He could not know, nor did he care, that it had been a valued, cherished possession of his former host, Raúl Mendoza. That bottle of Mezcal Desde San Baltazar Guelavilaen Oaxaca had come far to reach Nuevo Mexico, passing from hand to hand, trader to trader, freighter to freighter, on a journey from the village of San Baltazar Guelavila in the high country of Oaxaca, deep in Old Mexico. Mezcal from there was said to be the finest ever to caress the tongue of mankind. To esteem a guest with a taste of this rare and precious nectar was the highest honor Mendoza could bestow, the most signal honor, perhaps, in all of San Ysidro.

But Richard had offended in his lack of appreciation of the proffered drink, slugging it down as if it were cheap wine. Nor had Richard comprehended the quality of the stolen liquor as he gulped it down during his escape, then discarded the empty bottle as common garbage. And now Mendoza was left only to mourn the loss of his revered Mezcal Desde San Baltazar Guelavilaen Oaxaca, with Richard left only with a thirst unsatisfied for want of more.

As the sky darkened, Richard saw a faint glow across the river and atop a low mesa to the east. It appeared to come from fires. The glow intensified as he drew nearer, and he could see a settlement seeming to rise out of the very earth of the mesa, and he could hear faint singing or chanting drifting in the still desert air. He came across a trail that led down to and crossed the Jemez River and he followed it. The path climbed the side of the low escarpment. Topping out, Richard saw what looked like a miniature version of the pueblo he and Melvin had passed through near Taos. Like building blocks, adobe houses were stacked atop one another, the building on the ground level supporting smaller structures on its roof, with still more atop those. Ashes from the fires he had seen still glowed in an open area between structures, but whatever celebration or ceremony they accompanied looked to have ended, for there were no people in evidence.

Under a *ramada*, a sunshade with a brush-covered roof supported by upright posts, he found some discarded tortillas and bowls with scraps of a soup or stew made with corn, beans, squash, and other bits he could not identify, but ate anyway. As he walked through the small pueblo, a dog would occasionally bark at his presence, but it did not seem to arouse any suspicion among the residents. A woven wool blanket draped over a rail caught his attention and he draped it over his shoulders. Another dog started barking but he paid it no mind, continuing his stroll through the pueblo. Then he heard a voice, and saw a man on a roof, silhouetted against the starry sky. Another voice answered from a building across the way, this one more strident. Richard ran back through the center of the village and followed the pale ribbon that was the trail down off the mesa.

For what he guessed to be another two hours or so, Richard followed the road as it followed the sparse river. The stream flowed into a canyon that narrowed the sky above. Richard, bleary-eyed, called a halt for the night and, wrapped in his newfound blanket, rolled under a pine tree, wallowed himself a hip hole, and fell asleep. His last thought was a wish that the bottle of mezcal had not run dry so soon.

When the light of the sun penetrated his eyelids to awaken him, Richard raised up on an elbow to look around. The motion disturbed a scorpion crawling across his blanket, and the creature skittered away on all eight legs, its venomous tail curled over its back. Richard rolled out from under the tree limbs and scrambled to his feet, waving the blanket to shake off the possibility of other unwelcome visitors. He drank from the stream, then climbed out of the canyon to get the lay of the land. He walked to the top of a hill and saw where the sluggish Jemez River looked to trickle into a much larger stream. Richard assumed it to be the Rio Grande.

A few miles below the confluence lay a settlement, holding the desert at bay with a patchwork of green fields and orchards. Richard rolled the blanket and draped it over one shoulder and started walking. The nearer he came to the town, the more signs of settlement he encountered—trash and refuse clinging to brush and tipped into ravines, footpaths and cart tracks and wagon roads intersecting the main thoroughfare, *acequias* contouring the land and carrying water to crops, grazing livestock, and scattered houses. He passed pepper patches, fields of corn and beans, wheat and barley, melons and squash, apricot and apple orchards, and vineyards.

Then he started seeing people working in the fields and moving about with carts and wagons. What looked to be a family of Indians stopped on the road to watch him pass. The woman talked to him in a language strange to him, seeming to berate him, and started tugging at the blanket slung over his shoulder. Richard grabbed the blanket and pulled away, the man restraining the woman, the children watching with blank faces. He walked on, looking back to see the Indian family still watching him, the woman still talking and gesturing his way, trying to pull away from the man. He looked again after a few minutes to see the family walking back along the road he had traveled.

Walking about the outskirts of the town, Richard watched men working at granaries and haystacks, women tending kitchen gardens, and boys moving bands of sheep to graze fresh pastures. He stopped at one building where men loaded casks and barrels onto a wagon. As he watched, an old man shuffling along, staff in hand, stopped beside him to watch.

"*¿Que es esto?*" Richard said, testing the limits of his knowledge of the language.

"*Es una bodega. Hacen vino aqui.*"

"*¿Que?*"

The old man stared at him through rheumy eyes, as if Richard were daft.

Richard shrugged and said, "*No hablo español.*"

The man smiled, showing what looked to be the only tooth in his mouth. "*Vino,*" he said, mimicking drinking. "*Vino.*"

"Aah," Richard said with a smile. "*Vino.*" Then, "*¿Donde está esto?* What is this town?"

"Bernalillo," the old man said, and limped away, leaning on his walking stick.

Richard stayed, watching until the laden wagon pulled away from the winery. The double doors swung shut, but Richard watched from the shade of a tree across the road as workers came and went. And he noticed another building two doors down where wine was made or stored. He waited throughout the afternoon and into the evening when all the workers left, and, finally, when the man who must be in charge came out the door and locked it behind him, then looped a chain around the double doors and fastened it with a padlock.

After night fell and traffic in the neighborhood faded away, Richard crossed the street. He gave the chain on the double doors a tug, and tested the lock on the entry door. Around the side of the building, he checked the shuttered windows and found them tight. Out back, an alley passed behind the building, and outside another locked door were piles of junk: barrels falling apart, broken jugs and bottles, damaged tools, and piles of rotting pomace, the leftover skins, seeds, and stems from winemaking.

Richard rattled a shuttered window and found it loose. He rummaged through the trash and found a broken barrel stave, slipped it into the gap in the loose shutter and pried until it broke loose. He hefted himself up into the window, gritting his teeth and hissing breath through clenched teeth at the stab of pain in his sore shoulder, imagining he could feel the cut of the arrowhead inside. Dropping into the building, he found himself in a storeroom of sorts. Pawing around in the dark, he found a box of matches on a table, struck one, then found a lantern in its glow.

With the light turned low, he left the storeroom and passed presses and other winemaking implements he did not recognize. Farther along were rows and stacks of casks of various sizes. On a long shelf along one wall stood rows of jugs and bottle. He stuffed a bottle into the waistband of his pants and picked up a jug, carrying them back through the warehouse to the storeroom and open window. He put the lamp back in its place and extinguished it, then waited until his eyes could find the window in the dimness. Once outside, he pushed the shutter to, hoping no one would notice it was loose.

Richard followed a path toward the edge of town, and walked a ways off the footpath into a shallow ravine to huddle with his bottle and jug at the base of a tree. Wrapped in his blanket, he emptied the bottle, listening to the wine gurgle out as he swallowed it in long draughts. He then uncorked the jug and drank from it, balancing it on his forearm and hoisting it to his mouth. Satisfied, for now, he set the jug aside and curled up in his blanket and fell asleep.

So deep and drunken was his sleep that he did not hear the approach of the young men. Three in number, they, too, were in their cups—but only to the point of feeling jovial and adventurous. One of the men saw Richard sleeping under the tree as they staggered along the path. "¡Mira!" he said.

The others looked. They stopped and watched, discussing in slurred voices the possibilities in what lay before them. One walked over to Richard and tapped at the sole of Richard's boot with the toe of his own shoe. There was no response. He saw and pointed out to his friends the empty bottle and the wine jug. "Está borracho."

"Sí," his friends said, nodding with great solemnity, agreeing that the man under the tree was drunk.

The man rolled Richard onto his back. He stood back when Richard groaned and squirmed, waiting to assure himself the hombre borracho would not awaken. Then he stooped to check the contents of the pockets of Richard's vest, and feel for what might be concealed elsewhere. He found nothing. With a long sigh, he sat and contemplated the sleeping man. As his friends giggled and offered useless advice, he pulled off Richard's boots. A silver peso spilled out of one. He grabbed it and held it aloft to show his friends, exclaiming at his good fortune. He stood, pocketed the coin, and asked the others to help him lay hold of the blanket.

The three young men grasped one side of the blanket and lifted and pulled, rolling Richard out and off and into the dirt. Again, he muttered and writhed, but did not awaken. The men set off down the path, laughing at their good fortune in finding a blanket, a pair of worn but useful boots, a jug of wine, and even a silver coin. Surely they were blessed, they said, to find such valuable items left for them by providence on this night of nights.

The day was well underway when, finally, Richard stirred. He sat up and scrubbed the sleep out of his face with the palms of his hands. Still sagging, through squinted eyes to ward off light too intense, he looked around. He wiggled toes exposed through holey socks and wondered at the absence of his boots. He felt around for his blanket, but it did not come to hand. He held his head in his hands to stifle the throbbing. Seeking relief, he reached out for the jug and felt only empty air. He fell back into the dirt, forearm shielding his eyes, mind reeling in distress and disquiet.

When his breathing steadied, he sat up again, realizing he had been robbed while passed out drunk. Rising slowly to his feet, he stood until finding his balance, and walked, one unsteady step at a time, toward the town. He passed the *bodega* he had relieved of the wine behind his misfortune. The smell of food reminded him of his hunger as he passed through *Las Cocinitas,* the neighborhood called the little kitchens. He detoured through an alley, and found a waste barrel from one of the kitchens. Pawing through the soggy garbage, he found a tamale, still wrapped in its corn husk. He unwrapped and wolfed it down and when he swallowed the last bite he dug through the barrel looking for more.

The back door of the kitchen opened, and a woman stepped through, tossing dishwater out of a pan onto the ground. She saw Richard, and, taken aback by what he was doing, shook her head and muttered something under her breath, then went back inside, slamming shut the door.

What the hell am I doing? Richard thought. *Eating garbage like a stray dog or a wandering hog. How in God's name has it come to this?*

Walking through the streets barefoot, wondering what to do, he saw a sign above a door. MERCANTILE, it read. Beneath, in smaller letters, was the Spanish equivalent, LA TIENDA. Beneath that, in smaller letters yet, it read, LEWIS & PATE, PROP.

Still as a statue, Richard stood in the street reading the sign over and over, as if his eyes were seeing something that was not there. Foot traffic dodged him—giving him a wide berth—and carts and wagons veered to miss him, the drivers cursing him as they passed.

He opened the door and entered the store, stepping aside to look around. A woman stood at the counter, her back to Richard, as she waited for her parcels to be wrapped. The man behind the counter tied the final knot, smiled at the woman and thanked her. He looked at Richard, and continued to stare until the woman was gone.

He said, "*¿En qué puedo ayudarlo*, señor?"

Richard shook his head. "What?"

"Ah! You do not speak Spanish. I asked how I can help you."

"My name is Pate. Like on the sign."

The man screwed up his face. "Yes?" he said, shaking his head in confusion.

"Pate. Your sign says 'Pate' on it. That's my name."

"Yes?"

"Is there anybody here named Pate?"

"No, señor. Only you."

"What about the name on the sign?"

The storekeeper shrugged. I do not know Señor Pate. Only Señor Lewis."

"Would that be *Daniel* Lewis?"

The man nodded. "*Sí.*"

"Is he here?"

"Oh, no, señor. He comes by only on occasion. The store, it is under my management."

Richard thought for a time. "Where might I find Mister Lewis?"

The storekeeper shrugged. "Perhaps in Santa Fe, at *el almacén*—the storehouse from which our goods come."

Richard asked more questions, and the man told him Santa Fe was a two-day journey by wagon, but if one had a sturdy horse, he could easily make the journey in a day. Then he said a supply wagon was due from the warehouse that very day, and would likely start the return journey when emptied of the goods. He said Richard might be able to ride along, if the driver was willing.

When the wagon arrived, Richard approached the driver even before he stepped down off the seat, and offered to see to the unloading in exchange for being carried to Santa Fe.

CHAPTER TWENTY-SEVEN

The knock was gentle and tentative. Mary Lewis looked up from the ledgers on her desk. "Yes?"

The door opened slowly. Mary stood quickly, sending the chair rolling back on its wheels. The emaciated man in the doorway was bedraggled and unshaven, his feet covered only in filthy stockings more hole than fabric, trousers smudged and stained, shirt tattered and torn. His face was wan, eyes bloodshot and bleary. "Richard?"

"Mary."

"Richard! What on earth happened to you? You look awful!"

Richard dropped to his knees and sobbed. "Oh, Mary, Mary, Mary . . ."

Mary put down the pen in her hand and walked around the desk.

"Richard, what is it?"

"I've come to nothin', Mary. My life ain't worth livin'."

She reached out and took his hands, lifting and urging him to his feet. "Sit, please." She led him to a chair facing her desk, turned its mate toward him, and sat. "Tell me—how did you come to be here?"

Richard told the story of seeing the sign on the store in Bernalillo. And, how, having nowhere else to go and lacking the means to get there, convinced the supply wagon driver to let him ride along to this place.

"You-all are runnin' more than that one store down there, he told me."

Mary sketched out the network of stores her father had built, supplied primarily from the warehouse in Santa Fe and supplemented with local goods from each locale. She told of Daniel's near-constant travel, seeing to contracts for merchandise, dealing with freighters, keeping contact with his storekeepers, and dealing with bankers and the like.

"What about Pa? His name was beside Daniel's on that sign—on the one out front here, too."

Mary smiled. "Your father did his best for the firm, but he is not cut out for the mercantile business. His dream was to get back to the land."

Richard smiled and shook his bowed head. "Pa always was one for dreamin'."

"You will be pleased to know that dreaming served him well in this instance. Your father is now something of a land baron."

Richard's head snapped upright. "What?"

Mary related the tale of Lee's rescue of the woman and children threatened by road agents, the resulting appreciation from the government official to whom the family belonged, and the award of the land grant on the Pajarito Plateau and the rancho there. She told how Abel and his vaqueros had been busy over the months and years gathering wild cattle and selling them off, the result being a small fortune for the Pate family.

Richard sat silent, lost in thought over the story.

"Richard?"

He came back to the present and looked at Mary, smiling at him with a particular twinkle in her eye.

"You will also be pleased to know that you are now an uncle, Richard."

"What? Me? An uncle?"

"Yes. Abel and Emma are married, and have two little boys—Luke."

Again, Richard drifted away on his thoughts.

Mary let him sit for a few minutes, then clapped her hands once and stood. "Come along, Richard. Father is in town and will be eager to see you. We will leave for the ranch in the morning. I am certain Father will concur. But, first, you will come with me. I shall introduce you to Arturo, and he will escort you to the *barberia* for a hot bath, shave, and haircut. Then, he will outfit you from head to toe in proper clothing. To speak frankly, Richard, you look a fright. But fear not, Arturo will set it right."

She stood and again reached for Richard's hands. He did not respond to the invitation, only looked up at Mary, his eyes pooling.

"You said somethn' about goin' to the ranch. I can't do that Mary. Pa and Ma, well, they won't want nothin' to do with the likes of me. Not after what I've done."

Mary reached down and grabbed his hands, forcefully lifting until Richard stood.

"I am confident you are mistaken, Richard. You are, after all, still their son."

"I don't know . . ."

"Hush. And come along."

Richard submitted to the renovations Mary had outlined for him, and confessed to Arturo he felt better for it. He craved the calming effects of alcohol, but determined to resist. He sat for supper with Daniel and Mary, and heard more of his family, including the whereabouts of Melvin. They insisted he stay the night in their house, and, lacking an alternative, he agreed.

Come the morning, he accompanied them to the warehouse, where the merchant outfitted a buckboard with supplies for the ranch. The three of them climbed onto the spring seat, Daniel at the lines. With the snap of a buggy whip, he set the team of mules in motion and along the road up to the top of the mesa.

And a homecoming, of sorts, that had Richard's stomach roiling.

"Lee and Sarah will be pleased to see you. It has been some time."

"I don't know, Mister Lewis. You know that Pa and me never saw eye to eye."

"True enough, I will venture. However, you do not know how they mourned after you and Melvin left. Your mother was beside herself, and your father . . . Well, your father feigned acceptance of the situation, but the truth is, the absence of his two eldest sons ate at him. It still does, I believe."

"Well, so long as Abel was around, I don't reckon Pa was bothered overmuch by our bein' gone. Abel always was his favorite."

Daniel thought before answering. "It is true Abel was a comfort for your parents. And you know as well as I—better, I suppose—that Abel was less of a—challenge, shall we say?—for your father. Still, your leaving was harrowing to both your parents."

This time, Richard thought for a time before speaking. "What do you suppose'll happen when we get there? What'll Pa do?"

"Only he can say, Richard. What would you like him to do?"

"I don't know. Ain't like I can expect to be welcomed with open arms. It'd be enough, I guess, if he'd let me stay on and work on the ranch. If I could just be one of the hands, one of the workers, that'd be good enough. More than I deserve."

Mary asked if he really thought that would be enough, looking to the future.

Richard chuckled, a laugh with no humor in it. "What with where I been and what I've done, it damn sure better be. Like I said, it'd be more than I got any right to expect."

They rode on in silence, stopping frequently on the long climb up the canyons to the top of the plateau to let the mules blow. After topping out, they continued along the road through the woods and parks. When the buckboard reached the edge of the broad meadow that was headquarters for the ranch, Daniel stopped to allow Richard a look. He sat transfixed, studying the big stone house across the way, the other houses around it, the barns and outbuildings, the pens and corrals.

Richard let out a long, slow sigh. "That's quite the place they got there."

"That it is," Daniel said. "Mind you, it did not look so prosperous when granted to your father. The rancho had been abandoned for some years, and had become somewhat dilapidated. Your father has done a fine job of rejuvenating it. And, it must be said, Abel has done well with the cattle herds."

"I ain't surprised. There ain't no denyin' the boy's a worker. And he's got a good head on his shoulders besides." He paused, still looking over the hacienda. "Won't surprise me none if he tells me to get the hell out of here, even if Pa don't."

Mary laid a hand on Richard's thigh. "Do not borrow trouble, Richard. Let us wait and see what is in store. You may be pleasantly surprised."

Richard snorted. "Well, I won't get my hopes up. If I do get run off, it won't be no more than what I deserve."

Across the way, Lee and Sarah sat in rocking chairs on the porch, enjoying the cool shade of early evening as the sun cast long shadows. Lee drew a deep breath, savoring the spice that seasoned life on the ranch. "Can you smell that, woman?"

Sarah drew back, brow wrinkled, as she turned toward Lee. "What on earth are you talking about? What am I supposed to be smelling?"

"I don't know what you'd call it. Contentment, maybe. Could be happiness if you breathe deep enough."

With a laugh, Sarah chided her husband for his fanciful ways. "I will confess, Lee Pate, that the dreams you had for this place turned out a hell of a lot better than I ever expected." She reached out and placed her hand atop his where it rested on the arm of his rocker. "You're a good man when you put your mind to it."

Lee smiled. "I've said it before, Sarah, but it bears repeatin'—coarse language does not become you."

She laughed and patted his hand, their chairs rocking in unison.

Through half-veiled eyes, Lee saw the buckboard come out of the pine forest across the wide clearing and stop. "Who do you suppose that is, Sarah?"

"Can't say. Bad as my eyes is gettin' I can only just see there's somethin' out there. Damned if the years ain't catchin' up with me."

They sat and watched as the buckboard came along the two-track road across the parkland. As the wagon drew closer, Lee said, "I do believe that's Daniel comin'. Looks like he's got Mary with him. And someone else."

Sarah perked up, leaning forward to look. "Someone else? Who might it be?"

"Can't say. He's a man." Lee kept watching. He grabbed the arms of the rocker and pushed himself upright. "Lord above! I do believe it's Richard!"

He jumped off the porch, not bothering with the steps, and ran as fast as his old bones could carry him along the rutted road. When he drew near, Daniel reined up the mules and stopped the wagon. Richard stepped off and stood beside the road. Lee kept coming, saying nothing, stopping when he reached his son to throw his arms around Richard's neck and hold him tight.

Tears would not stop flowing as Sarah fixed a make-do late supper for the visitors, not bothering to summon the woman who usually did the cooking. She and Lee did not question

Richard; Sarah only put more and more food in front of him while Lee answered his questions. The visitors, tired from travel, were soon tucked up in their beds. Lee and Sarah retired as well, but lay in their bed holding hands well into the night, unable to sleep.

Abel squatted in front of the campfire; palms held into its glow to warm. He should sleep, he told himself. Before long, it would be time to replace one of the vaqueros and take his turn watching the cattle through the night. Even after all this time, the herds on the plateau were skittish, always wary of humans. He and his riders had gathered thousands of cattle from the *barrancas* and meadows and forests and hills and valleys and mesas and nooks and crannies of the plateau. The best cows and heifers they kept, along with the strongest bulls, young and old. Young unwanted bulls and bull calves were castrated and allowed to grow into beef steers, then taken to market, along with weedy females not fit to throw calves that would improve the herds.

Now, the herds running on various parts of the plateau were shaping up into prosperous stock, and steers carrying the Pate brand were sought after in the markets. Still, the cattle were leery of horseback men and hard to handle, having been feral for generations with wildness bred into them.

But Abel had seen significant improvements, and the day was not far away when the cattle might once again be worthy of the label "domestic." Comforted by the thought, he rolled in his blanket. He closed his eyes and pictured Emma and Luke and little Jamie waiting for him at home, then drifted off to sleep knowing that come tomorrow, he would see them again.

His shift night riding proved uneventful. The yapping of coyotes stirred the cattle on occasion, but there had been no apparent threat from *el lobo, el oso,* or *el puma.* While Abel often found evidence of kills by wolves, bears, and cougars, those predators faded into the forests like a disappearing mist whenever humans were present.

When the first hint of dawn paled the eastern sky, Abel left the herd to the *vaquero* he had shared the shift with and rode into camp to rouse the sleeping herders. But he found them already stirring, the fire built up and the coffeepot spitting steam. He indulged in a cup of the foul brew, thick as syrup and bitter as chicory. The *mozo* packed up the camp for the last time, at least for this trip, and started for home, pack mules in tow and the *remuda,* the spare horses, following. Abel and the others pushed the bedded cattle into a tighter bunch and started them on the path for home.

It was another long day in the saddle, and relief washed over Abel as the herd started down the last incline before reaching ranch headquarters and the pens there. As they drew near, he heard snatches of scratchy fiddle music over the bawling of the cattle. The old man who did the chores around headquarters was a fiddler, and Abel assumed he was treating himself—and whoever else might be in earshot—to an evening serenade.

But when he broke out into the open meadow with the herd, he realized it was something else altogether. The rock ranch house was alight, the glow of lamps shining through every window, upstairs and down. The fiddle he heard came from the house, and through the lower windows he could see people milling about and dancing. He reined up his horse and stared, for it was a sight the like of which he had never seen before.

Abel helped the men ease the cattle through the gate into the big pasture where they could graze through the night, ahead of moving into the pens come morning to be worked. With the gate rails slid into place, he rode with the vaqueros to the barn to unsaddle and turn out their mounts. As he pulled the latigo through the cinch ring, he listened to the fiddle, wondering at what was going on at the big house.

"Abel?"

He turned to find Jane, standing with hands clasped behind her back and rocking up and down on her toes. She wore her best dress and a big smile.

"Good to see you, Janie." He nodded toward the house. "What's up?"

Jane's smile widened. "It's Richard. Richard's come home!"

CHAPTER TWENTY-EIGHT

Jane came back to the house alone.

Lee said, "Was that Abel comin' home?"

Jane nodded.

"He be in soon?"

Jane shook her head. "No. He is not coming."

Lee stiffened. "What? Why not?"

"He didn't say. I told him to come, but he said no."

Lee found Abel by the barn, sitting on the top rail of the horse corral, watching the house. "Abel, Son. C'mon in the house. Richard's here."

"I know it. Jane told me."

"Well, come in. Ain't no sense sittin' out here."

"No, Pa, that's all right. I think I'll just go on home. Tell Emma I'm back," Abel said, sliding off the fence to stand on the ground.

Lee put a hand on his shoulder. "What is it, Abel? What's the matter?"

Abel nodded toward the house. "Him. Richard. That son of yours."

"I see. No, I don't see. Surely you can't bear him a grudge after all this time."

"It ain't that. Well, some. But that ain't all. He comes home and you throw a party. When me and Emma got married, all you done was send us back to work."

Lee thought for a minute. "Times were different then, Son.

239

You know it."

The silence stretched long before Abel spoke. "Still, he went off and left us. We needed him. And he run off. Took two good horses. Your Kentucky rifle, too. Snuck off in the night like the thief he was."

Lee nodded. "All that's so. Melvin, he went too."

"Oh, Pa—you know Mel didn't know no better—he just went along with whatever Richard said. Besides, he didn't come here expectin' somethin'."

"Richard don't expect one thing. Says he only wants to work, and have a place to live and food to eat. Things haven't been easy for him."

Abel scoffed. "Dammit, Pa, you think it's been easy for me? I been here all along, workin' my fingers to the bone. Wearing blisters on my butt ridin' every inch of this mountain huntin' cows. I been put in jail. I been shot at. I been beat near to death. Hell, I've even killed for this family. What's Richard done? Not one damn thing. Sure, he'll work—for a while. Then, first chance he gets he'll run off again and get drunk. Likely he's been drunk ever since he's been gone."

"Pretty near," Lee said, "from what he says. He ain't proud of it. Says he's give it up for good."

Again, Abel scoffed. "He says. He says! Richard will say whatever he thinks will get him whatever he wants. He don't mean a word of it. I just can't stomach him bein' here, just waitin' for his chance to claim what he thinks is his. Damn him! He don't deserve so much as a breath of air on this place. He's gone against everything you ever stood for!"

"Son, your boys maybe ain't of an age where you can know it yet, but being a father ain't easy. Things don't hardly ever turn out the way you hoped, the way you planned, the way you prayed. But supposin'—just supposin'—when Luke gets some years on him, his mind and heart take a turn off the road you hoped he'd follow. Or say little Jamie does. And one of 'em goes off like Richard done. And supposin' he comes back, knowin' that family was where he belonged all along. Think on that. And tell me what you'd do."

Abel said nothing. He looked at his father, where anxiety and apprehension deepened the lines that mapped his face. Then, Abel shook his head and swallowed hard. "I got half a mind to load Emma and the boys in the wagon and go off and start over for ourselves somewheres else, away from you and Ma and Richard and the whole damn bunch of you. Leastways then I'd know what I worked for was mine."

"No, Abel! You can't even think such a thing!" Lee took a deep breath, held it, then let it out long and slow. "Listen to me, Son. Could be we ain't always done right by you. I can only say we did what we thought best at the time. You've done well, and your mother and me, we . . . well, we . . . Son, like I said, we did the best we could. Maybe not as much as we ought to have. Maybe not as much as you expected."

Lee sniffled and wiped his eyes. "As for Richard, I can see how you don't expect much from him. And I can't say as I blame you. But he don't expect nothin' from us, either. Like I said, he wants to go to work like any ordinary hand on the place."

Abel snorted, and spat. "For now. Like I said, if he sticks— which I don't think he will—he'll want more soon enough. He never missed a chance growin' up to remind me he was your oldest son. And that he was in line for more'n me on account of it."

"Oh, Abel. Richard's still family, but he knows full well he gave all that up when he left us." He stretched both arms wide. "This—all of this—is yours, Abel. Everything we've built, all we've got, is yours when I'm dead and gone. Fact is, it's as much yours as mine already. Richard knows that. You should know that, too. You can't think of leaving it, Richard or no Richard!"

Abel looked to the house, from which happiness and joy seemed to radiate. He looked into his father's face and saw the glow of light from the house reflected in the tears trickling their way down his wrinkled cheeks. He looked again to the house and saw his brother standing with Mary in the back yard, haloed in the glow of light falling out the open doorway. He saw Mary reach out and take Richard by both his hands, and, after a moment, Richard fold her into the embrace of his arms. As he watched, tears welled in his eyes and he could feel the beat of his heart.

Lee cleared his throat. He spoke so softly Abel strained to hear. "There's one more thing you should remember, Abel. Something you should never forget." Lee paused and swallowed hard. Father and son looked toward the house and Richard standing there.

Lee sniffled, and again cleared his throat. "You call Richard *my son*. And that he is. But that ain't all he is—never forget, that no matter what, *he's your brother.*"

ABOUT THE AUTHOR

Writer **Rod Miller** is a four-time winner of, and six-time finalist for, the Western Writers of America Spur Award. He is also a two-time winner of the Western Fictioneers Peacemaker Award, as well as a four-time finalist. His writing has also won awards from Westerners International and the Academy of Western Artists. A lifelong Westerner, Miller writes fiction, history, poetry, and magazine articles about the American West's people and places. Read more online at writerRodMiller.com, Rawhide Robinson.com, and writerRodMiller.blogspot.com.

The employees of Five Star Publishing hope you have enjoyed this book.

Our Five Star novels explore little-known chapters from America's history, stories told from unique perspectives that will entertain a broad range of readers.

Other Five Star books are available at your local library, bookstore, all major book distributors, and directly from Five Star/Gale.

Connect with Five Star Publishing

Website:
    gale.com/five-star

Facebook:
    facebook.com/FiveStarCengage

Twitter:
    twitter.com/FiveStarCengage

Email:
    FiveStar@cengage.com

For information about titles and placing orders:
    (800) 223-1244
    gale.orders@cengage.com

To share your comments, write to us:
    Five Star Publishing
    Attn: Publisher
    10 Water St., Suite 310
    Waterville, ME 04901